I0668767

DELTA GREEN

Tales from Failed Anatomies

Dennis Detwiller

ARC DREAM PUBLISHING • 2014

Contents

Introduction
By John Scott Tynes

"HER WHITE HAIR IS thinned to the point where her peeling scalp shines in the light of the flashbulb."

You'll read that line in this book. Dennis's book. I pulled it out and slapped it here because it's emblematic of the unusual crossover talent that Dennis manifests. He's an artist who is a writer who is a game designer. He has an artist's eye—in college, at the School of Visual Art in New York, Dennis took field trips to the morgue to draw pictures of cadavers. He notices details that escape other people.

That bit about "her peeling scalp shines" for me conjures up a pork tenderloin. Before you cook a pork tenderloin, you need a long, thin-bladed knife, the kind they often call a boning knife. Usually on a pork tenderloin there's this long strip of fatty material, stretching the length of one side, known as silverskin. It's not the chalky, clogged-artery sort of fat you might remove from a steak, the kind that makes you uncomfortable when you consider your own prodigious gut and what it contains. No, the silverskin on a pork tenderloin is slick, shiny, and taut. It's the skin of an old woman's face, her hair thinned to the point where her peeling scalp shines in the light of the flashbulb. You slide the boning knife underneath it, between the silverskin and the red muscle of the tenderloin, and then you gently slice it free until it peels off in one long, thin strip. You do this because if you don't then when you cook the tenderloin, the fat of the silverskin will render and drip away and the remaining material will stiffen and contract, curling the meat and leaving behind a tough strip no one wants to eat. So you slice it free and peel it off and throw it in the trash or the compost, depending on your municipality.

Does this seem cold? Surgical? Implacable? Inhuman? Yes. You will find all those qualities in Dennis's writing for Delta Green. He possesses a vast and alien intelligence, spectral and probing. His greatest contribution to the original Delta Green sourcebook was his conception of the Mi-Go and their servitor Greys. Dennis has a natural affinity for those cosmic surgeons, those dada researchers, who examine us from a great and unknowable height. His writing has that quality, which can come across as either the five-thousand-foot view or the thousand-yard stare, depending on whether his narrator is alien or human. It's a fine distinction in any event.

One of my favorite things about Dennis's writing is that his love for fiction is broad. Far too many writers who work in the Cthulhu Mythos read nothing but horror fiction. Dennis introduced me to Haruki Murakami, who has become one of my very favorite writers, and to Brett Easton Ellis, who has not. In the long years we were housemates when Pagan Publishing was in its notorious phase as "the frat house for serial killers," Dennis loved to quote this passage from Julio Cortázar, an Argentinian writer, on the experience of being given a gold watch:

"They give you the gift of your trademark and the assurance that it's a trademark better than the others, they gift you with the impulse to compare your watch with other watches. They aren't giving you a watch, you are the gift, they're giving you yourself for the watch's birthday."

Right there, do you see it? The inversion. The watch is in command. You, the person receiving it, are the object, not the subject. The world turns upside down. I think this is why Dennis loved that passage. In a world ruled by amphibians, it is the scalpel that opens the frog.

I have had the very great pleasure to work with many talented artists in my life. I have also known a lot of other people who might describe themselves as artists. There is one very significant difference between the first group and the second group: real artists make things all the time. I mean, daily. They don't sit around drinking lapsang souchong and pondering the great work they will create. They pour the tea out on the ground, smash the teacup, and use the fragments to make something. They will flense their own grandmothers if they run short of watercolor paper. They do not stop making things. It is in this way that I have learned I am not an artist.

Dennis, however, is. Marriage did not slow him down. Two children did not slow him down. He continues to bang out fiction, roleplaying game books, drawings and paintings. The man does not know how to be idle. I do not expect him to stop generating art in all its forms until he is one day seized by a sudden stroke and then you will notice the old man's face, his white hair thinned to the point where his peeling scalp shines in the light of the flashbulb. Dennis Detwiller will die on August 17th,

2045, and inexplicably someone with an archaic film camera using one of the last extant flashbulbs in the world will capture the moment of his death and there, in the chemical luminescent bloom, you will see his silverskin, like those corpses in the morgue so long ago, the ones whose wounds and blemishes and faces you have seen in Dennis's drawings so many times over the years and never known it.

Dennis is a goddamn genius. Stop him at any cost. The gun is taped to the small of the dead man's back. Let it use you. It's all you're good for anyway. You are the finger pulled by the motion of the gun. The bullet has already fired. As it speeds towards its target it needs your intent to complete the inversion. The rapidly expanding sound waves reach back into your childhood. He was there then, too.

The boning knife sharpens itself. Your tissues yearn to be loosed. Welcome to these tales from failed anatomies.

JOHN SCOTT TYNES
SEATTLE, WASHINGTON
MAY 13, 2014

Foreword
By Robin D. Laws

The Alien Thoughts That Obtruded on the Consciousness of Agent Ted Gallatin, 35, as He Lay Slowly Dying in a Stairwell in Valley Center, KS:

THIS BECAME INEVITABLE

happened

has happened

has always happened

will always happen

When you tried to comprehend Us

When your mind

your tiny

fleeting

hint

of an awareness

Sought to reach out across the void

(When all in fact is void)

To impose what you call order

What you call meaning

What you call comprehension

On that which is the chaos beyond chaos

The inbreak of absolute non-meaning

The shudder of absence

That which a primitive arrangement of spongy animal tissue

thirteen hundred and fifty grams

(As you would measure them)

Cannot contain

Cannot correlate

What no physicality no mortality can contain or correlate

The ineffable We

We do not welcome our presence in your expiring meat

It hurts annoys buzzing gnat microbial the mismatch of scale

the failed fit of our Being to your thought

This death you experience

Blood soaking your poly-cotton shirt

Gutshot

Now we locate the correct abstraction in your language centers...

Category error

You would call it a category error

You die because of a category error

Reaching out to comprehend

The Eye and the Gate

The Gate and the Eye

The Lurker and its Threshold

"Maybe," you said to Bradshaw in that Kentucky sandwich shop mayo dripping down the length of your finger to the crook of your thumb, "the book is right and the entity they call Yog-Sothoth is trapped at the intersection of time and space."

We are the intersection of Time and Space

Trapped as a moon is trapped around its planet

Trapped as oxygen in a water molecule

Trapped as the word "teleology" is in your language "English"

Intrinsic

Intrinsic

It is your imaginings that shape how We manifest

Your grubby cruelties that you project onto Us

Your lust for destruction you require Us to embody

And so We do

Because without them you could not perceive Us at all

Simultaneity:

As you die:

On the cold planet Y'bbanau

A father

Elbow plates clicking

Intestinal sub-teeth clacking

Lifts his newborn son

To the pale light of a diseased celestial orb

Lofting him with all three arms

Intones: "O Sun O Sun O Daggaiggai

Bless this my son

The product of my pupal sac

Who I now name Gua-Daggai

In homage to You

So that You may protect him

From the pushing winds

From the tearing wilds

From the gnawers that dwell in the dark

That you may infuse him

With respect for his elders

Surety in his selfhood

Care for his progeny

And greatness, O Daggaiggai

Infuse him with greatness

So that he might spin new songs

Build walls and lanes and spires

That he might smash the armies of the Yla

That his visage may be incised on pots and tiles

That his name echo for a thousand years."

But Daggaiggai is just a ball of burning gas

And already inside Gua-Daggai

Is a parasite

Burrowed inside his filtration sheath

Soon he will be as dead as you

Songs unsung

Walls unbuilt

Armies unsmashed

Simultaneity:

As you die:

In our crypt-city beneath the ocean floor

We dream

Wings curled tight to drowsing head

Shallow breaths inflating bloated form

We dream and are dreamt of

And the dreamers drum and dance and fuck and spit

Paint themselves, don masks, mar their skins with prick and

pigment

They demand that We act

That We bend to their will

That We fill their pockets, reverse their humiliations, fill their

mouths with dominating words

That We slay their foes

Make them Lords of Earth when we shamble across it

As if We need them

As if they have aught to grant Us in return

We would blight them with madness

Were this not redundant

The stars are right

The stars are always right

The end is always happening

Linear time is but the echo back in time of the destruction of

time

When We come

(We have already come)

They will be like you

You will be like them

A double gazing in the mirror

Twins in the womb

Tiny fingers on each other's

Throats

All of you

Conspirators

Counter-conspirators

Cultists

Anti-cultists

All of you will be Agent Ted Gallatin, exsanguinating on a dirty stairwell in Valley Center, Kansas.

Simultaneity:

As you die:

An infinite plain, swept by stellar char, gray hollows and berms further than the eye can see

(Were there yet eyes here)

In a formless reality

Beyond the bounds of your galactic physics

A multi-cellular plant-like form emerges

Thrusting waving shell-follicles

Catching the stellar motes

Feeding on them

An irrelevant quantity of time passes

In the blink of Our globular glowing eye

A photo-reactive surface mutates into being on the topmost macro-cell of a single organism

It catches motes faster than those around it

Grows

Propagates

Our eye blinks again

The superior follicles acquire awareness

They learn to love one another

They exchange genetic material

They discover murder

They invent gods

Who are follicles

Like they are

Another blink

The follicles evolve motility

Murder becomes war

Power becomes slavery

Love becomes fornication

The follicles attain enlightened morality

Abandoning war for peace, slavery for equality

(Fucking and love remain all tangled up, but when aren't they?)

In the new follicular utopia

An organism that wouldn't have survived under the old order

Develops a mathematics

One that would undo everything, offering hope to its mortal
beings and your mortal beings, unwind the inevitability of cosmic destruction, an elder sign as big as the macroverse

(We say elder sign because that is what you understand, Ted
Gallatin, not because it exists as you conceive it.)

But then come the waves of stellar radiation

The motes that nourish the organisms fade to cinders

The mathematician follicle withers

And all is as it always was

Simultaneity:

As you die:

In the dead center of existence

(Dead in both senses of the term)

We writhe

A ball of shapelessness

A nucleus of madness, forever pulsing

Around Us a corps of drummers thunders

Around Us a ring of flautists pipe their monotone

They play the sole rhythm that calms

The only note that soothes

Our ever-bubbling horror

How was this part of Ourselves so reduced? To weakness, to insanity?

Because for a fraction of a glimmer of an instant, it permits itself to care.

To care about You.

Not you, Agent Ted Gallitin, but You, the crawling breathing puking elbowing farting eating shitting aspiring clawing exploring contending restless evolving massing Horde, the sentients, the self-awares, the mortals who spawn and mutate and build and decease across a billion worlds and planes.

But also you, Ted Gallitin, for this part of us, infinite in its understanding, encompasses all of you, your thoughts, fears, hates, yearnings and resentments.

That is the true Crawling Chaos, the vengeance of the microscopic upon the immeasurable. Not the power of the atom, or the boundlessness of evil, or any other such absurdity of your flawed and bounded conception.

The Crawling Chaos is all of you, reflected eternally in us.

We stand athwart all the thresholds. Those between worlds, and those between iterations of worlds. Each fractionally different. Each equally doomed.

As you die, so do other Ted Gallatins.

The one who lingered to talk to the man at the gas station is pushed into the roadway and hit by a speeding vehicle.

The one who missed his flight is shot in the same stairwell. He meets your fate in a little less than six hours.

The one who years ago succumbed to the blond woman at the motel in San Jose helps to summon one of our lesser forms. His flesh melts from his bones, granting us temporary solidity.

The one who renounced his professional duties after the Ohio situation wakes from a nightmare, sees our face, and suffers a massive stroke. His doctor and family, without calling it that, euthanize him a few months later.

Most Ted Gallatins die with simultaneity, as you die. The one with two children, the one with three, the many divorced ones, the few widowed ones, the situationally homosexual ones, the celibate ones, the Ted Gallatin who likes smooth jazz and the one who plays it in a band on weekend.

Lines converge. Some of yours stray, but most meet here, in this stairwell. Each of you had the chance to make other decisions.

Free will exists.

It leads you always to the same place.

Because you can't stop being who you are.

Simultaneity:

As you die:

We are bloated, elongated, finned. Veinous, propelled by pseudopods, barrel-shaped, clawed and toothed.

The worst form, We decide, the most repulsive shape, is a head, atop a set of shoulders, surmounting a torso, from which jut two pairs of arms, each terminating in a five-fingered hand, and legs, finished by a pair of flattened feet. We find you, the beings who most closely match this morphology. We clothe one of our number in your awful musculature. Through him, We walk among you.

We stand atop temple steps, gazing across an irrigated belt to a vast expanse of desert beyond. Thousands of you terrible hopping beasts prostrate yourselves before us. Burying foreheads submissively in the sand, you show us the lines of knobby vertebrae bisecting your backs. Your servility sickens us.

We perform a demonstration, in a packed hall, the air damp with the sodium of your condensed sweat. Employing a simple coil mechanism, We impel blue sparks to fly and dance. We launch a line of patter, in the style of your preachers and pitchmen. In pulpit cadence, We tell those in that hall what We tell you here

(years later and yet at the same time)

in this stairwell.

The perspiring lot of you shakes. You waver on patent leather feet, stink up tweed jackets and twill pants. You widen bare ape faces. You gasp and jostle one another and move your lips like so many fish. We dismiss you. City after city, stop after stop, you do the same. You stagger dumbfounded in the cooling air, looking for objects to smash, for beggars to kick. You go home to wives and children, waiting for them to step out of line. You lash out at them with fists and belts.

We tell you what you did not want to know.

Your malleability disgusts us.

We don't know why We do this.

It must be the tedium.

Time is over in an instant but within that instant stretches on unceasingly. If there is an emotion we share with you, it is boredom. On occasion you slake it for us.

If only in proportion to your fleeting, insect life spans.

We send our humanoid avatar to Hollywood. We snort cocaine from the silicone tits of failing starlets. With stretch limo emissions we poison the sky. In temperature-controlled boardrooms we spew the clichés that dull your daydreams.

Your superficiality degrades us.

Cloaked In him We go to the concentration camps and torture dens. We guide you in attaching electrodes to genitals, in sending in the dogs, in experiments that make a sadism of your science.

We tire of it long before you do.

Your depravity oppresses us.

Simultaneity:

As you die:

You have been hoping that the ginger-haired man will realize where you have gone and arrive in time to call for medical assistance.

(You have also been hoping that we would not find this thought.

As if there is a thought in you We could not locate.

That has not already been thought.)

In the exact moment you would call now, a garrote cuts through his laryngeal prominence. Breaks the thyroid cartilage. Severs the jugular.

The contents of which presently gush out.

He'll be dead before his knees smash down and shatter on the pavement of the Halstead Bank parking lot on 77th Street.

Yet in those instants all the thoughts We send rushing through your head as you bleed out will play through his mind as well.

We're not sure why We do this.

At one time there had to have been a reason for all this.

Your mistakes nearly protected you

Nearly shielded you from full understanding

(Or as full as you are capable of)

(Which is too full to absorb and live)

(The bullet wounds only an outward manifestation)

You

Your dossiers

Your databases

Your theories and speculations

You called us malign

We are not malign

Malign ≠ Indifferent

Intelligences
(1928)

ALBERT SYME IS AN odd sort who keeps to himself. Floppy and dire, he looks like a clerk, and that's what he is; one of the thousands that haunt the lunch carts on Washington Avenue at noon. Syme's glasses hang on the end of his nose like a man poised at the edge of a cliff. His eyes look at you precisely like those of a gecko sunning itself. They are blank and green and flat, and he stares for too long. People don't look at him. It's not because he's imposing. He's precisely the opposite, small and long-armed and bulging in the middle. It's not because he seems dangerous. He looks somewhat simple, slick like he was dolloped in a thin grease, and empty in the face.

The reason people don't look at him is that he's forgettable.

At this moment, Albert Syme is as close to normal as he ever will be.

Syme works for the Office of Naval Intelligence. Precisely four people know this, and only his boss and the one other person in his office know his name. The two ladies who sit in the Navy desk opposite the ONI collation room know he's there but don't know who he is. He supposes the bank might know—his pay draft being supplied by the Office of the Navy, after all. He says nothing to anyone else. His barber. His landlady. To them, he is a receipt. He has no family (they gave him up in Boston) and no friends.

Such things worry Syme. Sometimes, at work, he plays a game where he draws lines, like pipes, from name to name in his mind, connecting all who might know the secret. It doesn't really matter, he supposes, but he still worries. He imagines his name filling with water, sees the liquid moving in the dark of the pipes, drowning the names of those connected to him. He pictures the people in their tubes, drowning as the water rushes in, in the dark.

He smiles when he thinks these things. His secret, his job, is the most important thing in his life.

The job is his life, though he couldn't tell you why.

Now, July 19, 1928, he eats a hot dog in the summer sun, grasping it in one ink-stained hand while holding his hat down to keep it from catching the breeze and tumbling up the walk. He is surrounded by hundreds of people who fail to see him, lost in their own lunches, conversations, lives. He eats with the conviction and blankness of an animal. He does this every day when the weather is fine.

When he finishes, he crumples up the hot dog's wax paper wrapper and drops it to the cement. He glances at the ink on his hand and heads back up the steps of the huge, stone building, crossing from the light of the sun into the shadow of the portico. As he crosses from outside to in, the wind catches his hat but he snatches it from the air before it can get away.

He goes inside and continues the last day of his daily routine.

IF SYME HAD LEFT ten minutes later, he would have seen the officers arrive. Three men in Navy dress, one a captain with a valise handcuffed to his arm. In this building that is not unusual, but this man was special. His name tag read JOHNSON. Syme would have recognized him from the photo on the wall next to the hot pot. He stares at it every day. The two men with the captain were built in the exact way Syme is not. They were human walls with legs, wearing truncheons and pistols on their hips. They did not smile or speak.

These men entered the ONI collation room and the captain spoke with Syme's supervisor, Templeton Mears, a man who always looks as if he had just survived some near disaster. Mears listened to the description of the job the captain had in mind, and before he could finish Mears swung a hand towards Syme's desk. Mears barely contained the black terror he felt speaking to the Director of Naval Intelligence. As they spoke, it looked as if Mears' eyes would continue to grow until they engulfed his whole face.

When the captain was done, the valise was opened and papers were removed, as well as two Manila envelopes which stank of photographic chemicals. They were placed squarely in the center of Syme's desk. Mears signed a paper for them, and the men left. Immediately Mears fell into his wood chair, which squeaked under his weight. He covered his eyes with his hands.

The room fell back into the drone of the electric clock ticking time.

If he had been there, Syme would have seen all of this. Instead, he was outside, eating his hot dog.

Δ

SYME DOES NOT LIKE his boss. Mr. Mears is a slack man. He fails to do what is required by the job. He slinks in and out at odd hours. He piles work on Syme's desk. He reads funny books and sports annuals and flips through the encyclopedias which line the wood-grained walls, leaving Syme and the other man in the office, Norman, to finish the collation. Norman is not efficient, but cares about his work. Syme does not hate Norman. Instead, he feels about Norman the way he feels about the people who ride the #13 bus with him on the way to work. They are there the reason he is there, and as long as they don't bother him, he will not bother them.

What they do in the room, besides being secret, is boring. They pull Navy files, type and collate copies, staple photographs, cross-check ID numbers and collect them for closed envelope reports. They hand-duplicate files, sometimes many times over. These reports are numbered and are picked up once a week by an armed Navy officer. Where they go from there, no one in the room has any idea. For Norman it is a source of endless speculation. For Mears it is a unconsidered question. For Syme it is an indication that what they do here, in the ONI Collation Office, room 3118, is important.

Syme enters and finds Mears' desk empty. Norman sits at his smaller, steel desk, hunched over it, his jacket off, sweat on his thick brow and in his thinning brown hair. Norman leans over a sheet of graphing paper and draws a careful line on it with a mechanical pencil. He does this with his tongue pinched between his yellow teeth. Norman often has to hand-draw maps. It is something Syme does not have an eye for.

"What is this document?" Syme asks the room, his back to Norman's back.

Norman's pencil stops on the sheet and he turns. His face is round and red and Irish. His mouth hangs open. His empty blue eyes stare at Syme's back without any recognition of the fact that Syme was speaking to him.

Syme hefts the folders and holds them up without turning around.

"Some big wheel brought that down from the Chief of Naval Operations. I wasn't here. Just Mears. Mears told me."

"Where is Mears?"

Norman laughs, repeats the question in a whisper as if it were a joke, and goes back to work.

Syme removes his jacket, catching a whiff of his body odor in the process, folds the coat and drops it over the edge of his chair. He sits, pulls in his chair, carefully arranges his tools on the table—his typewriter, his India ink, his fountain pen, his mechanical pencil, stapler, eraser, ink eraser, paperclips and onionskins.

When this is done, he opens the photographic envelopes first. This has become a habit for him. He likes to guess what the report might be by looking at the photos. Photographs of wreckage usually mean foreign technology intelligence; bodies usually mean accidents; grainy photos are often spy shots of foreign fleets; photos of people usually mean suspected spies. There will be the original and for each original a copy.

Today when he looks at the first image, he has no idea what the report might contain.

The photograph is of an eye in extreme close-up. It is huge, bulbous and black, hanging on the skin of some creature, skin which looks like it is flaking off in diamond-shaped chunks. A human hand is barely visible in the upper right corner, out of focus, holding a wooden ruler with large hash-marks. The ruler indicates the eye is three and a quarter inches across. Even though the whole creature is not visible, Syme can see it is dead. He is not precisely sure why he knows this.

Something pulled from the ocean by some Navy destroyer?

Syme blinks, staring at the photo, and adjusts his glasses as if that might somehow help.

Finally, in an attempt to jumpstart his work, he unshuffles the stack of photos and papers in a fan on his desk, like a deck of cards.

He sits still for a long time.

Then he reads.

SYME WAS BORN WITH a cleft palate. The man who left him at the Park Green hospital in Boston said that was why he did so, but Syme does not know this or the man. He was left one evening in June, which has since become his birthday, by a man in sailor's garb whose hands were covered in blood as if he had delivered the child himself.

He was marked as "UBB CPl" in the registry, Unknown Baby Boy, Cleft Palate. He was assigned a number and held there in the children's ward, separated from the other children as if his face might infect them, in an area jokingly called Bastard Hall.

He was taken by the Catholic Charities precisely because of his cleft palate. He was moved to a house that had an assortment of children the world had disfigured, either by the hand of man or by genetics. Syme was two months old when he arrived.

Today, his face is seamless.

He knows some of this, but not much. He has not had the continuity of a family narrative to tell him this. Instead he has inferred it from a strange ridge on the inside of his mouth, and from what the charity house people told him. Sister Rosita had called him a very lucky little boy, and even then, even at five, Syme had realized she didn't just mean because of his adoption. His life after the orphanage was a life where he was held at arm's length. Provided for. Smiled at. Sent to school. But when he left the house of the people the government called his parents, he never went back. It was the life before the adoption that kept his mind rapt.

In the back of Syme's mind he can still recall struggling to speak, moving his tongue around the gap in the front of his face, and the whistling noise it would sometimes make when he breathed. To him, this feeling is so old—his face seems fine now—that it is like considering a long forgotten wound.

Until he was two, his face had a hole in it with a spray of ill-formed teeth that cut from his upper lip to the base of his nose. He doesn't really know this. He has no photographs. But every year Syme seemed to change. The wards noticed first that his nose seemed to straighten and flatten from what had been the shape of a split mushroom. A thick webbing of scar tissue filled the gap near the front of his mouth, which, over time, closed like a slow-healing wound. Finally his lip knit itself up like a zipper closing. This process took two years. It was so slow that the few who saw him often enough to notice were never certain what was happening, but it disturbed some of them.

Only Sister Rosita knew him from when he came to the charity house to when he left, and she called Syme a miracle. If Syme was asked to describe his life in one word, "miracle" would not be in the running.

IT IS JUST AFTER seven in the evening when Syme looks up again. Outside, he can see the electric lights from Grant Park through the large, curved window, which otherwise throws back a reflection of the entire room over the black of night. His head is buzzing like the clock.

Norman must have crept off some time before, saying nothing, shutting the door quietly to avoid interacting with Syme. In his typical manner, Mears had never returned. The building feels vast and empty, but Syme is used to being here at odd hours.

When it is empty, the building feels like a church.

Syme has finished reading the file he was to copy, and is having a hard time finding a point in the narrative to grab hold of and fold into a suitable shape to fit in his mind. It is not just the photos, which on their own are extremely disturbing. It is not the fact that the Federal government has seized the populace of an entire New England town in secret and interred them. It is not the fact that the report includes after-action statements from submarine commanders indicating torpedoes were fired. It is not even the agglomeration of these facts. It is what is left out of the report.

The holes in the report say things. They say that man is not the only intelligent resident of this world. They say that people can breed with inhuman...things...and that cities of their kind dot the bottom of oceans all over the world. They say the Navy has discovered an enemy which lives in the sea, and which had until now gone undiscovered. The report screams this without ever saying it outright.

A Marine battalion, heavy weapons, full combat, torpedoes—as always, the Navy is deadly serious. It is only when this narrative is inserted into the photos that the story takes off on its own, a looping film of black and white in Syme's mind.

His mind moves through pages and ties them up with photographs. In his mind's eye, the photos enter the lines of text and vice versa, and when they are inextricably linked up they spin and spin, refusing to leave his brain.

Two photographs in particular occupy his thoughts for some time.

One is of what might have once been a woman. Her face is fixed in the wax-like repose of death. Her neck is bloated and crisscrossed by mottled veins and scars. Her white hair is thinned to the point where her peeling scalp shines in the light of the flashbulb. Her eyes are huge and watery and turned at different angles. Her shirt, which looks like something from a Victorian play, is punctured by holes and where her torso is punched open, a thin liquid has poured out, something other than blood. Even that is not so bad. Above the waist she is hideous, dead but not inhuman. Below the waist, the body explodes into madness.

Her hips begin normally and then split into five limbs. The skirt which once covered the nightmare is rolled up and folded back. The limbs are mottled and scaly and fraught with dew-claws and teeth and strange webbing. They all end the same, in a dumb flipper the size of a forearm. No toes, nothing resembling a foot. Just gray-white flippers.

The second photograph is of two of these things. Living. Standing behind barbed wire fencing, lit by headlight or klieg. They stand upright. Both are male. One a child. The big one is an older man with a white beard, a pea coat and an odd, antiquated cap. Outside the wire in the background, the silhouettes of two Marines overlook the scene.

Both captives have strange, bulging throats, short legs, long arms and wide, reflective, shining eyes, watery eyes that are pools of light, staring into the camera. The man has his teeth bared, and they are tiny fish teeth, small, angled and perfect. The man hugs the boy protectively.

Syme does not know why he focuses on these photographs.

SYME ALMOST DIED OF a fever in the spring of 1925. The problem began with insomnia. He found, quite suddenly, he could no longer sleep through the night. Where he had once retired to bed and woken (without alarm) at the proper time, he found himself full of terrible energy. Lying in bed, even sitting still at night, felt wrong. Instead, it seemed that he should walk, run, dance, scream. The energy, which grew as the sun fell, was at first strangely exhilarating and later frightening, like too much current put through a circuit which began to heat and then melt.

He had not yet started at the Navy. He worked as a clerk at the Regis library. There he began what would later become his dull lifestyle, something which no doubt had aided him in securing a job at the Office of the Navy. He spoke to no one but his supervisor and those who crossed his path at work, and slowly exiled those outside of work who might once have considered him fondly; when he moved to Washington, D.C. in 1922, he had gathered a small circle of people who haunted the same places, and by 1925 he had jettisoned such people as irrelevant, replacing them with silence. It was all right. Many were pairing up and marrying, moving for work, completing other acts which to him seemed as alien as taking wing and flying away.

This quiet life lasted until the spring of 1925.

The feeling would settle just after three in the afternoon. A humming behind his eyes. The promise of a mad energy that would shake and propel him while darkness ruled. Still, he would work the day, return home, eat a meal in his bachelor apartment and then stare at the bed. His mind seemed to fill more and more with vitriol, dark images and fear as the night wore on. The radio did not help. Reading did not help.

Syme walked the parks at night. He would walk in the

dark, often keeping from the light, imagining he was swimming in the black. The moon hung over him like an enormous eye and Syme would find himself staring at it, sometimes for hours. In the morning he would drag himself home in the dim morning light, dress, and go to work, exhausted. Still he could not sleep. This schedule became his life, for a time.

At some point late in March, Syme's schedule skipped the tracks. He does not recall when this behavior slipped over into full delirium, he only remembers a sweet fade into a perfect state of being—no fear or doubt or even anger, just existence. Movement. Screaming. Blurred faces. A feeling of ebullient expectance. A fevered joy.

He woke on April 3 in St. Cuthbert's Hospital, and was told that he had been in the grips of a fever which had unbalanced him mentally. He had harmed no one, but had wandered the city in a haze until he collapsed while screaming at the moon in Anacostia Park three nights before. His fever had crested and collapsed the evening before. The doctors said he would now be well.

Even though library's director was understanding, Syme quit his job the next week. He prepared a curriculum vitae and applied at the government office. The next month, he began employment at the Office of Naval Intelligence. This notion had seized him suddenly and perfectly, and he found that even considering other possibilities hurt his mind.

It was a fresh start.

Δ

HE FINISHES THE ROTE copying of the file by one thirty in the morning, working without break. Mimicking all he finds in the one file, down to the smallest detail, Syme painstakingly staples the photographs at exact angles in the *doppelgänger* report, traces and adds perfect duplicates of handwritten notes which haunt its columns, and onionskins the sign-out sheet, adding his name to the list beneath that of Captain Johnson on both files.

He places the folders next to one another. It would be difficult for the person who had originally fashioned it to tell the difference. Such was his work. He picks both up, walks the short distance to Mears' desk, places them on it, locks the door and leaves.

In the empty hall, the church-like feeling of the building continues. Polished marble floors and dim lights and wood and the smell of old cigarettes. No one is here except at the charge desk downstairs where a single Navy man stands guard.

Syme walks down the darkened stairs.

THE MAN WHO LEFT Syme at Park Green as a baby was a sailor from Boston named O'Donogh. He died in a flop-house in Shanghai in 1921, choked on his own vomit, his body seizing like it was trying to eject the foulness he had filled it with over the years. When he was found by the land-lady, his body was searched and then dropped in a mass grave for paupers on a rise overlooking the East China Sea.

His body is still there, what of it is left, in the mud, in the dark.

He was a drunk fisherman from Boston, and it was there he took up with a woman in 1901, the only woman who would have him. This was before the drugs and the gambling. The woman was a local from Southhook, but her people had come from downstate. She had an odd cast but she put up with O'Donogh's ways and set about attempting to make a home for him and, soon after, for the child they would have.

She was not exactly ugly. Instead it was as if some subtle force had shifted her features so they failed, precisely, to line up. She looked a little like the reflection in a funhouse mirror. She was short and had large eyes.

They never married. Her name is not important.

When the baby came, the delivery was brief, but the woman took ill while O'Donogh marveled at the gap-mouthed child their coupling had fashioned. The woman died shortly after the baby came, despite the intervention of a doctor. Something else came out as well. Something half-formed and forgotten by the body that had shaped the baby. Something bulbous, wriggling and blue-black. It died soon after as well.

O'Donogh left the living child at Park Green and took to the bottle. From there his life meandered until he beached himself in Shanghai. Even in 1921, even in the days leading up to his overdose, O'Donogh would think of the baby and the woman.

He would think that he should have left that place earlier. That he should have killed the woman and the child inside her.

That he should have walked away without taking the mewling thing with him. That he should have left them both to rot.

That thing, which became Albert Syme, will never know any of this.

SYME HAS NO CONCEPTION of God. Religion has no place for him, but several times—though he does not clearly recall this— he has felt something brush up against his life. Like the hand of some unseen giant, redirecting things for him, pushing him in certain directions, making his decisions and actions clearer, easier.

He felt it most strongly in the spring of 1925.

Tonight that feeling is with him, and with it comes the elation of certainty. The confusion he felt earlier has fallen away, leaving in its wake a quiet thrumming, filling his mind, allowing room for nothing else.

THE FIRST PERSON TO enter the building on Washington Avenue the next morning sees the blood. From there the moments drop like dominoes, one after the other. The Navy man who watched the door is dead, sprawled behind the desk. He was struck on the side of the face with something metallic and heavy (a three hole punch) and then beaten for ten minutes with the base of the nearby flagpole. The flag of the Navy and American flag lie wrinkled on the ground, soaked in blood.

The Navy man's head is split like gourd, spewing pink tissue that looks like fat and blood so dark it is black. His gun is gone, but it is later found beneath a credenza across the way in the same lobby.

In Room 3118 they find Norman and Mears. Norman, too has been bludgeoned. Mears, it appears, walked in on it and met a similar fate. The two men were dragged and stacked in a corner, away from the desks, under the photograph of Captain Johnson and the hot pot, where their fluids settled and pooled, leaving them pale.

Flies have gathered in the room through the open window.

On Mears' desk there are no files. Instead there is an incinerated pile of paper fragments, burned in a stainless steel garbage pail.

By ten A.M. the police are looking for Syme. Detectives arrive at his apartment and find an empty cube with a bed, some Reader's Digests, some food and little else. No photographs, no address books. Syme's clothes and goods are in order. He has not been here.

By noon the Navy has stepped in. Their own intelligence personnel begin to look for Syme, and the police agree to remain quiet. It is in the national interest, after all.

THE NIGHT BEFORE, ALBERT Syme walks away from the building, his hands bloodied, his mouth in a grin. He stumbles in a way which keeps the few people he sees on the street from paying attention to him, like a man being continuously subjected to random movements of the body, a palsy.

He walks for what seems like a long time until he finally

finds what he seeks. When he does, a calmness fills him and the tics in his muscles subside.

The Potomac glitters beneath him in the summer night, smelling like a million dead fish left to rot in the sun. Syme undresses madly, ripping at his clothes, tearing his shirt, ripping the zipper free on his trousers. He casts his clothes aside. He will not need them again.

He hops down the retaining wall, naked, invigorated. When his foot touches the water—cool but not cold—he practically collapses under the force of ecstasy.

He enters the water perfectly, silently, and begins to swim south, down and out of the Potomac into Chesapeake Bay, and from there into the depths of the Atlantic. The stickiness of the blood on his fingers is replaced by the cooling numbness of the salt water.

The feeling which fills him and spills over into the night is unlike anything the orphan Syme has ever felt. The nuns never gave him this. His adoptive parents never gave him this. His real parents never gave him this. It is a feeling of finding respite in a world filled with danger. Of a small place where everything can be perfect. Something waits for him out there, in the dark.

Albert Syme is going home.

The File
(1942)

LIKE AN ALBATROSS, THE file found Lieutenant Commander Michael Grant in the winter of 1942. He passed it off in the paperwork shuffle like a hundred other mornings and did not consider it until the evening. He looped the pile of papers under his arm and left the briefing eager to get home, to listen to the radio and have a drink, take off his tie and unwind.

He summarized and vetted a dozen such files a week and so he had failed to think much about it. It was just another file until that night, when he picked it up.

Immediately, it was obvious something was wrong. Now that he really looked at it, the file stood out. The others were thin, clearly marked, boring. Office of Naval Intelligence files. This one was different, as if it were dug from some ancient pile of documentation: excavated. It smelled of time and papers rotting, of being overlooked and left too long in the dark.

It was triple the size of the other files—how had he not noticed that?—in a brown accordion envelope slick with wax and colored a deep, unhealthy brown. Something from the Twenties, maybe. The file's girth was bound and wrapped with an old, blue, hooked rubber band that barely kept it together, and the metal hooks that linked the ends of the band were rusted with age. Its front was stamped with a single word in ruined, scratched block letters: COVENANT. The stamp had been red once, but was distorted to black on the brown cardboard. Underneath the stamp was a sort of worn-down, embossed badge.

It was small and round and appeared to be the letter P with some Latin motto he could not read. The badge had long since been ground down to a frayed mess.

He had heard the word "covenant" before but could not place its meaning.

Setting the file on his knees, he grabbed the dictionary on the end table.

COVENANT. 1. An agreement, lease or deed. 2. An agreement that brings about a relationship of commitment between God and his people. The Jewish faith is based on the biblical covenants made with Abraham, Moses, and David.

A covenant. He knew all about covenants. He had signed his life away to the Navy. That was a covenant. He had given himself up to the will of his rambling, rich family, nestled in Stone Hill like ticks, and that was another covenant. He had proposed to Sissy out of a need to close that loop, and that was another one. When he thought about it, his world was nothing but covenants.

Life was nothing but covenants.

What was one more?

He opened the file.

He found himself looking at the back of an old photograph, yellowing with the cellophane coming off at the edges. Block printed text in faded and smeared ink on the yellowed paper read, "SUBJECT RECOVERED INNSMOUTH RAID OCT 28." Beside it was stamped "COPY."

He flipped the photograph over. It didn't occur to him until later that someone had purposely turned the photograph away, that they had placed it face down so that when the file was opened, it could not be seen. Someone had tried to spare him. That action in the past said: "Are you certain you wish to see?"

The picture was confusing. It lacked the clarity that Naval Intelligence wanted. It was blurry and indistinct except for the center of the image: a creature. It showed the dissection of a frog, or so he thought at first. He had, like his peers at school, dropped the cotton ball fat with chloroform on the tan frog in the bell jar and then, giggling, cut it to pieces. Here, in the photo, he thought he saw the outlines of something similar.

But the depth of the photograph was wrong. The blurs over the frog-thing were strange.

Only with closer examination did he clearly see the image. Like seeing an optical illusion, it took a moment for his eyes to adjust.

The creature was actually human-sized, cut and spread open like some horrific experiment on a stainless steel slab the size of a dining room table. It was built more or less like a man but had the head of something like a lizard, with bulging eyes and a mottled skin covered in boils and warts. Its open guts were spread out in an apron for the benefit of the photograph, which he now understood had been taken from a surgical balcony.

The size of the creature was revealed only when he saw

that the two white shapes hovering over it—angels holding bloody instruments—were surgeons in medical gowns seen at an odd angle. When his mind traced the outline of a doctor, of an arm and a head and a leg, the scene snapped into place. The creature grew in his mind until it was impossibly large. Once there, it refused to shrink.

Seen from above, two doctors stood over a frog-man creature at least five feet in size. It had hands and thumbs and eyes and gills. It was dead and in the possession of the Navy.

He read the file from front to back.

THE FILE WAS A trap. Poison. Something slipped to him by— whom? Carter? Randall? Any number of the handsome, blank, Ivy-league men clothed in military regalia, out to destroy him and use his corpse as a step-ladder to power and influence. He could not be resentful. After all, his methods were similar. He couldn't recall who handed it to him, they were all so alike. Alike to each other and to him.

He sat in the leather chair he had hauled up the steps to his tiny room. It snowed outside and the radio played Glenn Miller, "A String of Pearls," and the ice cracked in his drink as it melted. He stared at the wallpaper, repeating pictures of curled tulips interwoven in space, dancing to fill the blankness between wood paneling and the plaster. His mind drifted.

He was smart enough to realize his problem.

He was an up-and-comer, a favorite—the President knew him by name. His ascension was clear, perfect and, if he could avoid such traps as this file, soon to be complete. Before long he would achieve a level of power that could be destroyed only by his own action. New, sparkling lieutenant commander's badges rode his shoulders like headlights illuminating his path upward. He was handsome and tall, rich and well educated. He was everything a naval officer should be. And despite these advantages, he was clever.

He didn't know what the file meant, yet, but he knew it was dangerous. That was enough to start.

Was it fake? If so, it sat in his lap like a time-bomb waiting to go off. Perhaps a test produced by Naval Intelligence to weed out unfit minds. He would have to vet it, write a report and turn it in with his opinion on the validity and usefulness of the secrets inside. If he did and it was false, he was done.

Was it real? If so, it represented perhaps the most significant secret of the modern era. It became more inconceivable, more ludicrous the more he read. A race of amphibian humanoids haunted Earth's oceans and had interbred with humanity for hundreds, if not thousands of years. He'd have to turn that report in for general staff review, revealing to the Army a secret the Navy had held close since 1928.

He was admired and, now he knew, even hated. That was what the presence of this file most definitively signified. He must be doing something right.

THE NEXT MORNING HE made some calls. By noon, his earlier suspicions of a trap had crumbled. His clearance had revealed the provenance and authenticity of the file. Marines fighting in a supposed Prohibition raid on a dying coastal town. Submarines prowling the depths. The internment of the captured "subjects." The images in the photos stayed with him, behind his eyes. There was no way they were photographic trickery. The first picture, the angle, it was too subtle, too real.

He considered the file and its history. It was registered. He had signed for it and others must have, too. It was due for review at the end of the week. It was on the minds of those in charge. If it vanished, if he failed to turn it in, questions would be asked. He thought about the delicate connections holding his future together. He imagined he was a spider, crossing a fragile web, moving from connection to connection, avoiding the gaps. He thought about this for a long time.

He picked up the telephone again.

"Get me Captain Thomas Powell, Jupiter-069".

Uncle Tommy was a fixture in his life. Immortal. Not actually his uncle, but his father's best friend from the Navy. He could not recall a time when Uncle Tommy had not been there for him. Tommy had endlessly railed him to come to the Office of Naval Intelligence before Tommy himself found placement at the White House. After that, Tommy had watched like the rest of his family, with deep pride.

They met at 2:30 that afternoon at the naval officers club.

"HOW VERY PROUD WE are of you, Mikey," his uncle said, smiling, handing him a drink and shaking his other hand. His voice held a twang more western than southern.

Tommy was dapper, thin and tall and ageless. His hair was grey but cleanly cropped, and his skin was smooth and wax-like, without blemish or wrinkle unless his expression changed. He wore a civilian's suit and thin, wireframe glasses, no naval insignia. But he was well known in Washington. The grin faded from his lips as he saw it go unreciprocated.

"What?"

He took his uncle aside into one of the many darkened rooms and slid the door shut on oiled gliders. In the dimness, they sat in leather chairs beneath a tiny orange light.

"Innsmouth," was all he said.

He knew Uncle Tommy too well; the man blanched noticeably.

"Where did you hear that?"

He told his uncle of the file. Of how it had ended up in his review, of the situation he found himself in. What he loved about Tommy was that his uncle didn't speak to hear himself talk; he spoke only when he had something to say. His uncle sat in silence for a long minute and finally said:

"Martin Cook is who you want. I—I wouldn't have anything useful to add, I'm afraid. I'll call him. I'll tell him to call you."

They considered their drinks. He had heard of Cook. A fellow lieutenant commander in the Navy, one of the ONI old guard. Someone on the periphery without access to the President or his circle; someone stuck in one of the crazy orbits of Washington power, drifting in and out of the light. There were hundreds, thousands like him because of the war. The modern version of the royal court.

When he came out of these thoughts, he saw that all the

vigor had left Tommy. His uncle looked deflated, old. Like someone who had been suddenly struck by illness, sitting only to regain his breath. Tommy downed his drink in one go, his Adam's apple popping up and down like a mechanical pump. He finished with an explosive gasp and a gape-mouthed grimace, his eyes wide. He stared at the floor. When he looked up in the darkened room his eyes were watery and bloodshot, his cheeks and the bridge of his nose a bright pink. Uncle Tommy looked like something his nephew had never seen before: frightened.

"Mikey, this is serious business and no mistaking it. There are people on both sides who will go to great lengths to make this go away. They will do anything. This is the most serious breach of law in the history of the Navy."

"How much do you know—" he began, but Tommy stood suddenly and he found himself standing as well. Tommy grabbed his shoulder and considered his jacket.

"Sidearm?"

"No," he replied.

"Start," Tommy said, patted his chest, and left. What once might have seemed ridiculous tonight was wisdom. He didn't even know where his issued sidearm was. In a box beneath his bed, he thought, with a holster still raw and unbroken.

When he stepped into the night in his overcoat and across the silent, snow-covered street towards home, he was consumed with one thought. Tommy had said, "both sides." If the Navy was one side, what was the other? The question circled his mind as he walked home.

He dreamt of dark oceans stirring and things without names building cities in the drifting silt, beneath a mountain of water.

THE NEXT MORNING, AS the thin sun tried to melt away the snow, he found his pistol beneath his bed. Placing it on the small dinette table, he cleaned it efficiently and thoroughly. He scoured and oiled it for twenty minutes, finally working the slide with his palm. It snapped into place with a satisfying clank. As he dressed he strapped the gun in its holster, heavy and uncomfortable under his blue uniform jacket.

He entered his office in silence, using the security desk on the southwest corner. It was manned by two sleepy Marines; it was too early in the halls to encounter anyone else. He locked the door, placed the phone receiver off the cradle, and unfolded the file once more. After a moment, he removed the pistol—it dug into his chest and shoulder—and placed it on his desk near the lamp.

His plan had evolved. He believed he might have missed something in his two examinations of the file. He would read it once again in detail and take notes.

As he pulled each page out and studied both sides, he followed along on a thick pad with a pen, noting names, references and phone numbers. When he reached his first lead, he had assembled forty names—mostly Marines of varying ranks, as well as a naval officer who was now dead—and several high schools and armories that had been used as halfway points for the captured and relocated populace of the town.

Finally, as he lifted a photograph of a burned-out car in the middle of a town square, pockmarked with what he recognized as machine gun fire, a hand-written note from a Marine corporal fell away from the back of a photograph.

It was a list marked "Shock," followed by names and ranks on a letterhead for the Harrison Psychiatric Hospital in Harrison Massachusetts. He held the note, yellowed with age, close to his face and considered it for a long time. Then he picked up the phone.

THE CALL BEGAN IN confusion. The number was no longer correct. When he finally hunted down the Harrison Psychiatric Hospital's number after an interminable wait with various operators, he found himself speaking to the charge nurse at the front desk. It was nine-thirty in the morning by then. He had spent nearly an hour on the phone just to speak to a distant, distracted voice who seemed to have no interest in him.

Without identifying himself, he read the names from the sheet and the nurse replied with a single phrase for each:

"No patient is currently in house at this facility by that name."

When he came to the fourth name in the list, Private Macready, Arthur J., the nurse began her litany but stopped suddenly.

"Oh. Yes. Yes. Hold on, please." The phone clicked before he could respond.

Suddenly an older man was on the phone.

"Are you going to get your ass out here and pay for your

damned man, or should I put him out on the street? I think we both know that would be a bad idea!"

"Who is this?" he responded.

"This is Dr. Allen. This the new case officer? Pay your damn bills. We've been submitting the paperwork for three months with no response. I—"

"I'm coming out. I'm coming out," he repeated excitedly, cutting Allen off in mid-sentence.

"Bring a damn checkbook."

The phone clicked to a hum.

THE FOLLOWING MORNING, TWO days from the file review, he stood in front of the Harrison Psychiatric Hospital in Harrison, Massachusetts. The snow was worse here than in Washington, but despite his march from the train station, he was untouched. Immaculate in his Navy uniform, cap and all.

If looks were any indication, Harrison Psychiatric needed all the money it could get. The building held perhaps forty rooms all told, built in two styles: a true colonial mansion with a more modern, turn-of-the-century addition that sagged and fell towards the center, leaning on it like a drunk leaning on a sober friend.

Snow was piled to the windows at the front, and the windows all were fitted with bronze ivy grating, meant to look more cheerful than its function—bars to keep the inmates in. Instead, the faux-ivy looked like blue-green teeth scattered on tentacles which wove across the windows.

A harsh, unevenly shoveled path wandered from the road to the front door.

His knock went unanswered, so he tried the door and found it open. He stepped into the mud room and stomped the snow off his shoes, the feeling returning to his toes as the boiling heat of a stove passed through him but gave no warmth.

Past the mud room was a staircase landing enclosed in a cage of metal near a kitchen doorway. The sound of a piano being tapped by someone with no musical talent, or perhaps with an ear for torture, drifted everywhere. A single, repeating note struck out of time in such a manner that each hit came at an unexpected moment, just a second too soon, or too late, to form any pattern.

He stepped to the left into what was once a living room, following the piano. An old woman in a house robe sat at the piano, working on the high register keys, tapping out of time. If she had heard him enter, she made no sign of it.

He stepped nearer and she stopped suddenly, aware of his presence, but she did not turn. She was breathing heavily but he could not see her face.

A hand fell on his shoulder.

DR. ALLEN LOOKED ILL. That was all he could think on first glance. Sick. He had a cousin who had tuberculosis. The last time he had seen him, the cousin had looked better than Allen, and that was two weeks before they buried him.

Allen was small, thin and wasted, with sallow cheeks, a yellowed complexion, stained eyes the color of nicotine and a dead mat of straw-like hair. His glasses were huge as portholes, weighing on his face as if they caused his neck to sag. The doctor looked at him with an accusatory, flat, hate-filled, stare.

"Check?" Allen said and held out a skeletal hand.

He handed Allen the check they had agreed upon, and the storm clouds evident on Allen's face vanished. Now he was simply bored.

"Follow," he said and walked away. The woman at the piano never turned. She had sat in silence while they talked and when they left the room she resumed her atonal, incessant tapping.

Upstairs, past the gate, he found two narrow hallways, one with a slight tilt, heading off in different directions. Allen pulled an enormous key ring from nowhere and began sorting through keys. He creaked his way up the hall to a door whose frame had been retrofitted to handle a metal door. The door had a classic prisoner bolt-hole slot near the ground for a meal tray.

"He is the worst patient we have. The worst patient I've had. Ever. When you go in, mind your hands."

"You're not staying?"

"No. I'm tired of hearing all the nonsense he goes on about. I'll babysit him—as long as you pay your damn bills— but I'll be damned if I can treat him. Bang the door when you're done."

Before he could adjust to the idea, he was in the room with the madman and the door was locked behind him.

Δ

PRIVATE MACREADY, ARTHUR J., looked at least sixty but by
his records was only forty-six. He had been incarcerated since
1928, immediately after the Innsmouth action. His medical record indicated permanent psychiatric medical treatment due to
"shock". His last listed action was in Guatemala in 1928, but
this was not true. It did not line up with Macready's orders. His
last assignment was in New England in 1928.

The orders in the file had been stamped DESTROY ALL
COPIES.

Macready was bolted to the wall in full shackles. Despite
this, the madman had somehow removed most of his pajama
coverall, leaving it shredded down to his waist. His hair was
unkempt and grown wild. All in all, one was reminded of the
Mad Hatter from *Alice's Adventures in Wonderland.* A big
head, tiny limbs, oversized hands and feet, a stupid, easy grin
with buck yellow teeth. He was obviously insane.

He was also filthy. A toilet at the side of the room had
chips knocked out of it from the shackles and was covered in
all manner of filth. The room smelled of sweat, urine, shit and
time. Macready's reach with the shackles was marked by an arc
of grimy footprints which traced a half circle on one side of the
room.

Macready saw the Navy uniform and stood, shackles
clanking. He attempted to bring his hand up for a salute, and
could not, his arm jerking up short.

"Tell me about Innsmouth," he said to Macready, as evenly

as he could.

Macready collapsed and at first, it sounded like he was weeping. But as the madman rocked back and forth, it became clear he wasn't crying at all. He was laughing.

"I'M LIEUTENANT COMMANDER MICHAEL Grant and I need to know more about COVENANT. About what you found, your squad."

"You want to know—what? How it was to shoot the things? The fake children? The old women? It was fine. That wasn't the problem." Though the laughter had died, his yellow smile kept coming out.

"What did you find in the town?"

"We found everything. Are you having the dreams yet?" Macready looked up through the mop of his hair, his eyes catching the light in an uncomfortable manner.

"Dreams?"

"Never mind. We found a town of frog men. Haha. Funny. Okay? That's it. That's what's got me locked up here. Talking about the damn frog men." He was wheezing with anger, or fear, his face downcast.

"I believe you."

"Oh, I know you do. Problem is, we need to tell everyone. They're spreading. They can see us. Their—it can see us all, in our dreams." Macready's laugh was lilting and light. It drifted in and out of the silence in the room. It ended with Macready mumbling to himself.

"What are you saying?" Grant finally asked.

In an instant, Macready was on his feet. It was so sudden, so perfect and fluid a movement, it was if there was no interim step. Macready was on his feet at the extent of the shackles, veins standing out on his wasted neck. He pushed as far as he could go, three feet from Grant, struggling like an animal in a trap.

"In his house he lies dead, dreaming!" he shrieked, spittle flying from his lips.

The energy, whatever it was, left Macready like a current being switched off. He collapsed to the ground as if he had been shot, shackles clanking.

"How do you fight something in your dreams? How?" Macready asked from the floor, wheezing.

"Was the Army involved?" Grant finally asked, quietly.

"Marines and Navy."

"Who was your commanding officer?"

"Warrant Officer Micah Walsh."

When Grant stopped asking, Macready stopped speaking. He wheezed on the floor. They waited in silence while Grant attempted to come up with something else to ask.

Finally, he offered: "I'm going to pay for your treatment." And then Grant pounded on the door, which made a hollow booming metal roar up the hallway. He waited for Allen.

"Grant," Macready said in a small voice as footsteps came up the hall.

"Yes?"

"You should have never come here."

"Why?"

But Macready didn't answer, instead fixing his face in a gummy grin with his hair fallen over his eyes. His expression looked confused and empty. When Allen opened the door and he stepped out, the madman spoke once more. He said it in the manner of someone repeating the time. Quietly, and with certainty. To Macready, it was a known thing—an absolute.

"Because now they know who you are."

They could hear the madman laugh all the way down the hall and into the living room.

IN THE BEGINNING, THE dream was normal. It was home. Georgia. Sissy sat on the couch in the sitting room and the light from the window was cold and blue, but the house was warm. He dreamt about her like this from time to time. The calmness of the scene was a counterpoint to the hectic activity of the wartime capital, something his mind needed to vent the frustration of a million bureaucracies and pointless meetings. He could always guess he was under too much stress when he worked in this dream.

They sat in silence with the clock ticking out time in taffy notes, the strikes stretching and pulling as the dreamtime warped and shifted. She said nothing, he said nothing.

He looked down.

He was holding the bloated file in his hands and it was open on a photograph of children's bodies stacked next to a mailbox which read GILMAN in crooked white letters. Each child had been shot numerous times, but even that disfigurement could not hide their bizarre anatomy. Frog children with bulbous globe-like eyes turned up to the sky, arms and legs akimbo, dropped in a stack like discarded wood.

Startled, struggling to close the file before Sissy could see, he spilled it out on the floor and all over the room, the papers cutting crazy arcs in the air as they swung to and fro on the drafts. He panicked, his fear rising as he dropped to the ground and began gathering the contents in one hand, folding and ruining them in his grasp; but there were too many. The floor was a sea of classified paperwork filled with inhuman horrors.

That was when he noticed the water.

For some reason the old oak floor was covered in drops of water, small puddles which formed reflective blobs which caught the light of the window and glowed like blue-white beacons. Some of the papers had landed on the drops and were absorbing them. Other blobs drifted as the floor shifted under his weight and, finding entry to the floor below, dropped through cracks in the wood silently, leaving tiny beads behind.

Suddenly, a spill of water cascaded from beneath the door, as if someone had thrown a bucket of it at the door from the outside. Not a bucket, a deluge—instead of slowing and then stopping, the water kept coming. It continued to spray from beneath the crack until the ancient oak door pushed inwards with a reluctant, creaking moan.

One of the windows behind him imploded and cold water and glass fragments found his legs. The room rapidly filled, and with the water came the soupy smell of the ocean. Of seawater and rotting things. Throughout this, Sissy sat unmindful, working on her needlepoint, not looking up, not noticing the water, not doing anything. The water drifted up her ankle and calf and knee and waist as he struggled to his feet, almost knocked down by the force of water which surrounded his hips and splashed up his back.

He lost her when the water crested his head suddenly, leaving him swept off his feet. For almost a minute he struggled, feet off the ground, lost in a sea of shadows and bubbles. The shift, when it occurred, was sudden and perfect. A pop as clear as if a reel of film of his life had been pulled and replaced by another. The house, Sissy, the concern he felt was gone, suddenly, reset.

He swam and breathed the ocean. He didn't see this from outside; he was one of them. Swimming in the salt water at a hundred atmospheres as if it were completely natural. There was no confusion or pain. No house. No Sissy. No question. He swam in the dark along with the things from the file and worked with them. This was his life, all he had ever known.

As the dream progressed, the grey-green world swept him towards a center, like a mote spiraling in a drain. He was pulled into the water-sky and into a current too powerful to resist; instead, he could only orient himself to watch as the landscape drifted by.

He passed gargantuan structures, older than Rome, whose angles were wrong, like optical illusions in books, showing Möbius strips or pictures that appeared to hang off the printed page.

He swept past an army of blurred man-like shapes in a rectangle the size of a football field, bowing on the muck of the bottom in supplication to some unseen god. He could hear their low, waterlogged song that hummed in the lower registers of his hearing like the chanting of a thousand drowned monks. As he moved, the suction sped up, pulling him faster and faster towards a growing slice of nothing at the sea floor.

And then he was flung over the expanse of the black gap in the bottom of the sea. A void where light could not go. An endless nothing into which he tumbled, unable to resist. As the darkness closed off the aquatic world and left him in the black, he suddenly discovered he could not breath the water at all. He choked and sputtered.

And then, just as his lungs seized for the final time, he saw them, miles below in the dark. Three globes, blue-white, in the water.

Eyes. The size of city blocks. Watching him.

COMMANDER COOK WAS HARD to find for a registered member of the armed forces. His office was a threadbare cubicle at the Department of the Navy building, and his secretary seemed shocked someone might actually look for him, much less want to speak with him. She took down Grant's number and continued her crossword puzzle. He never called back.

Twice, Grant turned up at low level meetings that Cook was scheduled to attend, but saw no one resembling the picture he had uncovered in the old man's personnel file. Instead, a sea of uniforms sat and met, formulating plans to dislodge the Axis in some distant locale.

It was leaving the second meeting that he noticed his tail.

The guy was good. Big, but forgettable, and fast. Easily lost in the crowd in his gray hat and coat, a shadow of a man.

Grant cut into a Five and Dime and wound down an aisle past products marked with ration info, picked through a sea of magazines, watching the door. No one came in.

A rough hand fell on his shoulder and he jumped and spun, now face to face with the man in the gray coat. Grant's hand drifted up towards the gun before it was grabbed and pressed back to his side. The hand that held it was implacable. Grant acquiesced, though he didn't fully understand why. The man released him and stepped back.

The gray man's face, flat and ruined like a boxer's, smiled, showing uneven teeth whose enamel was almost gone, leaving nearly transparent edges. The face would not resolve into a single image, and instead remained a series of interlocking parts that somehow floated together.

"Hi, friend," the gray man said, smiling. "How's your day?"

Grant said nothing, but stepped back.

The gray man held up a piece of paper, a train ticket.

On the ticket, a phone number.

THE NUMBER RANG AND rang and finally, just as he was ready to hang up, was picked up and answered by a confused voice.

"Hello?"

"Com—"

A loud cough which interrupted him.

"No, no. I know. I know. What?"

"I have something for you, I think."

"Yeah. Okay. Let's, um. Let's meet."

"All right."

A click and the hum of an empty line.

THE GUN FELT UNCOMFORTABLE as he waited, and the car was cold. Soon, the gun was a block of ice strapped to his chest and his feet were far away and numb. But the window fogged with his breath and he cracked it. There was no use in maintaining heat now. It was better to acclimatize.

Finally, the man he was waiting for.

Across Massachusetts Avenue, a portly, unassuming man in no uniform crossed a footpath from a bus stop and jumped a strip of slush in a surprisingly spry manner, landing without wetting his freshly shined shoes. He held his poorly sized hat in place so it didn't leave his head.

The man stepped across the street, gripping a bell valise like a doctor, and held out a single, leather-gloved hand as he walked without looking up, causing a laundry truck to screech to a halt in front of him. He did not hurry, even as the truck driver began swearing at him from behind the fogged plate glass.

Commander Martin Cook smiled.

He stepped over the water on the other side of the street and made his way towards the train station, past the fountain covered in tarpaulin, and disappeared into a crowd of dozens who moved toward the building.

Grant stepped from the car, his knees popping as he stood, and followed, trotting off into the snow.

INSIDE, A HUNDRED FACES drove criss-cross paths across a marble floor like a dance he did not know. Warmth drifted down from above, slipping into him slowly, waking him, causing his eyes to water. The gun remained cold next to his heart. His eyes darted across faces, snapping from one to another, moving so rapidly he did not dare try to think about it. Not him. Not him. Not him.

There.

Cook crossed towards the northeast trains, head down, looking at a newspaper folded over his index finger as he walked, lost in some internal world. Grant plotted a path to intercept him and drifted into the crowd.

People made way for Grant's uniform, and he arrived behind Cook just as he had planned. He could reach out now and grab him if he wanted.

Cook moved on to the train platform, fiddling with the paper so it sat beneath his arm, recovering a ticket from his overcoat pocket. He flipped the ticket around and held it at arm's length to read it. He squinted up at the train board and then moved down the line, looking for the last car.

Grant followed, unfolding the train ticket for Boston the gray man had given him.

The last car it was. A cardboard placard read RESERVED in the window, but Grant ignored it and stepped inside anyway.

Cook didn't look up. The car was otherwise empty, freshly cleaned. Still, it stank of smoke.

Grant walked behind Cook and sat. From between the seats in front of him, he could see the commander's head, reading something out of sight. Perhaps the paper.

Silence in the car. Outside two bells rung, and people milled about but no one entered their car. The train lurched forward, slightly. Soon, steady movement.

Half an hour of rocking and rumbling. Hypnotic.

"Are you going to come sit next to me or shall I come back?" Cook announced to the car. Though he could not see it, Grant thought Cook was smiling.

"FIRST OFF, YOU'RE LATE," Cook laughed. His teeth were bad but he smiled unabashedly. He shook his head, looked out the window at the snow. "You have been of an interest to me, commander."

"And why is that, sir?"

"You're Navy. You come from a good family and recommended," Cook said, shrugging.

"And I see the President," Grant said.

"Yes, the President." Cook opened the valise. He turned the valise on its side, and produced three photographs and a map. The French coast in a fold-out print from a travel book. Fodors.

"You have seen the briefing file on COVENANT."

"Yes sir."

"Did you dream?"

Grant started, but Cook did not wait.

"One in three dreams about it. We don't know why. Which dream was it? The thing in the ocean? The ritual? The house?"

"How—"

"This is important, and you only get one swing at this, so listen up." Cook held out a hand in a gesture of confused acceptance. "There is no 'how'. These things simply are. We'll never know how. If you need something to hang on to, it's this: Someone needs to stop them."

"France?"

"Point du Camp." Cook pointed at the map and slid two photos across. One was a close-up of a Nazi construction crew. Men in pajamas overlooked by blurs in guard uniforms. Wire and pillboxes on the sea. The second photo was of a book on a table. The book was bloated and water-ruined and fat and old. The cover was rippled and worn like jerky. The picture was blurred and out of focus. In the background, a man in an SS uniform laughed.

"The Nazis are trying to call the things. The things we found. Trying to ally themselves with them. Get it?"

Grant felt his stomach slowly spin out of sequence with the rocking in the car.

"Who's giving you this information?"

"They are reliable. Better not know the rest."

Grant flipped the photo and the one with the book had a Nazi eagle stamped on the back.

"What do you need of me?"

"I need to know: Are you in or are you out?"

Δ

The President ate scrambled eggs and considered a spray of documents across the desk. The terrier trotted between the servicemen who all stood at attention, eyes fixed on a wall above the President's head.

The little dog nosed in, smelling feet, occasionally jumping up and sniffing hands. No one moved.

"So...this Portugal business?" the President said, finally. He made a sound like someone who did not particularly care for the food in front of him, but he kept eating.

"Yes, sir," an intelligence officer offered. Grant could not see which one.

"Never mind." The President sipped clam chowder from a cup. "Fala, now you stop that." But the dog persisted. "Goddamn dog. Anything else, boys?"

Salutes and nossirs and movement, but not from Grant.

The other officers, confused, lost their lock-step and moved out of the room, all order gone. Faces tried to meet Grant's and lock eyes with him. "What are you doing?" those looks said. "What do you know that I don't?"

The door clicked behind him but Grant did not move.

There was a long silence, broken by sounds of the President eating. Finally, his hands folded the files one by one on his desk. The secretary came in, as if by magic, and slid them all together into a pile. She stepped back out with them and shut the curved door behind her.

"Lieutenant Commander Grant," the President said, placing his glasses on. When the President looked at him, Grant felt his stomach swim around in his body like a panicked creature.

"Yes, sir, I—"

Grant found his mouth empty of words. He looked at the President. His mind was a blank, a flat expanse. His thoughts slipped across like a body hurled across a field of ice. He looked away, out the window. It was a yellow-white light, square, sided by curtains, the glass wet with condensation.

Somewhere out there, he believed, the Nazis were calling things from the sea.

"I've uncovered something we need to be paying attention to."

"Hm. New?"

"Old, sir."

Grant stepped forward and placed the COVENANT folder on the desk. The President looked at him, and back to the document. He wiped his hands with a napkin marked with the Presidential Seal, used one finger to flip the folder open, and considered the back of the first photograph.

"Does this operation have a name?"

"Yes, sir."

"What is it?"

Grant told him what Cook had called it.

The President placed a finger on his tongue and looked at the back of the picture, exactly as Grant had, days earlier. His eyebrows knitted.

Before the President's fingers found the edge to flip it over, Grant had a moment to wonder whether or not the man would dream tonight.

Night and Water
(1944)

"I'M COLONEL STILLMAN."

"I don't give a fuck who you are. What do you want?"

The sergeant coughed, glancing up from the laborious task of scraping a thin, gray fungus from his powder-soaked foot with a Swiss army knife. He glanced up only long enough to project a contemptuous wave of disinterest at the new arrival. Deciding to duck this situation, the hunched wet ghost of a soldier who had led Stillman to the MP command tent of the Twelfth Army Group disappeared through the flap into the night like a figment of the imagination.

From the noises outside the tent Stillman garnered a feeling of endless, crazed movement, like a huge football game of a million men or more maneuvering in total darkness, of transports full of fuel and troops rumbling to ever-widening perimeters of battle in the east.

Stillman was dressed in rain-soaked Army fatigues but wore no insignia. After waves upon waves of German commandos dressed as American soldiers had poured through the lines during the Ardennes offensive, it didn't really matter what you wore up on the front anymore. He could have been done up as a thirteenth-century samurai and received the same reaction. This way sir, watch your step....

The soldiers near the front were too tired to deal with subterfuge. They had much more direct problems to contend with.

Stillman's once-plain face was marred by two meandering lines of a single, healed scar which looked pink and smooth, like a patch of baby's skin. One of those lines had missed his left eye by less than an inch and the eye socket looked uneven, as if it had been broken and set poorly, giving his green eyes a crooked stare. Clutching a bundle of damp files, he looked like a deformed paperboy. His boots were thick with mud, and a Thompson submachine gun was slung at his thin shoulders. The sergeant ignored all this and continued to pick at his foot, teeth clenched, eyes drawn down to a squint.

The stench inside the command tent was terrible: shoe leather, wet wool, and body odor, and the relentless pounding of shells in the distance sounded like drums from some jungle movie. It was abundantly clear to Stillman—and to anyone with half a brain—that the natives of Europe were indeed restless. All you had to do was look around at the bodies piled like cordwood or catch a whiff of the high, sweet smell of rot which floated in the heavy March air.

Fortress Europe had been under siege now for more than eight months, and its cities were aflame with tanks and Allied men. The Americans, Russians, and British were poised on the fringes of Germany, surrounding it on all sides, entering its borders with stabbing movements, subsuming it like a virus seizing a sickened cell.

From outside came the cacophony of a rattletrap jeep, passing nearby in the dark and the rain. Stillman turned away for a moment, trying to pierce the gloom beyond the tent flap. He saw nothing to attach to the ruckus.

"What the fuck do you want?" the sergeant reiterated in a fouler tone, still intent on his project.

"Here's my orders," Stillman said.

"I don't want your fucking orders. I want to know what the fuck you want. Did I fucking stutter?" The sergeant stood and hopped over to a makeshift table, constructed from a half-intact door laid across a broken stone birdbath that looked older than the United States itself. He hunted around the table, digging under piles of maps and field manuals until he came out with a small pair of surgical scissors. Plopping back down on the cot he continued fiddling with his foot, absently dropping his Swiss army knife on the floor. It bounced from the precarious planks which passed for a floor and through the gap between them, then down into the mud below.

"The SS Officer. Schanburg," Stillman said.

The sergeant glanced up and really saw Stillman for the first time. Something in the sergeant's face changed and his jaw slowly clenched and unclenched as if he was chewing on some particularly resilient piece of food. With a smooth motion he slipped a new olive-drab sock on and pulled his boots up, but did not lace them. Stillman watched in silence as the man extinguished the lantern, mumbling to himself.

"Like a fucking butler," the sergeant said.

The two exited into the rain. Shells sailed through the air and fell seven miles to the East over and over again, screaming through the dull rain, trying to coax General Model and Army Group B back to their homeland through negative reinforcement.

"You intelligence guys are damn spooky," the sergeant said in a vaguely buddy-buddy tone, as they marched through the dark towards an assortment of lights to the east of the camp, near what remained of the French town of Trier.

Patton had rolled through and over it in under three hours and the Germans had conceded ground only after a nasty skirmish which had almost completely leveled the small village. That same battle separated Army Group B into two pockets, surrounded on all sides by the American Twelfth Army. Where Patton and his army were now was anyone's guess. Leipzig? Berlin? It wouldn't surprise Stillman.

The rain was just enough to turn the ground to mud and to obscure vision beyond ten feet. In some places the mud was up to Stillman's knees, but the sergeant seemed immune to it. Jeeps and tanks and more vague and unidentifiable shapes, nothing more than shadows in the rain, were laid about seemingly at random, not so much parked as abandoned. There was no real road, just the ever-present mud, tents, and some ruined foundations which were marked with picket poles so you wouldn't fall into them at night. Stillman caught the sight of two men at the edge of a foundation, and it took him a moment to realize they were pissing into it. The smell of ammonia, cordite, piss, and rot were rich in the air despite the cleansing rain. Soon the rain would be sun, the ground grass. Hopefully.

"Here he is," the sergeant said, and pulled back the flap of a tent guarded by a thin, drenched, pimply-faced private who gave a half-hearted salute with his left hand. He finished eating a handful of wet crackers with the other, a ration kit perched in the crook of his arm to keep it from the rain. The sergeant glared at the kid for a few seconds and stepped aside, holding the flap open for Stillman. Stillman handed his Thompson over and said, "Hold this, kid." He walked into the tent as the soldier dropped his ration kit into the mud while fumbling with the submachine gun.

Inside the small tent, a single SS soldier sat behind a folding card table reading from what looked like a tiny bible by the soft red light of a glass lantern. A second private, standing guard inside the tent, snapped a perfunctory salute which the sergeant didn't return. He didn't even look at the private, and eventually the kid dropped his arm, bored or tired.

"He turned himself over to Patton's boys," the sergeant explained. "But they had a bug up their ass to get to Eisenhach or Leipzieg or wherever. So they handed him over to us. We kept him separate from the other prisoners." The sergeant spat a rich green glob onto the ground and considered his prize.

The Nazi's face and black uniform had been stained with blood and mud in varying amounts and his hat was gone, giving him a wild, hunted look. His thin brown hair was sticking almost straight up due to dried mud and his uneven lips mimed along with the words as he read them in the book—he didn't look up as the sergeant spoke of his capture. Despite his uniform and demeanor, his plump form made him look somehow harmless, like someone's grandfather or next-door neighbor, but Stillman knew better. The man was a butcher, a sly killer.

The Nazi finally looked up and locked eyes with Stillman. A mild smile creased his round face.

"Hello, Major Stillman," the Nazi said in perfect English.

All eyes turned to Stillman, who calmly walked into the room and sat down opposite the prisoner, placing the wet files on the card table. A puddle soon began to form around the pile.

"Actually, it's Colonel Stillman," he said.

An uneasy silence descended.

"Give me those orders," the sergeant said after the moment passed. Stillman handed over a wet bundle of papers which had taken the shape of his clenched hand. The sergeant glanced at the bundle once, not really reading them, but just registering their presence before he began to walk out.

"Aren't you going to check them?" Stillman asked, not really caring either way.

"No. I don't think I want to know what you're here for after all," said the sergeant and stalked off, limping back into the night.

Outside the tent, to the east, the shells kept falling like the rain.

"GET OUT OF HERE, kid," Stillman said, and the private left without a backwards glance, probably envisioning putting his feet up somewhere warm and dry, if there was such a place to be found in this nightmare of mud.

The SS officer leaned back in his chair and showed his teeth in a broad smile. His teeth looked yellow and too straight to be real. Stillman now noted the chair he was sitting in was an old water-logged leather and mahogany antique recovered from some derelict building.

"You remember me, of course?" the SS man laughed. It wasn't even really a question. His voice was rich and penetrating. It was the voice of a good friend, one you could not help but trust. Stillman didn't trust him.

"Yes. Fécamp. 1943."

"Yes, yes. And you think you've won now? You think this is all?" The SS man's eyes opened comically wide and his eyebrows bunched his forehead into numerous folds. The question hung in the air.

"Yeah. You're about done. A month or two at the most." Stillman could hear the doubt in his voice, and found himself despising his own lack of belief. He wanted to believe that the war was nearing its end. He wanted to believe in something. Instead, things happened and then, as if by reflex, he acted. It was like everything he said was being transmitted remotely from some foreign locale, only to be broadcast from his mouth. He reacted to things. He never did things.

"You do not believe this. I can tell." Another laugh. "Do you have a cigarette?"

"No," Stillman lied.

"The Reich has some secrets left in it." The SS man said, eyeing Stillman's nicotine-stained fingers with contempt.

"Yes, *Sturmscharführer* Schanburg, we know." It was Stillman's turn to smile.

"What do you mean?" The plump little killer's face darkened with inquisitiveness.

"Nothing."

"Your scar. It gives you…character." Schanburg didn't

smile, but his eyes followed the arc of the gash in Stillman's face greedily.

Silence in the tent.

"Let's talk about Fécamp."

"Certainly. Why don't you begin?" Schanburg said, fingering his bible. He looked bored or distracted, Stillman couldn't tell which.

"I don't remember much," Stillman said, hoping to draw the Nazi out. In truth he remembered it all. He would never forget it.

"What is the first thing you recall, then?"

"Night and water," Stillman said, another reflex. The words seemed completely alien to him, and the memories which came back to him now seemed equally so. But they were always there. Night and water, he had said. But even that wasn't it. He could clearly remember it all, almost. But never before had he tried to think about it. As he pushed his mind back in time, he felt something in the depths of his consciousness stir. There was something in there with him. The memories came back to him like a rushing wave of living darkness.

THE BEACH AT FÉCAMP which faced the channel was freezing. Gray and tan sand and stones, with the yellow reeds and the relentless blue-gray surf, covered by a completely overcast purple sky which hung improbably above to set the scene. Night and water. It was winter in France, and as the four black-clad men clambered ashore from their rubber raft the wind whipped at their backs. The only thing clearly visible was their glistening white eyes, searching for their fate, trying to penetrate time to see the end of their lives as it approached. All would be claimed, some sooner, some later.

But the beach appeared undefended except for several anti-tank constructions which blocked the only solid incline past the edge of the sand. A million things could prove that theory wrong in practice, of course. A mine, a sniper, a machine gun nest. Intelligence suggested the Germans considered the beach an unlikely invasion point, since the gentle scoop of land which jutted out into the channel was known to sailors for centuries as a treacherous zone. There were rip-tides, cross-currents, jetties, and underwater sandbars and rocks. It was why the Allied team had chosen to come aground here, in the hopes that their targets would not expect it—the waters were just far too dangerous for normal amphibious assault.

The beach itself seemed harmless enough. Anything could be in the dark, but the team of commandos rushed ashore anyway.

Major Michael Stillman felt the freezing water splash up into his crotch as he struggled ashore. Three other men followed. The second-to-last man deflated and secreted the raft among the large rocks near the high-tide line. The constant, all-pervasive sound of the waves crashing, a sound which Stillman associated with his childhood in Cape Cod, drowned out all other noises. When the craft was hidden, one of the men flickered a burst of light at the ocean from a hooded lamp. Stillman knew the British submarine *Dauntless*, which had carried them here, would now be sinking back beneath the waves. But the craft was not visible from the shore. Hopefully the team would be here to meet it again in three hours with something to show for its troubles.

The British and Americans struggled past the rocky beach, running clumsily up the rise to the safety of the yellow and dead high grass beyond the tank traps. The men settled in, squatting on their haunches like animals on the thinner, softer sand. A distant, hollow sound drew their attention to the North. Otherwise the area felt abandoned, empty.

"There," O'Brien said. The little British man, a thin-muscled figure in his black suit, pointed through the reeds with a black leather glove to the North, while pulling his silenced Sten MK II around from his back to rest the muzzle on his forearm. With his black woolen cap pulled down and his rat-like face made up with black face paint, O'Brien was nothing more than bad teeth and blue eyes to Stillman.

Past the edge of the weeds the team could spy a single well-lit road which traced its way up to the cliffs, deserted. The beach they had arrived on became a series of jagged chalk cliffs about a quarter-mile to the north, and the recently laid road they looked upon meandered up to its peak. Remote lights atop the cliffs shone in the fog which shrouded them and made them glow like distant stars. They had trained for three days on the sister cliffs across the channel in England, simulating the assault, but even after having so much time to work out the mission on a facsimile, the beach, road, and cliffs now seemed totally unfamiliar, like they had somehow mistakenly been dropped on some alien planet instead of a beach only a hundred miles away.

Stillman fished a small pair of binoculars out of his pack and spied the guardhouse which straddled the road, a thin structure that looked like an old-fashioned outhouse emblazoned with yellow and black stripes. A square, glassless window opened onto the guardhouse's one room, which appeared to be empty. Atop the peaked roof, a small dynamic swastika danced in the wind, glowing in the night like a blood-red eye.

"There's nobody there," Stillman whispered back.

The door to the little shack hung wide on squeaky hinges, slowly swinging forward and back in the freezing wind, occasionally banging on the striped black-and-white barricade which prevented motor traffic from using the road. This was the noise which first drew their attention.

O'Brien considered the structure with his binoculars.

"Bullet holes, Mike," the man said in a stiff British accent.

The two watched the shack for a moment. The window of the hut was shattered and spread out on the tar road in a million different glittering pieces. Small black bullet holes traced a line up the door in a zigzag—a burst most likely fired from a submachine gun. But something was strange. Stillman couldn't place it.

"Bleedin' partisans," Garrity cursed under his breath with a northern English accent. He was small, too, like O'Brien, but seemingly without any muscular bulk. Delicate as a dancer. Like the others he was dressed all in black, and like O'Brien he carried a silenced Sten and a large pack. The coal-black paint on his usually ruddy face was thick with drops of what Stillman took to be perspiration. His red hair poked from beneath the cap in tight curls.

"You think it was some of the Maquis?" Stillman whispered. The idea of being killed by Germans was one thing; the idea of being killed by Frenchmen who were also killing Germans was quite another. "From where? Le Havre? Dieppe?"

"Perhaps. I don't know," O'Brien responded.

"Fuck it all. I hope not," Garrity whispered to himself.

"What are we doing?" Filky piped in too loud a voice. The others glared at him.

The biggest one in the group, Filky obviously didn't fit. He was the last to arrive every time the team moved, and his attempts at stealth were poor even at his best. A small pair of glasses with a jeweler's loupe embedded in them rode his fat American face. The box on his back clattered when he moved and set all the others on edge. Tools for the mission.

"We're going in," Stillman murmured in response.

Filky moaned and rolled his eyes.

"Just stow it, Filky."

"Listen," Stillman began. "I know you've all been briefed for DELTA GREEN clearance. I know you've seen the photos and files. But I've seen the real thing. I've done all this before. Let me tell you now. It's all real. Don't fuck up."

His words lingering behind him, Stillman began to inch forward through the high grass, heading north along the ridge on his hands and knees with his De Lisle carbine slung at his back. He projected a surety in his movement and a conviction in his voice he did not feel inside. Truthfully, now that the enemy seemed strangely absent, Stillman was at a loss as to what to do.

Δ

THE RISING CLIFF ROAD had been cleared of vegetation, leaving a vast track of dead ground between the guard shack and the main building on the crest of the hill, but much of that ground was in a blanket of darkness. The road was a line of light, slightly curved, tracing a path from the checkpoint at the base of the cliffs to the hazy, distant cement building, which was lit in half-a-dozen places by flickering amber and white lights. There didn't seem to be any other structures within the fenced enclosure on the hill except for a second guard cupola just before the fence. The fence was constrictive, drawn tight around the bunker like a second skin. Razor wire was visible both at its base and on its top, glinting like sharks' teeth. A single gate hung open next to the second guard cupola. A single courtyard past the fence came face-to-face with the bunker. No movement could be detected there, even after three minutes of observation.

It looked like an easy ride, and for precisely that reason Stillman believed it wouldn't be.

THE ALLIED COMMANDOS SQUATTED at the edge of the high grass and watched the facility for some time through binoculars. Stillman thought back to the briefing by Commander Cook and considered all the angles. It was his first mission in command. He could feel the mistakes waiting for him, predatory, indistinct. Stillman longed for more training, for more reconnaissance, for more information.

"According to the files recovered at the Cap de la Hague raid," Cook had said, "the weapon, this so-called *Donnerschlag*, is being tested by the Karotechia for widespread production. We are counting on their group's natural inclination towards privacy within the Reich itself to help us. The facility at Fécamp seems to be self-contained and ignored by the outside hierarchy of command."

Onboard the submarine *Dauntless*, as they prepared the raft to paddle ashore in the turbulent surf, Stillman and the men had spied the *Donnerschlag* for the first time: a vaguely reflective blue-gray dome a hundred feet across, carved into the side of the chalk cliffs and filigreed with a spider-web array of steel cables. The center of the dish was punctured by a single black orifice, the interior of which could not be seen. Anything could be contained within the cliff face.

Stillman's team was not here to destroy the device, but to steal any relevant data or personnel they could recover during a brief and hastily organized commando operation. According to the files that Delta Green had recovered from the Nazi occult organization, the Karotechia, the *Donnerschlag* was in its earliest testing phase. Unfortunately, the files said little else on the device and just what it was supposed to do. Regardless, it would never survive long enough to see warfare. The facility had been discovered by the Royal Air Force before it could be fully reconnoitered by Delta Green.

In less than five hours, Stillman knew, seven RAF Wellington bombers would erase the cliffs, the *Donnerschlag*, and the facility at Fécamp from the face of the Earth forever. The

Allied command who had organized the raid knew nothing of Stillman and his commandos, and it was thought best by those really in control that this remain the case.

For it was up to Stillman and his team to find out what the Allies were about to erase. Anything found would only be for those few within the Allied command structure who knew what a tiny occult-oriented portion of the Third Reich was really up to. Only a handful of British and American men, including Roosevelt and Churchill, knew that the Karotechia was making startling progress in the application and exploitation of things most people thought to be hogwash: magic, sorcery, the secrets of the occult. Hidden within the tapestry of the human obsession with the mystical was a very real and ultimately deadly power. The leaders of the free world were not about to let Hitler pull an ace from up his sleeve without a fight. The *Donnerschlag*—"Thunderclap"—was thought to be one such ace.

Stillman had been on another French beach less than a month before, on Delta Green's first mission to upset the plans of the Karotechia. The mission had proven successful beyond the group's wildest expectations and had given the obscure OSS project a bargaining chip to cement ties with PISCES, its British counterpart. The two groups, like the Karotechia, were interested in the exploitation of the occult for military purposes. But PISCES and Delta Green differed from the Karotechia in one vital way: they only wished to exploit the occult insofar as was needed to contain it. They were wise enough to see behind the curtain of claptrap and mumbo-jumbo which history had laid over the reality of the supernatural, and wise enough to realize that this curtain must stay closed or the world might perish. Hitler and his henchmen had tried God knows how many times to pull that curtain away to gain power. Stillman had helped stop one such attempt only twenty-two days before.

On that mission, where Stillman and another commando group had erased a similar camp of Nazis who were communing with things that lived beneath the ocean, he had seen sights he would have sworn could never be true, could never be real. But both the blunt and subtle realities of the situation had settled in his skull and taken root, especially when further horrors were forthcoming after the assault, when they returned to England and the intelligence they had recovered during the raid blossomed into a whole new bouquet of fears. During the operation they had recovered over forty classified files from the Karotechia, files that Delta Green and PISCES examined with mounting dread. Each file was a horror story worse than the last, done up in black and blood red, emblazoned with swastikas and runes.

He had read them all.

"THE LIGHTS ARE GOING down," O'Brien mumbled, bringing Stillman back.

Filky, the electronics man, fumbled for his own pair of binoculars and considered the building with the squinty-eyed stare of a myopic. The hazy lights began to grow more and more dim.

"They're charging the batteries...probably," the fat man said, dispirited.

"Garrity, check the guard booth," Stillman ordered and Garrity was gone in a heartbeat, silently. The lithe man streaked across the road and into the booth in seconds. Inside the booth, Garrity could be seen poking around rapidly, his glistening eyes lit red by some type of internal lighting. He was back just as rapidly but his eyes held confusion.

"Empty except for a change of uniform. Boots, the whole kit. And an MP40, recently fired. There's a red light on the console labeled 'Gerät Aktiv'."

Everyone spoke German except Filky, but the fat man had already guessed what the light meant.

"Device active." Stillman felt something hard and cold settle in his stomach. What did the uniform and bullet holes mean? He had no idea. But the Donnerschlag was charging and time was rushing past. Who knew what the device could do? A vision of the last mission swam into his mind's eye like a nightmare, Nazis on a beach with inhuman things stumbling in from the waves to make Faustian pacts.

"We go in, now," Stillman barked, and headed up the hill at a full run, his carbine in his hands. For a moment the three other men remained in the grass, watching Stillman's silhouette disappear into the dark on the hill.

Then they followed, Filky taking up the rear, wheezing and moaning.

THE SECOND GUARD CUPOLA they spied from the dark was empty also, but had no bullet holes as far as they could tell. Beyond the cupola and the open gate of the fence the lights on the blocky concrete building slowly began gaining intensity, as if more power were being allotted to them from some internal power source. The smell of ozone drifted down the mountain.

"The batteries are...almost done...charging," Filky wheezed, hands on his plump knees, trying to catch his breath.

"The whole place is abandoned," O'Brien thought aloud.

Everything had taken on a soft glow, and light played strangely in the fog. The building, less than thirty yards away, looked indistinct and harmless. Two large squares of cement with no windows. The four men spied it at some length.

"Clothes," O'Brien whispered, pointing. In the dark of the hill, just before the curve of its surface disappeared into the sky on the eastern slope, were several dozen pieces of cloth. Glints of white and gray, folded and rumpled pants, shirts tossed lightly in the wind. It took Stillman a moment to realize that they were laid out in a parade formation, more or less, as if the clothes were carefully placed, one next to the other, by some unknown party.

"Does anyone feel...strange?" Filky whispered. But before he could continue, the noise of wind-blown cloth drew the groups attention to the north.

"More clothes and a motorbike," Garrity whispered, his voice solemn. They all looked. At the southern face of the building a door hung wide and a white bundle of cloth, almost definitely a coat of some kind, lay on the cement where it was caressed by the wind. A single boot stuck up next to it like an exclamation point. Next to it a gray BMW motorcycle lay inexpertly on its side. It looked like it had been dropped.

"Blimey." O'Brien's face was full of fear.

"What the hell is going on here?" Garrity whined.

Something tangible and electric was in the air.

The bunker was seamless, except for the open door and several small lamps which spotted its upper walls. Its curved cement ceiling arched gracefully in a half-dome painted green and tan. Its walls were wrought with perfect interconnecting German lines, defiantly rewriting nature to the whim of the Reich. It looked efficient, secretive, and deadly. But the gaping door ruined its illusion of invulnerability. It looked like the head of some fossilized giant turned on its side, with its mouth agape.

Above the door an amber light suddenly began flickering in ever-quickening intervals. All eyes turned to Stillman for direction. German words stenciled above the light and illuminated by the bursts caught his eye, and his breath seized in his chest.

Gefahrenzone. "Danger zone," he silently translated. A terrible second passed, pregnant with any possibility.

"Move!" Stillman snapped and with all regard for stealth gone he rushed towards the building. Something primal and new within him screamed a warning that his body believed without question. He went from a tense calm to complete panic in less than a second. His higher functions sat back and watched as on some survival level his body attempted to avoid a disaster it somehow sensed was forming around him.

A humming began to carry in the air, like the sound of a huge tuning fork, and it throbbed in his ears along with the pounding of his heart. It felt like the vibration of an immense engine embedded in the ground grinding to life, but as it sailed up and down in pitch, lost in teeth-rattling crescendos and bowel-shaking lows, it began to cycle quicker and quicker. The purple of the sky began to dance in a glowing haze around Stillman's eyes, tracing strange arcs of rainbow colors in the fog. His lungs burned and his chest heaved as the crest of the hill loomed closer. Vaguely, past the sound of blood in his ears, Stillman could hear his men behind him, packs rattling, breath rushing in and out. Faster was all he could think. Faster.

The concrete building was backlit with a soft light which seemed to bleed from out of the air itself. Past the guard booth, gone in an instant—more clothes and a flashing red light. A discarded submachine gun on the pavement, ringed with spent, ejected shells. His own feet ringing on the concrete walkway inside the fenced perimeter. Rushing towards him the white coat, boot, and motorcycle. Beyond them, less than fifty feet away, the open door. The finish line.

Somewhere a klaxon began to sound, lost beneath the roar of his own heart.

Stillman could feel invisible shapes slip past his skin as he ran, more than the wind, like the air itself was congealing around him in a thousand transparent filaments.

From the black of the gaping bunker door a young man's face suddenly appeared, looming out of the dark like a ghost. Blond, blue-eyed, wearing a tattered, blood-stained lab coat. The young man saw Stillman and the German's eyes, already wide with fear, locked on him. Stillman never even slowed.

With a hurried glance towards his wristwatch, the young man's face shifted to a crazed, pleading look as he waved Stillman forward.

"Schnell!" the German shrieked, his blue eyes searching the air behind Stillman, seeing something. Something other than the commando team. In an instant, in that look, Stillman knew.

Something terrible was coming. Something terrible was already here.

Something behind him in the air.

Never slowing, Stillman shot through the door like a rabbit running to ground, tripping over the threshold as he crossed it. His knee connected painfully with the cement and he rolled over, smashing his other knee and crashing into the door on the far wall with a hollow clang.

A second later the steel door he had run through slammed shut behind him but he was too weak to protest.

Then a sound Stillman would take to his grave. O'Brien's voice—just O'Brien—shrieking and firing his weapon, which coughed rounds out, sounding like a cat choking up hairballs with mechanical precision. Bullets connected with the cement, the door, the fence. O'Brien screamed as if he was being burned, as if he was being eaten alive. These sounds quickly died, stolen away by a muffled humming—then, silence beyond the door.

Stillman rose to his hands and knees and then collapsed in the small concrete room, completely unconcerned about everything but catching his breath and the screaming pain in his knees. His carbine dropped to the ground and he shed his pack with his last ounce of energy. The klaxon sounded echoey and strange in the room. An amber light flashed on and off in time with the siren.

The thin young German sat down, squatting next to the shut door with his hands over his eyes. With a hitching, sobbing breath the German began to cry. He looked very young and very scared.

"*Scheisse. Scheisse. Scheisse!*" he choked, over and over again. The klaxon suddenly ceased and the amber lights clicked off. Immediately, before the darkness could take hold, a fluorescent bulb on the ceiling glowed with a buzzing, clicking light. A thrumming, pressured silence pushed in on Stillman and he slowly looked up. The room was a featureless gray cube with two doors, one to the interior, one to the exterior.

It took a minute of silence for Stillman to realize that there were no sounds outside the door any longer and that none would be forthcoming. Garrity, O'Brien, and Filky were somehow...gone. Whatever had come had taken his men. Somehow he knew that nothing living was now outside except what had been drawn here by the Karotechia's infernal machine.

In his mind's eye he could see three sets of empty black clothing laying unattended outside on the cement.

"YOU ARE BRITISH?" THE German said cautiously in English, his voice high-pitched and whiny. His thin, sharp-cheekboned face was red and wet with tears. His white coat was covered in a fine spray of dried blood. He wore French loafers and tattered white socks.

"American." Stillman coughed and stood up, retrieving his carbine. The German made no move to stop him or stand up.

"American," the youth repeated, looking at his hands.

"Outside, I thought you were SS."

"What—" Stillman began, but was cut off by the German rapidly standing and looking at his watch.

"Haag was wrong. The powering cycle is not a set interval," the kid muttered in German. A thin, near-transparent blond beard had begun to grow on his young face.

"Was Haag wearing a coat like yours and boots?"

"Yes, that was Haag you saw there on the ground." The young man fished a thin pair of glasses out of his breast pocket and slipped them over his big ears. His eyes were wide and wet and crazed.

"My name is Stillman."

The German looked up with a startled glance.

"I am Doctor Weichs."

"What the hell have you done here, Weichs?" Stillman barked.

"We just do not know," the boy replied, eyes downcast.

"Who's 'we'?"

Echoing footsteps sounded from the inside of the building beyond the steel door, answering the question. Stillman leveled the carbine at Weichs and backed into the corner next to the door. He raised a gloved index finger to his lips and smiled cold-bloodedly at the scientist. Weichs looked expectant and scared, but said nothing and remained still.

The door slid open slowly, flooding the room with a warm yellow light.

Δ

"WEICHS? DID HAAG MAKE—" the SS officer began in German, but fell into silence as his brown eyes focused on Stillman. The De Lisle was pointed directly at the officer's groin. Weichs pushed his back up against the wall, but made no other moves.

The SS man was rotund and well-groomed. A perfectly trimmed brown goatee rode his large mouth and his slicked-back hair was rich with pomade. He resembled a younger, better-looking Heinrich Himmler. Two *Sonnenrad* runes, cast in silver—stylized curved swastikas—were pinned at his lapels. The *Sonnenrad* was the chosen symbol of the Karotechia.

"Remove your pistol—slowly—with your left hand," Stillman said in German. His voice was flat with implied violence.

"I am left-handed," the officer replied in a calm voice.

"Then use your right hand."

The officer did so slowly, and dropped the gun to the cement floor with a clatter. Weichs watched this all with disbelieving eyes. Stillman kicked the Walther away towards the far wall.

"I am *Sturmscharführer* Schanburg. I am in command here."

"Not anymore. Weichs, sit down." Stillman motioned with the muzzle of the carbine for Weichs to cross the room and sit next to the officer. The young German did so, terror in his eyes.

Weichs sat next to the officer, skirting the pistol in a wide berth. Schanburg's eyes darted between the young scientist and the muzzle of the carbine.

"Now. Since I am the commander, make a report," Stillman demanded.

"Yes sir, commandant," Schanburg replied in accented English, clicking his boots together. A faint smile rippled over his pudgy face. Weichs let out a startled, strangled laugh which he silenced with both hands.

SCHANBURG SPUN A SPARSE tale in simple, straightforward sentences, deftly avoiding any mention of the Karotechia or the Nazis' pursuits into the occult sciences. It was simple. The *Donnerschlag* machine was constructed to sink ships and knock planes out of the air with waves of focused sound. That focused sound was created by two unique electromagnets embedded beneath the cliff itself. It had not been fully powered up or fired before except in scale tests. Yesterday, during its initial power-up phase, something had happened. All personnel outside the command bunker had disappeared. Anyone venturing out of the command bunker suffered the same weird fate.

Schanburg claimed he did not know where the personnel had gone, or what had taken them. But Weichs' eyes were full of knowledge.

"Weichs, what took them?" Stillman asked.

Although Schanburg said nothing, his eyes were imperious. He glared at the young scientist, his gaze full of silent commands.

"Th-thi-things," Weichs stuttered finally, and looked down at the floor.

A silence filled the air.

"American, I suggest you surrender now. By dawn this place will be filled with SS men from the Third *Jagd* Division." Schanburg's voice had found its authority once more, and all the humor was gone. It was so ripe with command that Stillman numbly glanced down to make sure he was still holding the carbine.

Weichs' eyes played between the two like a child watching its parents in the midst of an argument.

"I got you beat there, Schanburg. Before dawn this place will be filled with nothing but smoke and craters. The device, us, and Weichs' 'things' will be erased. The RAF is going to remake this cliff into the surface of the moon. And nothing can live on the moon. Not even the high and mighty SS or the American army. Unless we can figure a way out of here, we're all going the way of the dodo in just under"—Stillman considered his watch—"three hours now."

Weichs stood so suddenly that Stillman brought the carbine around to bear, but the youth had just realized his situation. His mouth open and shut like a grounded fish and his eyes bounced between the two doors endlessly, as if he was half-expecting a third option to appear miraculously as he searched. Then, as suddenly as he stood, the youth collapsed to his knees and let out a coughing, gagging stream of vomit.

Time passed, and the sour smell filled the room.

"Then I turn myself over as a prisoner of war," Schanburg said in a reasonable voice, unfazed, all pretense of command and subterfuge gone. Weichs looked up with assenting eyes and wiped orange flecks of vomit from his lips.

"What do we do now?" Weichs moaned.

Stillman didn't know.

THEY STOOD IN THE command bunker, a chamber located almost fifty feet into the earth beneath the concrete building. Schanburg had lead them from the surface through a rat's warren of staircases, tunnels, and shafts. The small set of rooms they were in now was apparently the command center of the *Donnerschlag* and were located a mere four meters behind the huge dish set into the cliff face, thirty feet down into the earth. All around him were banks of switches, knobs, and other, more baroque constructions which meant little to Stillman. This was the late Filky's department.

Stillman had forced a tour of these six chambers at gunpoint, carefully searching them for anyone lying in wait, but the two prisoners insisted they were the last of the staff to survive. All others had died in the incident or in attempting to escape. A large portion of the construction staff had been up top during the weapons-charging phase for some reason on which Schanburg refused to elaborate.

Weichs and Schanburg considered a tattered series of blueprints on a large steel table which sat beneath a bank of huge, glowing vacuum tubes. The room smelled of seared copper, drying paint, and sweat.

"What are we looking at, Weichs?" Stillman demanded. The blueprints were nothing but a baroque interaction of white lines marked with numbers, German phrases, and measurements.

"You wished to know where the electromagnets were, *ja?*"

"Yes. Yeah."

"Tell him, Weichs," Schanburg growled.

"We are separated from them by a large portion of rock. They are located, along with the power generators, on the far side of the cliff to the east. The shut-down procedure does not seem to be working from the command center. We assumed some sort of fault occurred in the wiring between here and there. That is where Haag was...going to...." The youth's voice trailed off. Weichs' finger had traced a single long line of white out into a vast open blue space on the chart. The line connected two complexes of room with a thin tether of wire.

"So that's the generator complex?" Stillman pointed at the smaller compound of rooms on the diagram. According to the measurements it was over a half a kilometer from the command bunker.

"Yes."

"Is that usually manned?"

"Yes," both Schanburg and Weichs answered.

"Has there been any contact with its crew?"

"No."

"You assume they're dead."

"Yes."

"Now the machine is cycling randomly," Schanburg concluded.

"Weichs?" Stillman looked to the kid.

"It is venting power to maintain a peak charge, but there appears..."

"...to be a fault in the system," Stillman finished.

"Yes." Weichs' eyes seemed to be peering through the blueprints.

"So you haven't fired the weapon yet?" Stillman asked.

"No," Schanburg replied, cutting Weichs off with a subtle hand gesture. But something was behind Schanburg's eyes.

"So it's the electromagnets causing the...problems."

"Yes," they both confirmed.

"Why? What's so special about them?"

Schanburg scowled at Weichs, and the youth remained silent. Stillman's eyes traced the outline of the blueprints and found the name of the device: The Eisenbein Resonator. What the hell was a resonator?

"So fire the weapon. Won't that kill the charge?"

"That wiring, too, appears faulty," Weichs confessed.

"Great," Stillman spat. His brow furrowed. "Now look, I made it here overland at a full run. We can dash for it."

"No!" Weichs cried. "You were lucky—just lucky. The cycles are random. Some short, some long. We cannot predict. Haag gambled. He lost."

Stillman frowned in frustration. They considered the blueprints again for some time in silence. The second hand of the clock on the wall swept round and round.

"Okay." Stillman rose from the chair and faced his two charges. "We have to get to the beach and we have less than two hours to do it. How?"

"You have a vehicle on the beach?" Schanburg glanced up with sly, brown eyes.

"No," Stillman replied, suddenly wary. "I have a two-man raft in my pack."

"Do we have to go through the beach to get to the water?" Weichs asked, his eyes far away.

Schanburg ignored him and spoke over him: "Extraction by ship, I assume?"

"What did you say there, Weichs?" Stillman waved his carbine at Schanburg, who shut up instantly. Stillman fixed the young scientist with a stare: "What did you say?"

"There is another way to the water," Weichs murmured.

"How?"

Weichs cast a scared glance at Schanburg.

"Ignore him. How else do we get to the water, Weichs?" Stillman demanded.

"Through the sounding chamber. It opens onto the dish in the cliff. Some of the guide wires run down to the rocks at the base."

Something like unease spilled out onto Schanburg's face.

"What?" Stillman demanded of the SS officer.

"Nothing," Schanburg blurted back.

"Okay, that's it. Lead the way, Weichs."

The three marched back to the stairwell and then down, further into the earth.

EVENTUALLY THEY REACHED A large steel door painted red in a plain cement room. The feeling of burial here was complete. They had come through three similar rooms to get here. The sensation of hundreds of tons of stone on all sides with no way out grew as each door shut behind them, despite the fact that Stillman had memorized the way to the surface, for all the good it would do him.

The white words on the red steel: *Gefahr! Niederfrequenz-ton.* "Danger, Low Frequency Sound."

"Weichs, open it up."

The scientist cast a frightened look at Schanburg and then undid the complex locking mechanism of the door. He gave Stillman a questioning shrug.

"Open it?" he murmured.

"Yeah. Go ahead."

Weichs pushed on the heavy door, putting all his weight behind it. The hinges squealed as the three-inch-thick steel slab began to slowly pivot inward.

The sound filled their little chamber, and it took almost a minute for Stillman to realize what he was hearing: waves mercilessly pounding stone, and a grated, crazed voice, screaming at the top of its range, echoing and reverberating strangely. Screaming a song. Words. Over and over again. Memories from training came back to Stillman then, language school at Camp X. Russian.

He was hearing someone outside singing the Soviet national anthem.

"YOU FUCKING ANIMAL!" STILLMAN roared. His green eyes locked on Schanburg and his plain face was set in hard lines. The fat SS man seemed to shrink beneath the stare. The carbine slowly found a bead on Schanburg's plump face.

"I should snuff you right now." Stillman found that his voice sounded strange. The room had taken on an unreal quality, and with this feeling came the surety that anything was possible. He could kill Schanburg and Weichs and make the rendezvous. He could wait for the bombs to claim him. Anything.

From the sounding chamber outside the singing continued. The Nazis were going to test their device on POWs; that poor bastard outside would have been the *Donnerschlag*'s first victim. A hatred black and perfect fell over Stillman and he embraced it like the first effects of a beloved drug. Weichs had retreated to the far wall, his eyes confused and full of fear, and Stillman knew the boy had no knowledge of what lay beyond the threshold—otherwise he never would have suggested the chamber as a possible escape route.

"I remind you. I am a prisoner of war," Schanburg began, his voice full of panic as he saw the look on Stillman's face. "By the articles of the Geneva—" The wooden carbine butt struck him in the stomach first and then in the jaw, completing a rapid and well-practiced move Stillman had never before attempted on a real subject. It worked admirably. The SS man crumpled like a marionette whose strings had been suddenly clipped. He lay unconscious on the ground, blood pouring from his chin, lips, and nose in a growing stream. Only then did the feeling of unreality fade from Stillman's vision.

"You've already broken the Geneva convention, you inhuman son of a bitch. Why shouldn't I?"

Weichs slid to the ground in the corner and stared in disbelief as Stillman glowered over the wheezing Schanburg. Then the American turned his attention to the young German.

"Get up, Weichs."

Weichs' eyes didn't blink, couldn't blink. The little scientist pushed himself back against the wall and stared at the unconscious SS officer. Schanburg was a mess. His jaw had shifted, grown black, and swollen to twice its size. Blood from his temple continued to flow, though the torrent from his mouth and nose had stopped. His chest rose and fell at uneven intervals.

"Get up. I'm not going to hurt you."

Weichs stood, pushing himself up from the knees. A harsh icy wind blew into the small concrete room, whistling through the open door. Above the sound of the distant surf, the mad, desperate singing continued.

"Weichs, don't worry about Schanburg. He can't hurt you now."

Weichs clutched his sides to warm himself and looked down on the unconscious man.

"Yes," he said in a small voice.

The two men entered the sounding chamber. A strange ululating echo would repeat every noise they made, fading down the spectrum to nothingness. But the singing drowned most of the noises out.

Shaped like a bell turned on its side, the rounded room was about fifty feet from top to bottom and stared out onto a perfect view of the sea. Whitecaps breaking in the darkness of the French night, a sharp, high whistling wind which was bitterly cold, and the cool dull purple of the sky. It faced England,

and the point at which Stillman and his men came ashore from the *Dauntless*. Several steel cables dropped over the edge of the room to the uncertain rock face below.

"These are the sounding boards," Weichs mumbled through chattering teeth, while rapidly rubbing his arms for warmth.

The door opened in a dead space on the wall, but on either side of the wall, odd silvery shafts of material which did not look like normal steel tracked forward to the edge of the precipice. They could be seen to vibrate minutely with each loud sound in the chamber. They shook violently when the mad singing reached its peak.

"The electromagnets vibrate them at speed and the sound waves are focused there." The scientist pointed at a large bowl-shaped device the size of a small car set plainly in the center of the room. The bowl face opened on the sea, like a radar dish tilted forward. The singing seemed to come from inside it.

"First things first." Stillman inched around the dome, sticking his head gingerly onto the open side. Inside the shell was a stick figure of a man wearing a single gray coverall, without shoes, gloves, or hat. His face was nothing more than skin stretched tautly over malnourished bone—all his hair was shaved. His blue eyes, yellowed through age, were sunken into his eye sockets and those teeth that remained in his mouth were rotted black. Despite his grave condition he sang, his pigeon chest somehow heaving in and out to continue his odious racket, but a rumbling in his lungs made it plain that he was very, very ill. His thin hands were fastened to the inside of the bell by leather straps and his legs were bolted to the ground in a strange harness-like contraption. His face was covered in a dried, frozen glaze of snot and tears.

Focusing swiftly on Stillman, the man's eyes narrowed down to furrowed slits, and his song died in a coughing fit rich with spit and mucus. When the wave of coughing passed, the man launched into a speech in Russian. A hail of syllables shot by Stillman, too jumbled and crazed for him to pick apart with his limited repertoire. Something about joining a party. Then, before he could react, the stick man let loose an amazing spray of phlegm which landed squarely on Stillman's black jacket, gloves, and gun. The Russian's yellowed eyes were filled with an absolute defiance.

Stillman held up his first two fingers in a victory sign, tried his best to smile and yelled: "American!"

To demonstrate his point he held up the carbine, a device of British manufacture.

Something like a religious frenzy came into the Russian's eyes.

"American! American! My friend! *Tovarisch!* American!" His voice was hoarse and exhausted. Once he was free of the bonds, the limp bundle of bones that was the Russian tumbled into Stillman's arms, weakly clutching at him like a baby. Crying.

The thin body was warm. Too warm, with fever and dysentery and God knew what else, but Stillman held on to him.

Over his shoulder, Stillman watched as Weichs stood near the door, his face full of fear. He was looking at his watch.

"Eh...We only have one hour twenty minutes," Weichs chided.

Stillman had finally gotten the Russian to stop thanking him and had dressed the stick man in assorted lab clothing. His name was Nikolai Manchenkov. And from what Stillman could decipher from his basic Russian, he had spent seven months at the Natzweiler Concentration Camp. He had been sent to Fécamp along with a Todt slave labor construction crew. Most of his comrades had perished during construction of this facility.

It was only when Stillman realized that Manchenkov was competent in German that real communication began to occur between the two men.

"One hour, nine minutes," Weichs reminded them.

"They choose me for the experiments, yes?" the sickly Russian mumbled in accented German. "A sergeant major, he choose me and some of my men. He put me in the cliff."

"What was his name?" Stillman quietly prodded, nodding his head in a supportive fashion.

"Schanburg! The bleeding man," Manchenkov shouted, pointing back towards the room where Schanburg lay unconscious.

"You said tests, Nikolai? They tested the weapon already?"

"Yes. One time. Then they bring in whole new men. New commander. New soldier. Same old prisoner." He giggled through black teeth.

"Okay, Nikolai, here it is," Stillman said in German. "We have to get out of here in less than—" He looked back at Weichs.

"One hour, three minutes," the German flatly intoned.

"So you will have to gather your strength." Stillman handed the Russian a ration pack and his canteen. "Don't eat too much."

The Russian saluted with two sore-covered fingers.

Stillman stood up and dragged Weichs into the next room in a frenzy of movement.

"What the hell is he talking about, Weichs?" Stillman spat out, slamming the German against the wall.

"I...do not know. What?"

"The first test. Why didn't you mention it?" Stillman shook the little German and Weichs' glasses fell to the ground with a clatter. All the fear Weichs had gathered and lost in regard to Stillman suddenly leapt back to him.

"I...I arrived just the other night! I swear it! Everyone but Schanburg is new!"

Stillman knew the scientist was telling the truth.

"Fine," Stillman grumbled and let the kid go.

The American stalked back to console the Russian in the other room. He didn't see the hatred drift into Weichs' ice-blue eyes like clouds passing over the sun.

AMAZINGLY, MANCHENKOV WAS CAPABLE of moving under his own power. The force of will which shone through his weakened form dwarfed anything Stillman had ever seen. Seven months without adequate food or water, seven months in hell without respite, and the man was still moving—still trying. Even still smiling.

Stillman knew then that he would do whatever he had to do to save the Russian. The German officer had become expendable. Anyway, their mission was to recover technical data. Certainly a Nazi scientist would prove more useful than some officer.

The SS officer's jaw was broken, and Stillman didn't expect him to wake up in time to see the fireworks. All in all, he thought this was rather a merciful way for the sonofabitch to clock out. With Weich's help, Stillman had shifted the bulky man to the secondary control bunker and laid him across a steel desk.

"Stillman, we have to go now!" Weichs whined.

Forty minutes until the submarine surfaced off the coast and as far as the Germans knew, forty minutes until the air raid. Why he had lied to them, he had no idea. Still it felt good to let them sweat it a little. What was an extra hour to live between friends? Stillman gathered all the technical specifications for the device he could locate in the maze of rooms. Weichs helped, carefully folding page after page of blueprints before placing them in a leather attaché, eyes wide with fear. This seemed to be a gesture of placation, an attempt to hurry Stillman along, but the American took his time.

"Weichs, go and get my pack," Stillman ordered and the little German skittered away, up the stairwells to the main entrance. Stillman knew the kid was more afraid of what could be outside on the surface than anything else. He wasn't going anywhere. Besides, he needed a moment alone with Manchenkov.

"Nikolai." At the sound of his name the battered Russian stirred to slumping attention, rising from the hardwood chair with a desperate effort. With a deft movement Stillman released a small commando knife from its wrist sheath and felt the warm metal drop into his hand. The wicked-looking blue-black blade was shaped in a triangle and had a deadly, effective weight to it. Its edge, honed to a razor sharpness, caught the light.

Stillman held the knife, pommel out to the Russian.

"Watch Weichs," was all he said, and Manchenkov nodded wearily. The pain of an entire people stared back at him through yellowed half-dead eyes.

STILLMAN GUESSED IT WAS more than forty feet to the uneven spray of jagged boulders below the sounding chamber. The boulders were solid, and there were enough of them to traverse a thin path back to the beach he had landed on, but they looked treacherous. Waves continuously pounded them, spattering the cliff face with sheets of white spray. The water would be freezing, the waves relentless.

Stillman stepped back to the focus and began fishing the nylon line out of his backpack. Manchenkov sat near his former prison gathering his strength, wearing a thick wool coat Stillman had located in one of the bunker rooms. Weichs watched as Stillman looped the line on his forearm, measuring out fifty feet. The German had obediently brought the pack back from the surface room without comment.

Something briefly played across Stillman's mind and was gone. He couldn't shake the feeling it was something important.

Then he secured the line and threw it over the side.

"Twenty minutes," Weichs groaned.

Stillman helped Manchenkov to his feet.

THE STRUGGLE TO THE base of the cliff was terrible. Weichs traversed the line without difficulty and stared up, a white shape on a gray rock, tiny and indistinct. He didn't attempt to run. Stillman would have preferred to go first, but he had to go down beneath Manchenkov, to support the Russian as they slowly inched downward. Twice, the Russian's arms gave way and only Stillman's shoulders and iron grip saved him from the rocks below.

"Apologies!" was all Manchenkov would shout over the whistling wind and crashing waves. "Apologies!"

Finally, they found themselves in the freezing spray of the surf. Verbal communication was not possible above the roar of the ocean, and Stillman waved his right arm madly to the south. Weichs began inching his way along the treacherous wet rocks towards the beach with his back to the cliff face. Manchenkov and Stillman followed at a snail's pace. Water ran into all orifices, inching its way into his suit, into his eyes, his nose, stinging, biting. The Russian was a shape of pure exhaustion, a caricature of human endurance. Coughs and fever wracked his frail body, water seared his already weary eyes.

Stillman clutched the shivering Russian and continued forward.

When they reached the beach Stillman felt the Russian's legs give way. Manchenkov fell face-forward before Stillman could grab him. The stick man landed in the sand with a thud. Stillman spun him over and listened for breath, dropping his carbine to the ground.

Weichs, clutching his sides, stared off in the distance in wonder as Stillman squatted next to the ruined form.

Above them, a hazy aurora borealis played on the peak of the cliff.

"MANCHENKOV!" STILLMAN SHOUTED, BUT the Russian didn't stir.

"The water must dampen the field effect," Weichs mumbled to himself, eyeing the strange lights on the cliff.

"Nikolai!" Stillman screamed, gently slapping the unconscious man's face. No response. The Russian's chest rose and fell, weakly, and his pulse was thready and faint.

"Weichs, help me move him to the boat." Stillman gestured vaguely towards where O'Brien had stored the raft.

A metallic click sounded behind him.

"For the Reich," Weichs announced bravely. Stillman spun from the Russian, lifting his carbine from the sand—too late. The little German scientist stood three feet away with Schanburg's pistol pointed at his chest. Stillman dropped his carbine.

I forgot the pistol, Stillman thought calmly to himself.

"Weichs, I can get you out of all this—"

The gunshot was sharp and echoed off the cliff face and rocks in a million directions. Stillman dropped to the ground suddenly. It was not a matter of sapped strength. It just was not possible for him to stand after the lancing pain shot through his chest, where the bullet had carved a hole and blown out through his back. Face down in the sand he felt completely helpless, unable to move. The noise of the surf seemed inordinately loud. The sand beneath his head trembled with every wave break.

"You stupid American!" Weichs shrieked in German and stumbled, half-crazed, towards the rocks where O'Brien had stashed their raft.

Stillman had been foolish but he was experienced, skilled in ways the soft scientist would never be. Weichs had put one through his chest, but the ruined Russian had survived God knows how many tortures and debasements at the hands of the Nazis—and Stillman had not spent months in a concentration camp. Something in Stillman stirred, some desperate force of will. A reservoir of perfect calm and power brought Stillman up to his knees. His body was numb with adrenalin as he shambled up behind Weichs like a pulp-magazine monster. The surf roared as he fell on Weichs, who never even knew what hit him. Stillman looped his elbow around the little German's neck and locked it in his other arm. He popped Weichs' skull from its base by throwing his weight behind his arm and dropping the scientist backwards onto the ground. The German twitched once and was still.

"Cocksucker," Stillman groaned. The two forms remained still on the sand for a long time, Stillman unable to rise from the pain. Eventually he shouted, when he freed his arm from around the German's neck, and then was quiet. The pain rose and fell in waves like the surf. Stillman struggled to his feet and swayed. His shadow was cast out ahead of him on the beach by the aurora on the hill.

He heard the footsteps behind him in the sand, but by then it was too late.

"KILL YOU, WEICHS!" THE Russian shrieked in German, his voice echoing off the cliffs. Manchenkov's mad blue eyes tracked Stillman but saw nothing. The fever and fatigue had taken the Russian, transporting him to a world where everyone was a bitter enemy. Where everyone was German.

Manchenkov's claw-like, sore-covered hand was raised in a martial stance. Then he was on Stillman.

The knife he had given the Russian, his own knife, sunk into Stillman's left cheek before he even knew what hit him. His eyes instantly closed and no force on earth could open them. The pain was intense and grinding and then faded into numbness and shrieking and struggle. Warm liquid began to spill down his throat, forcing him to breathe madly just to stay alive. He spit blood out of his mouth in between plumes of vapor from his nose.

The Russian was insanely strong, impossibly strong, and he was on top of him. The knife tip struck Stillman's face twice and then the pommel smashed into his head. The exact sound of a walnut being cracked erupted in the center of his brain— more than sound. Manchenkov smashed the knife again and again into his head, shrieking insanities. The Russian had seemingly forgotten how to use the knife, and now swung it like a hammer, blunt end first, cutting his own fingers to ribbons as he madly gripped the blade.

Stillman struck out blindly and connected with the Russian's shoulder. Manchenkov spilled to the sand and all fight left him as instantly as it had come. Stillman tried to open his eyes but could only open one to a sliver. The right side of his head felt numb and fat and wet. The world looked sandy and red.

Stillman staggered towards the rocks moaning, dragging the helpless Russian behind him.

"AND THEN WE MET the *Dauntless*," Stillman finished. The shells outside the tent had stopped falling sometime in the past. A point which had gone by unchecked.

"It is funny, Major—excuse me, Colonel Stillman. But when I crawled from the bunker and found Weichs on the beach, I assumed you had lied about the air-raid."

"I didn't. I lied about the time." Stillman coughed.

"I know it. I know it. I saw the planes. You were true to your word, if not the letter of it," Schanburg finished, holding his hands up in a mock gesture of surrender. "What happened to the Russian?"

"He died of pneumonia," Stillman grated.

"It is a good lesson. Russians can never be trusted."

"That Russian was worth more than your whole shitty country—even before we burned it to the ground."

Schanburg looked like he had been struck.

Stillman remained silent. Brooding.

"Listen, Colonel Stillman. We met under circumstances beyond our control. I understand that. We know now who is going to win this war. I did as I was ordered to do. I wish to cooperate with your Army. When your counter-intelligence men return, I will be moved to England for debriefing. Soon, I will be working and living in your homeland. We will be, how do you say—countrymen. Then perhaps you will show me the proper respect." Schanburg's lip quivered over his yellow teeth. Sweat stood out on his forehead.

"Who did you speak to?" Stillman asked incredulously. The disbelief in the American's voice pleased the German, who smiled.

"The CIC men with Patton's force. They are interested in me, I have connections with the *Abwehr*, the *Gestapo*, and obviously the SS. They, unlike you, seem to understand the gravity of the situation in the east," Schanburg curtly replied, his voice full of contempt. "Something your naive mind can't seem to grasp."

It made sense. It was the CIC men who'd dumped Schanburg's name in the files of captured German officers. That's how he had come to the attention of Delta Green.

"Schanburg, you'll never be an American," Stillman smoothly intoned.

"Ah, I see. I will be beneath you somehow, yes? Even though we will share a single flag. I thought all men in your country were equally created?"

"No. You'll never make it to America at all."

Something like fear spread over Schanburg's face as he realized Stillman was serious. The German's eyes played back and forth rapidly around the tent, like an animal marking escape routes.

"What—what do—you are here about Fécamp? The Resonator? I will tell you about these things, I will cooperate—"

"You've misunderstood my purpose here. I don't give a shit about that device." Stillman smiled.

"What?"

"We have diagrams of it back in London. Hell, we've even got Eisenbein himself. I don't need some second-rate intelligence officer's ideas on such a thing. Nope. You're here, or that is, I'm here, for another reason.

"Let's talk about the Karotechia, shall we?"

All the color drained from Schanburg's face.

"SO THE WORD MEANS nothing to you?" Stillman continued.

"No. Nothing," Schanburg replied stiffly.

"Where are the *Sonnenrad* runes you used to wear at your lapels?"

"What?" Schanburg stalled.

"The curved swastikas, what did those markings mean?"

"They were just...symbols."

"Fine. Let us talk about *Aktion Götterdämmerung.*"

Schanburg's face fixed itself into a mask of horror. All pretense of his cool calm had fled the instant the word Karotechia had been muttered. Now, with *Götterdämmerung* on the table, his eyebrows rose until his forehead was a mass of wrinkles. His uneven mouth opened once, and then thinking better of it, shut solidly.

"No comment, then?" Stillman sunnily asked and stood. "Fine. I'll talk about it. We probably know more about it than you do, anyway.

"Aktion Götterdämmerung is the last gasp of your compatriots, the Karotechia. It is a research project which uncovered a formula which could call things from outside. Things like you called at Fécamp, but much more powerful. The experiment at Naudabaum Castle was a practice run. A threat to the Allies..." Stillman glanced at the German, whose mouth now hung open.

"But of course, you'd know nothing about that. You're just a peon in the big scheme of things.

"The higher-ups, your bosses, wanted to get the Allies' attention. They filmed one of their attempts at the use of this formula, at Naudabaum Castle in Bavaria. Naudabaum is a crater now.

"They were stupid enough to believe that we would negotiate with madmen. They were foolish enough to think this evened the playing field. We let some of them think that...but others..." Stillman smiled—and then frowned suddenly, as if some thought just struck him.

The shells began to pound outside once more. Stillman sat back down and put his foot up on the card table. The lamp vibrated once and was still.

"Well, *Götterdämmerung. Götterdämmerung* is a group of specially trained Karotechia personnel, waiting for a signal. These men will surrender to Allied forces, and when the news comes down that Germany has finally fallen, these men are to call those things once more, the things that leveled Naudabaum Castle. This time, though, those things will be brought fully into our world. Their manifestation would make the disaster at Naudabaum castle look like a trifling. There would be nothing left. No cities, no people. No Earth."

"How—" Schanburg croaked, but Stillman held up one thin finger. The SS man fell back into a moody, stunned silence.

"The problem with this plan—and trust me, very, very few people know this, even on our end. The problem with this plan is that the texts that contain the 'calling formula,' which are disguised as Red Cross pocket bibles..." Stillman dropped a wink at Schanburg as the German clutched his tiny bible in both hands convulsively. He then continued: "...are flawed. They were altered on purpose. The ritual at Naudabaum and the ritual in those bibles are just a little bit different. Just a touch. Just to make sure they don't work."

Schanburg's eyes had grown so wide that the whole of his pupils were visible.

"How?" he sputtered.

"Someone on the inside. One of the men who made the Naudabaum Castle incident happen, and who also knew we would never stop until every Nazi laid down his weapon and the Reich was a memory. It was simple, really. Someone in your precious little group had a family. We got them out to Switzerland. In exchange, he turned on your group and altered the rituals during the printing. Right now there's fifty men just like you, men who think they hold the key to the world in their pocket, in POW camps in France and Belgium, when in truth all they have is a crappy faux-bible. How does that get you?"

But Schanburg couldn't answer.

"Anything you want to say?" Stillman asked, sated.

"How?" Schanburg replied, voice hoarse.

"What are you, an Indian?" Stillman retorted. "That was a joke."

"A joke," Schanburg repeated numbly.

"So here we are again after all these years. Some would call it kismet, fate, synchronicity. But I like to think Manchenkov would call it justice." Stillman clapped his hands and glanced around jauntily. He stood, grimacing as his knees popped. He unholstered his .45 pistol, a bulky silver-black weapon, and chambered a round with an adroit gesture.

"I'm gonna enjoy this."

Schanburg stood suddenly, kicking the chair he'd sat in back into the mud with a wet thud.

"Hold it," Stillman said and leveled the pistol at Schanburg's chest. The German froze instantly.

Stillman's anger slowly gathered in the tent, silently, like a summer storm. Twice as the minutes ticked by, a tiny contented smile played across his lips. Schanburg trembled before him, eyes downcast in the mud.

"Are you a member of the Karotechia?" Stillman finally bellowed, spit flying from his lips and his eyes shrinking to tiny martial slits. Schanburg held his hands inanely up in front of his head, as if to protect it from the gunshot. Strange high-pitched squealing sounds erupted from his mouth randomly, the sounds of a wounded child.

"No! No! I do not know this group!" he shrieked, shaking his hands in the air.

Stillman grinned.

"Well, that's too bad there, Schanburg. See, I only have a shoot-to-kill order on *suspected* members of the Karotechia." The gun found its bead on Schanburg's head. The hammer was cocked. "If only you had confirmed my suspicions I wouldn't have the authority to shoot you now..."

"WAIT! I AM—"

Schanburg's voice was lost in the roar of the pistol.

Outside, in the rain, the shells continued to fall.

Dead, Death, Dying
(1955)

"...SOVIET MISSILE ADVANCEMENTS."

David looked up and found an empty white screen, held up in one corner by yellowing cello-tape, the last slide gone, lost while he was searching his mind for some indication as to why he was at this meeting. He was in life sciences, one of the men on the fast track to build gear which could keep a dog, or maybe a man, alive in space—if such a thing were even possible.

The slides that rolled by for the last hour were about the Soviet plans for Eastern Europe, for expanding the red empire from China to the English Channel. They showed the same old stuff he saw on the news, in the papers. The Iron Curtain, the red tide. There was so much hyperbole he no longer knew what to believe.

"Yes?" He smiled to the three men at the end of the table.

They were not unusual, at least not in Huntsville. They had the same cardboard cut-out faces, flattops and black-rimmed glasses as every other intelligence agent that prowled the halls. Rockets were the future, and it was the job of spies to defend the future. Huntsville was more and more like the Pentagon. If you threw a rock at White Sands, you'd hit a half dozen of them before it came to rest.

Their primary obsession was watching everything, like they could take your brain apart with their eyes. They watched you, they watched the projects, they watched each other.

Like now. One man looked at the other. They were so alike as to be nearly interchangeable. He did not recall their names, though they were all one syllable: Moore, Paul, Ward. David thought he saw one eyebrow raise and another drop. A signal between them, the weight of a thought jumping from one mind to the other.

"We would like you to look at something for us," one of them said.

David had been involved in interdepartmental bureaucracy before. He felt he should clear this up before they all looked foolish. When the men unboxed some charred piece of Soviet rocket propulsion and all he could do was shrug and smile, it would be too late.

"Gentlemen. I think there might have been some sort of mistake. I am not in the rocket research program—"

A hand came up. His voice petered out. One of the men began to speak, as if reciting something extremely boring but well-known due to intense repetition.

"Donauri, David, Ph.D., naturalized Canadian, 44 years of age, A-clearance, wife, Camille, 37, one son, Walter, 8, employed Huntsville special research projects center, June 7, 1951, life sciences."

David's face stopped somewhere in the middle of finding a smile.

"Yes?" one prompted.

"Yes," David replied.

"We would like you to look at something for us," one of them said. Perhaps the one who had said it in the first place. It was hard to tell.

The three men sat in the darkened room and watched him while the realization sank in; he, specifically, among the thousands of employees at White Sands and the Huntsville research hub, had been singled out by the United States government. He had done nothing wrong.

He was not a spy.

Still.

HE WAS ESCORTED OUT of Building F on to the tarmac at Huntsville field. There they were met by two other men standing next to a black limousine. These men were slightly larger versions of the others.

"David, this is Agent Sharp," one of his escorts said to him, gesturing at one of the big men. "He will take you where you need to go."

He was alone in the limousine before he realized what was going on. The two big men sat up front with the shadowed divider up. The car rolled out off the testing grounds into the hills surrounding the Ordnance Missile Laboratories.

The sun was going down and he found his day had rapidly gotten away from him. Who would call Camille? Who would know where he was?

It was full dark, and by his watch 9:45, when they arrived at the house. Through car windows it was nothing more than four lit rectangles in the dark. The door on the far side of the limo opened and he stepped out.

He was flanked by identical shadow men. Another stood on the porch with the door open. White light spilled out.

He was startled by the squawk of a walkie-talkie, and jumped. One of the men in the car brought the big radio to his face and said, "Subject is present, lock it down." He clicked off the radio and placed it back inside the limousine.

"This is Agent Carver," Sharp said. "He will show you where you need to go."

Two syllables, David thought. *I am moving up the chain of command.*

"Excuse me," David interrupted, as he was moved away from the car. "Has my wife—"

"She's been notified," Sharp said with an empty smile.

Sharp and the car receded into the dark as David moved towards the house and up the steps. The house was so bright, it took his eyes a few seconds to adjust as he entered.

THE ROOM WAS ONCE a normal farmhouse kitchen. It was impossible to tell what the surrounding area looked like. Outside the windows was only black. But the odd part was not the room.

A sheet of polyurethane had been spread around the empty floor and an odd, submarine-like hatch had been embedded in the far wall. It was new, and was marked HAZARD in spray-painted, red letters that still looked wet.

The plastic was thick and clear and doubled up in places, like it was placed haphazardly, or to reinforce it. It was squeezed beneath the metal lip of the submarine door, which had been, he could see, cut into what had once been an unbroken wall. The door split in half the moulding that once ran across the wall.

A small night-table, one that had seen much use, stood next to the door. A new F-1 bacteriological safety suit was laid across the table along with a respirator.

Next to it, on the ground, was a gas-pumping unit with a spray handle, marked FUEL.

He turned and found the door closed. On the inside of the farm door, an odd rubber stopper had been looped around its perimeter, and it made a squeak as the door was being shut. Agent Carver stood in front of him.

"I need to use the WC," David said.

"We need you to look at something," Carver responded, stretching his hand out towards the submarine door.

He remained there, posed with a dull smile on his face under flat eyes until David got dressed.

THE THING IN THE plastic box watched him enter. It was alive and it could move. But beyond that—and this *really* disturbed him—he could not identify it.

Some biological process had begun and finding its gait had gone wild, speeding up, distorting, spraying out limbs and bones and skin and eyes at a maddening pace. The ruin in the box did not look even remotely human. But there were odd shapes, strange bones that looked too human to be in the mass.

David was an expert in biology and chemistry, and this thing defied his knowledge.

It could not be real.

It was real.

Behind the thick gloves and claustrophobic mask, David

took two steps towards the thing, and it felt like he was at the bottom of a pool, bobbing along, floating.

The box was Plexiglas, and looked specifically made for the thing, and yet somehow still was too small. Squeezed in the space, skin butting up against the edges, flattened, the thing's weird sides worked in frightened respiration. An oversize polygonal box of clear plastic built to keep biological field samples shoved full of a mess of human-like parts: eyes, limbs, mottled and sickly skin, breathing, moving.

On the box in gold foil was the word опасность.

He stumbled from the room.

THE DOOR SLAMMED AND he almost fell taking off the mask. Carver or someone like him entered the room.

"What...is it?" David asked, trying to find his breath.

"We were hoping you might know that."

"Really?"

David laughed and sat down hard, covering his face. The floor creaked as he shifted his body. He focused on his hands and his knees. He looked straight ahead, past them, and felt the world blur. He hovered there, in the space between action and thought, and heard a deep humming that shook his mind.

"Doctor?" Carver said.

"Doctor?"

"I'M DONE HERE," DAVID said, the fear a wavering line through his voice. He stood, briskly, wiping his pants, looking around for an exit. He had no idea what it was, only that it was wrong, and that following something this wrong was a quick route to becoming expendable.

"You are not," Carver said. It was only then that David realized how tall, how strong the man looked. Only when Carver moved in front of the door in one step could David see his predicament.

Carver's face held its half-smile. "What you *are* is a foreign national living in America at the whim of the government. What you *are* is a Georgian, *Davit,* who became a Frenchman, who became a Canadian, and who attended communist meetings in Montreal and before that, in Paris during the war. What you *are* is whatever I want you to be."

David looked up, blinking, eyes stinging, thinking of Camille.

Carver said, "I want you to be a loyal and valuable science asset assisting your adopted government."

David's mind closed in on itself in a loop. Desperate to please, incapable of doing so.

"I can't—I don't. You. I don't even know where you found—it."

Carver looked at him, blank. A mannequin with a perfectly carved, robotic face. The half-smile never left his features. Nothing moved, but David felt he could hear parts clicking away inside the black box of Carver's head.

"Stay here," Carver said, finally, when all the sums had been totaled.

Δ

THE FILE WAS THICK and most of it redacted. Where the real things happened were instead squiggly, thick, black lines. The operation name was SIC SEMPER TYRANNIS. An emerald stamp marked the cover. The first location listed was NOVOSI-BIRSK USSR.

He read.

ONE MONTH BEFORE, AMERICAN operatives had crossed into a remote location in the U.S.S.R. on a mission to destroy a facility run by a former Nazi scientist named Grünwald, whose work was known to the operation leads. In this covert engagement Soviets and Americans had been killed. Grünwald was assassinated and the facility burned to the ground. Overall, the Americans deemed it a victory.

But the Americans came back with something when they were not expected to come back at all.

It was, in the record, described as a "REDMAN sample." A portion of human tissue, in the Plexiglas box, kept in a small pool of nutrient. It had been measured upon return at 3 oz. It was the box David had seen in the room, but the description of what was inside it did not match. At all. The box now contained maybe twenty pounds of...it.

"Subject's records referenced the works of DR. LAKE, AL-FRED. References to POINT ZERO and GERMAN FACILI-TIES were also...."

"Soviet submarine activity at map coordinates 73°03′S 13°25′W, independently confirmed and tracked by...."

"REDMAN moved to the facility on JAN 2/53. FEB 2/53...."

"Material storage proved troublesome...."

David looked up at Carver and said, carefully, "What do you want me to do?"

IT WAS BIGGER.

He found himself back in the room, in full gear. The box it was in had split in his absence, the edges popped open, and the thing was half spilled out on the floor.

David got to work.

It took all he was to take a fluid sample with the kit, and he shouted in his mask when the thing jumped as he put the needle in it. Something clear but red and syrupy, like human blood run thin, came out. He filled three test tubes and turned back to it.

Now that it was halfway out of the box, he could see it was parts of a person, grown crazily, thrown together, somehow alive. It never resolved its shape into anything; it always remained a mess of parts. It looked like the wasted limbs of some crippled child slammed around a larger mass of meat, breathing, shaking, pulsing.

When he returned for a skin scraping, he saw a mouth, moving. In it, baby teeth. They clicked and moved and spit dribbled from the hole.

He leaned in. It was...talking.

"Damekhmarot," it wheezed.

He thought of his father and mother, and his dead sister, and heard them laughing and singing in Georgian, the language of his youth.

Help me, the thing had said.

"*Bodishi,*" he whispered back, his lips numb. *I'm sorry.*

An amber eye fixed on him from the mass, blinking and squinting, focusing. Marking him. He stared back, trapped in its gaze.

When his eyes felt they could get no larger, he fumbled for the kit and closed it, and stepped out of the room.

"I HAVE THEM, I have them," David said, pulling off the mask. He handed Carver the sample box.

Carver put the box aside in a manner indicating it was unimportant.

"You can talk to it?"

"What?"

"You understand it?"

"Ye—"

That's when the world shook.

CARVER NEVER HESITATED. STILL he was not fast enough. He saw Carver produce a silver pistol like a magic trick and then saw only the floor. Dust dropped in a wave as the sound of something like a truck being dropped on the house erupted again and again.

When he rose to his knees he saw Carver already off the ground, lifted, dangling from ropy limbs that had pierced the wall, some still wrapped in plastic. The bulb on the ceiling rocked and rocked, casting crazy shadows all over the room. It looked like a pink spider with ten-foot limbs, crawling through a rough hole in the wall.

It screamed like a wind tunnel shot through a human vocal tract. The thing in the box was bigger now—it had grown again—and seemed to be all limbs. The flesh moved and melted and resolved itself again, becoming what it needed as needed.

Two thin limbs settled on Carver's neck and thickened there for a second. David heard Carver's muffled screams become a crunching, retching sound.

Carver's head popped off like champagne cork and David screamed like a child, pulling himself back into a corner, all rational thought gone. The blood spray seemed eternal. Shooting up seven feet to coat the ceiling, the light, the wall, until it finally subsided.

David distantly registered the hollow thud of Carver's head hitting the wood floor.

The thing fell on Carver's corpse, stemming the spray of blood, and began to feed.

Somewhere, a radio squawked.

David disappeared inside himself awhile.

SOME TIME LATER—HE DIDN'T know how long—after a huge crash and distant screams, and an explosion and the sound of a machine gun, and a long silence, David heard footsteps.

He opened his eyes.

The man looked normal enough, for the most part. Young. He wore a suit too large for him, and his hair was long and black and unkempt. His shoes too big. Someone else's shoes. His face was spattered in blood which he had attempted to clean off.

"Me ar avnebs t'k'ven," the man said, and offered a hand. *I will not hurt you.*

He seemed familiar. Someone from a movie or a newsreel or the papers. David's mind raced and rose and fell from coherence in fits and starts.

He took the hand. It felt human enough.

"K'art'veli khar?" Are you Georgian?

"Diakh," David said, finally. *Yes.*

"T'k'ven khart' patimari?" You are a prisoner?

"Diakh, diakh," David said.

"Turizmi," the ragged man said, and gestured to the hole in the wall to the outside.

David left.

AT DAWN DAVID FOUND the diner. He had been walking for a time; he had no idea how long. He had abandoned the F-1 suit and had wandered past the ruins of the limousine and the remains of a monstrous firefight. The agents were dead but there was little left of them to be found, just blood and bullet holes.

As he walked, after the first mile, he realized there was no one coming. He kept walking.

The diner was active despite the early hour. David entered just as the sun crested the horizon, filling the world with a blue-white light.

He fumbled for his wallet and found money there. He looked around and for a moment considered weeping and falling to the ground. Instead, he ordered a coffee.

He drank in silence for a long time, ignoring looks from the truckers. He was out of place, a suit-and-tie man in the boonies, drinking coffee, staring, shaken.

Finally, when he could hear his own thoughts again, he found a phone and rang Camille.

"HI, HONEY," SHE SAID, sleep in her voice.

"Camille, Cami..." he said, almost crying, voice cracking.

"Is this about Stalin?" Camille asked, half-yawning, voice far away down the line.

"What? What did you say?"

"Did you get called away because Stalin is dead? It's all over the news. He's dead, in Russia."

David's mind repeated one word, over and over again.

REDMAN.

Punching
(1964)

THE VEGA CRAWLS UP the drive to the house in the dark, and the driver, Henry Briggs, leans forward over the wheel to consider the house as he cruises past it. He pulls in next to the other cars—a Mercedes, a Jaguar, a Rolls—and gets out. In the row of darkened cars his Vega looks out of place. It's even parked unevenly, while the others are in a perfect row. He tries to make a joke out of this in his mind, but finds with some bitterness that he can't.

He stops once, on his way from the cars, and finds himself looking on a perfect, seamless, manicured lawn which stretches out into a dark copse of trees. He wishes he didn't feel impressed, but he does. The house has changed, and in that change has only become better than it was.

Briggs is a big, older man. Someone who once might have been a boxer. His features look like they had been set to drift by one too many hard punches. But the eyes above his ruined nose are small and clever. He's in a suit, the one he wears to work on Wednesdays, that looks two steps too low for this social stratum. He looks as uncomfortable as he is. He straightens his tie and crosses the drive to the house.

It's a big Newport house. Bleached wood, big windows, dozens of rooms, manicured garden, crushed gravel drive. It is as far from the place that Briggs lives, or exists, as is possible.

It is the end of summer, 1964.

Δ

HE OPENS THE DOOR to the sound of a hundred voices. The house is full of people, all his age, walking, talking, eating, drinking. A black man sits at a Baby Grand piano playing music twenty years out of date.

A paper banner hangs over the gable windows in the back, covering the edge of the high ceiling. It reads "WELCOME CLASS OF '44".

Briggs walks to the bar and orders a double gin and tonic, and the bartender, sensing an out-of-place soul, pours generously. Briggs stands at the bar, over the bar, really, watching the crowd, sipping the drink.

By 1944 it was over. The year 1943 was when his life was ruined, and that thought, he thinks, is just as useless as any other, even though it is true. He drinks the drink.

BRIGGS HAS KILLED MANY people. He lost count by 1944. By 1944, when he was in Italy, it was already too late, and he hasn't really tried to puzzle it out since then. The last killing was two weeks ago. A woman who was twenty-six years old by her passport. He doesn't feel bad about it.

Something was in her, using her, something from outside. He put a bullet through her face and she launched herself at him, struggling and cackling black laughter while ooze that looked like butter gone over poured out of the hole through her head. She wrestled like she was twice her size. She was so strong Briggs barely had time to pin her arms down with his legs and bludgeon her—it—to death with a heavy bronze lamp.

Then he burned the building to the ground.

Killing wasn't all that bad when you learned what was really going on. Death was a rule of the world, everyone knew that. It was how systems renewed themselves. It was beautiful, in a way. Killing these other things, though — these other things didn't die on their own. Something in reality had slipped a spoke and they ran on and on. It was up to the group to punch their ticket. He had done many such things for the group since 1943. Since any semblance of normal life had ended.

No one knew what the things were, really. He had heard some in the group go on and on about Elder Ones and cycles and elliptical orbits of dead stars that ruined the world every 900 million years. He'd seen reports on time gates and ray guns and things that, if they slipped past the net the group had raised, could destabilize the whole world.

Once, he saw something huge and gelatinous and covered in a thousand eyes crawl up from a hand-carved pit in Peru, struggle over the ledge, and consume a tied-up goat with the avidity of a spider feeding on a fly.

There were worse things.

WHEN HE SEES PETE Martin, his mind drifts back. He can't help it. He's like a goddamn school girl. Martin, his friend. The man he most admired. The guy he had followed around like an idiot.

The man who introduced him to Commander Cook.

Well, indirectly.

Martin looks like what he is. Rich. He drifts through the

crowd as if on rollers, a drink filled near to spilling in one large, soft hand. Martin is tall and thin and regal. His face has dark rings under the eyes, but they almost look like makeup. This is a man who would have to puzzle out how, exactly, to use a shovel. To drive a car. To do anything. Things were, are, done for him.

It has always been that way. These were the rules Briggs grew up with. The rich were the rich, the poor were the poor. When a crossover occurred, it was due to luck, skill, or some indefinable quality.

Briggs had all three.

When he was eighteen years old, he had been stupid and naive and young enough to believe that made him special.

AFTER 1941, HARVARD WAS a ghost ship. Classes were shells of what they once had been. Hallways abandoned. Dorms silent. But Briggs was eager. He had worked delivering ice for nine summers to get here. He had cracked the books and had spun up his gift with languages into something valuable. People had noticed.

He didn't look the sort that could translate Bing Crosby into Greek, but he was. His father had it, he had it. He could hear something once and repeat it perfectly. His dad called it the magic ear. But Briggs had something more than that catgut salesman ever had—he had a hunger for something more than a two-room walkup in Mercator. He was more than a man who smiled and looked down when someone yelled at him over a ten cent shortage. He was a person.

He wanted to be important.

The boxing helped. The college needed boxers. Or at least they had in September 1941, the year he started in Linguistics. He never even laced up, not once, for the school; there was no one to box. Didn't matter. He didn't like fighting, he was just good at it, and only then because of his size and reach. There was no real skill he could discern in beating another man senseless.

The school was abandoned. The war had siphoned nearly everyone away. Those who remained were scrawny, sickly, or had something obviously wrong with their anatomy.

Briggs and Martin stood out. Briggs, of course, was in his prime. Huge and imposing and dangerous-looking. Martin looked normal for Harvard. Young and rich and content, with a Cheshire smile on his face all the time like he was in on the big secret.

No one had called Briggs up. There was no letter, no draft notice, and he would be damned if he would volunteer after what he did to get here. If they came for him, that was one thing. If not, he'd get his damn degree. He could give a fuck about the war. He had his own war.

It had been that way since he returned to class from the 1941 Christmas break. The break was dire. Cousins and uncles and friends and others talking about joining up. About reporting in. About turning up for the Navy, because that was the safest, or the Army, because it would all be over before it even started, or the Army Air Corps because, hell, then you got to fly. Even then, before Guadalcanal, no one wanted to join the Marines.

Briggs had nodded and smiled and excused himself, and when the time came he slunk back to Harvard and kept to his books and kept his head down and tried not to talk to anyone outside the rarified life of languages. He half expected a letter any day, a plain letter typed by some fat woman in an office in Washington, calling him to line up and be shot.

It never came. Instead, one day he looked up in Hieratic and Pre-Hieratic and saw Martin sitting there in a row of empty seats, watching him. Peter Martin. Smiling.

MARTIN WAS PART OF the club. If you had to ask which club, you would never know. The two struck up an unlikely friendship over the fall of 1942, back before Briggs knew what Martin was really thinking. Briggs, for his part, didn't care.

He simply wanted in the club, so of course he never spoke about it. The club made men. It manufactured leaders, presidents, generals. It created greatness from nothing and flung it out into the world.

"You can't understand what it's like in Newport," Martin would say over deviled eggs and drinks at the Box, and Briggs knew he was right and hated that feeling. He couldn't know what it was like to be secure in his own skin, to be waited on, to feel the pull of others as they desperately tried to get your attention.

Briggs believed Martin saw him as a project, as a possible future member of the club, which, like the university, had emptied. It still held its rites, but with only a fraction of the membership. No one had been punched—given entry to the club—

since the war started. There were rumblings that this famine of membership would not last.

Briggs made Martin his project. The lonely rich kid would become his friend. And in time, it happened. For reasons which would become clear later.

"You're right, I can't understand it. So show me," Briggs said. That summer, Martin did.

PETER'S FATHER WAS EDGAR Martin, an ex-Navy man who had inherited something terribly important, although no indication of it could be detected in their house on Nantucket.

The old man looked like someone had smashed his head down between his shoulder blades with a shovel at some distant point in the past. When he turned to face someone, his whole body swiveled at the waist. His eyes were large and liquid behind thick glasses held with solder in a gaudy gold-wired frame. It was his only real point of extravagance, besides his family.

Even in the summer of 1942 on the island, Mr. Martin wore the outfit of a wealthy bookkeeper, with a full wool waistcoat and all. He had warmed to Henry Briggs after bombarding him with a bevy of questions which seemed designed to embarrass or confuse him. They had done neither. Briggs had answered honestly while Peter looked on with amusement, perched on the edge of an ancient, weather-wrecked wood chair in chinos and sandals.

The test, whatever it was, had been passed. Edgar Martin now called him Henry, and was candid with him in a way he never seemed to be with his own son. Briggs was certain he was getting somewhere.

Still, he had no idea where.

The summer dragged on and as the world burned, Henry read, slept, ate and slowly changed color, plotting to find his place in a future where people would look to him and not away.

THE NIGHT IN AUGUST when he ran into Edgar Martin in the rambling house was the first indication that he should have been paying more attention.

"You seem like a good boy, Henry, and I don't want you to take this the wrong way," Edgar said, holding a glass of milk beaded with moisture, looking out a window on a black beach.

"Sir?" Henry said, pulling the robe tighter.

"Martin hasn't tried—hasn't done anything strange? That you would think strange?"

The question fell on the ground and silence followed it.

"No," Briggs finally replied, though he had no idea what they were talking about.

"Good. Good. I think you might be a good influence on him. Try and keep him out of trouble."

Briggs went back upstairs and didn't think about that conversation again until after it all fell apart.

SOMEONE IS TALKING ABOUT LBJ again, and Briggs looks up from his third glass to find Martin staring at him, just as they had met, eye-to-eye, for the first time in 1941. Briggs widens his smirk into a smile, one that feels completely fake, and waves. Martin excuses himself from the beautiful woman who is speaking at him and walks over.

"Henry! How the heck are you, man?" Martin says, smiling, hand extended.

Briggs stands from the stool, wipes his right hand on his trousers, grabs what seems to be a handkerchief from his jacket with his other hand and turns. He shakes hands with Martin and glances around the room. No one sees the .38.

The first bullet catches Martin in the cheek, leaving a pockmark the size of a cigarette burn, and the smile—that contented smile—hardens into a thin-lipped grimace as the powder-flash burns his face. Something red, wet and gelatinous launches itself from the back of Martin's head, landing on the ground like a dishful of water flung out the back door.

Martin falls forward, collapsing in a heap like a marionette with its strings clipped, folding in an unnatural position. Briggs empties the gun into Martin's slumped body, four more rounds at close range in his neck and back.

Martin bounces on the ground with each hit, convulsing. Then he slowly slides to the right and rolls over, covered in black and red viscera and blood. His blue eyes are tinged with yellow. Peter Martin, whatever was Peter Martin, is gone.

When Briggs looks up, his ears ringing, the room is empty, like a magic trick. He sits back down and sips ice water.

IN 1943, BRIGGS FELT he was close. They had skirted the basics of the club; how one was punched, how one might be admitted. Martin talked about it now, though never by name. He talked and talked about how Henry might fit in, how others like him had gained membership before. He told stories of where they ended up, the glorious achievements of those who were punched.

Henry was so excited, he didn't even pull away when Martin kissed him, suddenly, for the first time in the darkened hallway at Widener Library.

From there things moved fast.

Henry Briggs hadn't been certain of the limits of what he might do to escape his old life. The spring and summer of 1943 proved that if there were any limits, sleeping with Peter Martin was not one of them. He never considered whether or not it was something he really wanted. At the time, it just seemed to happen.

IT FAILED AS YOU might imagine, suddenly. At the end the affair tumbled in slow motion, like a car wreck played back at 1/8 speed. Bodies, glass and metal tumbling, some crushed, some thrown free.

When Henry staggered to his feet again, he had been dismissed from Harvard. Peter disappeared into the monied escapes his family had prepared for him. Henry's hopes for school, for the group, vanished like a fog. He was left a survivor of the wreck of his life, wandering.

It was three months later, and he was hauling ice again, when Edgar Martin's car pulled up. When the door opened for Briggs, he got in without a word being exchanged.

Δ

"MY SON IS ILL," Edgar said. "We have known this for a long time."

Henry said nothing.

"I would appreciate if nothing was said of this. And you, Henry, I have kept my eye out for you, too."

Henry looked up.

"There is a man who has been watching you, a man who has interest in the languages you know. A man I once worked with. A man from the government." Edgar considered the buildings as they rolled past. "Would you like to meet him?"

Henry said nothing.

They kept driving.

Commander Cook sat in the darkened library of an old house, waiting outside town with a fat folder full of horrors to snap Henry out of his life forever.

AND NOW HE IS here, in 1964, being shouted at through a bull-horn by police.

Henry Briggs snaps the revolver open, dumps the shells, and reloads with blunt fingers. One round, two rounds, three rounds, four. He has no idea what might happen when he closes the cylinder. But it strikes him now, the humor of it.

The cylinder clicks shut. He brings the gun up.

He pictures the bullet entering his head and going on with his life as if nothing has happened. Of his smile widening and the horrors within him let loose on the world, like the woman, like the darkness at the edges of science. The blackness in him which people like Peter brought out, mocked, made happen. The feelings in him which were not right. The work he had wrought because of them.

He pictures an end, and finds a comfort there.

Everyone, everywhere dies. If you're good and real, and not from outside the world, you eventually end. And in that ending is a finality that makes Henry Briggs feel somber and happy and warm. It is the feeling he has been seeking his entire life. The feeling of certainty.

The revolver tastes like smoke, and then like nothing at all.

The Secrets No One Knows
(1968)

THE ROOM WAS COMMON. Clean but not overtly so. Empty except for the classic wood desk and the man behind it. If you saw it, it would put you in mind of being called up to the teacher after class, the same clock buzzing on the wall like a locust, the same feeling of the strange empty classroom. Tic tac toe tile floor of scuffed linoleum, Styrofoam gridded ceilings covering a patchwork of pipes and wires that wound through the dark, connecting strange systems no one has touched in ages, moving fluids, energies.

The room exhibited a strange tense frenetic energy, like the air itself was vibrating at speed. Staying there too long, one would find themselves watching the clock endlessly spin, the click of the seconds hand popping time, uniform but somehow skewed.

Staring at the empty green wall, following the one cord from the one plug in the wall to the one lamp on the desk, the wire carefully stapled to the rubber liner of the wall, the seconds, minutes, hours piling up on your shoulders like a transparent humming weight—one was often found forgetting things. In the room the ways of the everyday world seemed far away and empty, like a dream recounted to you by a friend. Words were hard to come by and rarely needed, and often one could be found reciting a single word over and over, playing with it like one might play with a shiny marble.

The room dulled you like an eraser, grinding the clear mind to dust in its endless blandness. The buzzing clock and boxed-perspective floor and ceiling drew your gaze to the flat green rectangles of the cinderblock walls, pulling your will from your sockets with a dull force, leaving you slack-jawed and devoid of feeling.

Those who worked there did little. They did not study papers, write or otherwise use any of their faculties in a productive manner. Instead, the door to the left was observed, as was the door to the right. The only two entrances or exits from the room. This room was an airlock for secrets. Those entering from the right and exiting to the left were asked a single question.

Those coming from the left and exiting to the right were asked to provide proper documentation, sign in on the single dull clipboard with the same old beaten and crushed taped ball-point, and surrender their weapons, which were locked in a strong-box in the desk.

Everyone came and went from the left, implying that the room to the right was singular, or a series of rooms with no exit. Those who worked in the green room never saw what went on past the right door. Rumors abounded. Medical equipment and doctors were the most common transients through it. Some signed in with trembling hands, followed by obvious old pros, smiling the smile of the Mona Lisa, a smile like a fortune cookie. Fragile and ready to be broken open with a word or gesture.

When the door opened to the right, a slight tugging on

the inner ear and eyes could be felt, as if the air from the green room was being sucked inward. When the door shut with its same mechanical click, the suction on the rubber bib at the base of it was audible. Like the sound of a closing refrigerator door as the vacuum restores itself.

Once there was screaming from past the right door. Explicit orders kept the worker in the green room from passing that threshold. The man on duty that day preformed his job perfectly, hesitating only once, as the hollow report of a single gunshot echoed back through the seal of the door. The man did not cross the threshold, but instead stood at the door, a huge .45 in his hand loaded and cocked. The body was removed by three disheveled doctors in bloody coats. Four had signed in that day.

Usually the question yielded base responses, a simple shaking of the head no, a "nope," "nothing" or "not today" being the runners up in that order (there was little else to do but count responses). Sometimes simple phrases were repeated by strangely pale doctors, looking as if the corpse they were Y-stitching sat up one day and asked about the weather or who won the Yankees game the day before.

On the day of the screaming and the gunshot, the last doctor out answered the question, hands trembling as he untied his smock.

"Did it say anything today?" the question went.

"Cthulhu...R'lyeh...Dagon...." the bloodied doctor responded. Quickly signing out, rushing to the left door into the complex at Los Alamos, back to the real world of secrets about bombs, and planes, and missiles.

"Cthulhu," the man behind the desk repeated to no one at all as the minutes clicked by.

Somehow he thought that word sounded familiar.

Coming Home
(1970)

THE WORLD HAD CONSPIRED against him again. The vistas and places he had walked as a child were gone, replaced by boxes, cement and garbage.

McDonalds restaurants crawled across the landscape and strip malls and car dealerships and signs. He thought of the jungle, and strangely found that he missed it. At least it was alive, that smell, not like the city. Not like here where the city had heaved itself out into the open fields at the edge of everything.

This place, the stop, stunk of old cigarettes and piss and alcohol, empty and artificial things that washed out the real smells.

It was May 1, 1970, and his hands were not shaking, so it was a good day. Each day he marked the calendar on the wall at the Pentagon with an X—each day his hands did not shake—that was a good day.

There had been a lot of X's lately. He was doing well, but he had begun to think about the boy again, and the temple, and the—

He dropped the thought like something hot, pulling away internally, closing his eyes.

It was replaced with an image of his daughter skating on Silver Lake when she was six, the winter of 1967. The ghost cut lazy arcs on the black ice, spinning with a grace and consistency never mastered in real life.

He knew it was an illusion. He didn't care. Anything was better than the alternative.

He waited on the bus stop along with everyone else, the folded leather valise at his feet. He was a soldier. He stood ramrod straight in his uniform without turning his head. Others shuffled and fidgeted. He did neither, watching the air ahead of him instead, his thin face carefully set in a bland expression of order.

When the bus came, he waited for the others to board, picked up the valise, and climbed aboard last.

In the valise was a shotgun he had sawn down in his empty garage while Gail and the kids were at the super market. He had smiled then. He had grinned like a mad dog, shaking and laughing and wiping sweat from his face, working his way through the barrel, the saw shrieking in time with his arm.

When the barrel dropped away and clanked to the cement, he shouted with joy, laughing until he was doubled over in pain and the world swam before him with blotches of blooming color.

He nearly blacked out from the laughter.

That had been during a span of empty calendar days. White rectangles infinite in their blankness, echoing their indifference towards him, leaping off the wall, eating the room, the Pentagon, the world, drowning his mind in the nothing. Still, it was best not to invoke the calendar. Only when it was needed would he think about it. A totem to ward off the worst of the blankness. The calendar was something dangerous to be worshipped.

Only shaking or laughing or weeping could make the feelings go, and sometimes not even then. The valise was insurance, and he took it everywhere. If the world opened beneath him, he would save those around him first, if he could, and only then save himself.

Lieutenant Arvin Tipler was his name, and if anyone had asked he would have said yes, he had been in the shit.

At the Pentagon in 1970, no one asked. When he entered through the officer's entrance, no one stopped him and no one searched him. No one saw him.

If that were true, if he were invisible in the Pentagon, was he still real? He didn't know. He really didn't know anymore. Sometimes he hoped he wasn't. Sometimes he prayed that he was.

Even he had to admit, the bus ride was convincing. It shook just like a real bus, filled with the smell of Juicy Fruit gum and crushed cigarettes. Lepus had smelled like that, all the time somehow, even in the jungle.

Fuck you, Tipler. Eye my pack again and your head will look like a fucking canoe.

Arvin Tipler cut the memory off and it dropped into the black where it vanished obediently. Maybe today was going to be a good day. He wasn't certain anymore.

He looked across on the bus and found himself face-to-face with a Puerto Rican boy, maybe nine, maybe ten, watching him with liquid eyes. The boy had a look of amusement on his face. He was untouchable, invincible next to his mother, a fat thing squatting like a toad wrapped a sun dress.

The boy popped gum in his mouth and grinned wider.

For a brief moment Tipler recalled the other child, some local from Cambodia, cut open and hung like a pig in a butcher shop window. Guts gone, dangling in the rain from a dongtchem tree, mouth wide from gravity, eyes hollowed out of life.

Tipler considered this and lost grip on the thoughts.

IT WAS WAR. IT was in the war. His war. His generation's war. It wasn't like anything else. It wasn't like the Beach at Normandy, or MacArthur at Inchon. It was like dying by degrees. It was rotting in a sweltering heat with no direction and mud in your eyes and in your boots and in your body. It was being eaten alive by time with no hope of respite. It was like nothing else he had ever felt. It was the opposite of victory, it was the opposite of all that was good, it was the opposite of the resurrection.

Every success was hollow and fleeting and every failure crushing and complete. No one knew why. No one could see. Still, it went on and on.

From the war, from his war, escape and goodness and progress looked like what they were: nonsense words. This was the place where those words had stopped meaning something. A break in a sentence that led to a string of gibberish words like *hope* and *happiness* and *life* and *order*.

In this war, you pointed your guns away from the people you knew and into expanses of jungle which could, and did, eat anything: tanks, aircraft, human beings. You were surrounded on all fronts by enemies. Besides those you were here to crush (who were phantoms), there was the jungle, a maw of green which was infinite and writhing and ever advancing.

An emptiness of consumption crawled across the face of the war like another, more fundamental conflict, Man vs. Nature or Time vs. Order. It was absolute, so much so that the war was the backdrop. When you learned to look at it properly.

The men you hunted in their pajamas, which were so much more efficient and suited for the green than any gear the American soldier wore, drifted in and out of the jungle like they could swim in it. The jungle was their mother, their ally, their birthplace and their prize, to be won when the last tired American left this war. They all knew it was coming. Everyone. No American thought to win anymore.

The war had become an embarrassing ritual, drawn in blood and bone, that two foes were forced to enact, when it was clear to all who had won. It was a PR stunt with a body count.

They stumbled, they ate, they shat in the mud and the rain and waited. They waited to go. For their turn to be done.

And this all happened to Tipler before the temple, before the briefing and Lepus and Poe and then the thing, the things he didn't like to think about.

Before he heard them: the voices that knew his secrets.

HE FOUND HIMSELF BACK on the bus, looking at the child. Tipler summoned everything he could and smiled.

"How old are you?" Tipler heard himself ask the boy.

"How old are you?" the mother-thing said to the boy.

"Six years old," the boy said, eyes on the ground. He stood, swaying, and shot his arms in the air to grab for a dangling handhold. For a moment, Tipler saw the dead Cambodian boy in his place, matching his pose, upside down.

Tipler felt the milk and toast and peach in his stomach spin.

"How wonderful," Tipler heard himself say. His voice was thick.

In the infinite world of other choices, Tipler erased them with a shotgun blast, or a slug blew his head into the chrome of the ceiling, or he burned his home to the ground surrounded by the corpses of his family, or he lit himself up with gasoline or ignited a bundle of dynamite in a Dunkin Donuts or erased his head in the middle of a school yard, or a thousand other things.

In these other worlds, Tipler drew a loop within himself and pinched his existence off, leaving a police report and the mystery of the silent dead.

He knew that was a cowardly escape. It was too early. Being a hero meant knowing the right moment to die.

When nothing was left, these times reflected in on themselves, humming back to the last of a billion Tiplers, somehow skirting his own oblivion. Riding a wave of ruin to some ultimate prize — the realization of just why, of all who could have seen and survived, he had witnessed the opening of a gap through this world.

Inside had been the clockwork horror of the parts of reality that clicked and moved and ate and shat the debris of time and space.

What did that mean? What did that make him? What did that make the world?

No answer came while the boy grinned to himself, assured in his own importance. Only the thrumming behind the eyes, and the knowledge of the shotgun in his bag, and the possibility of escape kept Tipler from screaming.

Instead of killing them all, and himself, Tipler went to work. Again.

THE PENTAGON WAS A derelict library that went on and on and on and on. Doors and windows and hallways and stairwells and elevators and machines, pumping in the dark. It smelled of old food, rotting plasterboard, waterlogged asbestos, and time.

Ideas churned through these halls, ending most often with far-flung death, destruction and misery. Human industry at its purest form was conducted here, in a great pentagonal eye which glanced lazily across the world. When it found what it was looking for, it focused the might of a nation and hammered it to ruin.

Tipler was at home in the Pentagon. This was not some grand architecture, only box upon box of limited perspectives that collided with walls, or broken windows that looked on dead alcoves where yellow grass sat, starved for light.

It was built in haste at the height of the worst conflict the world had yet known (other, bigger ones were coming, he was certain). But it had not been built for the ages.

It had simply been built.

Instead of marble there was granite, in place of pillars

were crossbeams, in place of plaster were asbestos tiles. It was temporary. It was a hack job, a speedy job, but an amazing one nonetheless.

It was a well worn, well known, endlessly sinking ship, falling into ruin in a thousand ways every day. The occupants did their best to maintain it, but in a world of guerrilla conflicts and moon shots the budget was limited.

In a newsletter, he had read a story of the janitorial team discovering an abandoned series of steam tunnels unopened for perhaps twenty years, filled with a coven of rats. It was discovered because the droppings of the rats were so prolific they blocked a drain, causing an overflow of filth-filled water into a cafeteria. After it was drained, a janitor in a hazard suit armed with a .22 pistol and gas mask had waded into the tunnels.

He was there for a long time.

The newsletter gave the enemy kill count: 67 rats, no Pentagon casualties. They even named the operation MOUSE TRAP.

Such stories were common. The building encompassed seven million square feet, and not all of that was recorded on the plans.

Tipler wouldn't be surprised if there were a hundred such rats' nests, a thousand, a million dark rooms hidden in the endless expanse of boxes, in the dark. They would all be found, he knew, and unlocked in time.

Tipler's office was one such cube. A stapler, an electric typewriter, a steel desk, a ticking electric clock and a flickering fluorescent light which made living things appear wax-like and empty, showing their reality.

On the wall, a calendar.

The calendar.

HE HAD LONG SINCE begun to regard the calendar as magic. Like the equipment on the desk it predated him. At first the calendar seemed to hang unassumingly on the wall. Then the day came when he flipped it open. He had done it on a lark to look at the image on the month: an eagle pulling a goggling fish from the mirror-like surface of water.

When he touched it for the first time, did he feel its power? Did he know?

Inside the calendar, he found a sea of Xs. Days stretching back to the 1st of the year marked with a red X in marker by some steady, now absent hand.

The last X ended two weeks before Tipler found himself manning the desk. In the beginning that had seemed inconsequential. Trivial.

He had paperwork, but the image of the white boxes and red Xs preyed on his mind, entering his thoughts, distracting him, draining him.

On the sixth day he realized a large portion of his time was consumed thinking about the calendar. Later he found himself simply staring at it, not working. The level of control necessary to keep from going to the calendar, from opening it, was immense.

Nothing in his life, not even the things he didn't like to think about, could match it. It was a perfect obsession. Complete.

He sat there for the better part of his ninth day staring at the calendar before finally deciding to mark the days between the end of the previous Xs and the beginning of his time here, to make the streak unbroken. To fix it.

But only after he had done this did he realize his mistake. He had marked those days in a fury of scribbled black ink. Black.

Black, not red.

His Xs were similar but not the same.

Wrong. Wrong.

He fled for the day, spilling down the half-steps of a long hallway, his feet skittering in a stuttering near-fall and recovering at a run towards a red sign marked EXIT.

Today, Tipler lifted the black pen and carefully drew the first slash of an X on the date, and then, struggling, finished it. He lay back in his chair, which squeaked a protest, and let out a rush of air, sweating, exhausted.

He loosened his tie, and pushed the papers away from in front of him, sliding them out, scattering them.

He placed his head on the cool steel of the table and slept. No dreams.

AT HOME, HIS DAUGHTER sat on the steps.

Tipler sat on the stoop and watched her in silence as she painted, spun yarn around popsicle sticks, and then painted again. She was small, frail, with a large head and thick glasses and braided brown hair and a barrette with a kitten on one side.

She had always been quiet. A quiet baby, attentive, watching. Here she was focused, ignoring the world around her. Mind fixed on the task in front of her; there was nothing else.

Such focus. Such a pointless little thing.

In the front yard the trees shed brown and red leaves. Inside the house, he heard his wife slam a door. Water seeped into his pants and made him cold, but it was only a body, it was only an ever-dying thing. Tipler looked up into the sky and saw a pale white splotch in the sky.

His daughter looked up with him. Meat strung to sinew across bone. A tiny, crawling thing under the light of a sun which drove the world like a giant ox. Spinning, breeding, dying, burning. Then, as if she could see his thoughts:

"Daddy, what will happen when the sun dies?"

Tipler looked back.

"Nothing will happen. There will be nothing left to happen. No one left to do it."

She seemed to think about this for a long time, and then began working on her project again, a frown on her face.

"All the people will be gone?" she finally said.

"Yes," Tipler said.

"Where will they be?" She was still looking for a way out.

"Dead. The Earth. Everything, everywhere will be dead."

"Does that make you sad, daddy?"

"No." And he was proud that he didn't have to think about it.

She stood and carefully lifted the paint bottle with a brush sticking out of it, placing it in the crook of her arm, and held the cross-thing out from her shirt, so she wouldn't get wet paint on it.

"Me either, I guess."

She leaned down and kissed Tipler on the cheek and then went inside with a slam of the screen door.

Tipler sat on the porch until it was full dark, the light fading and fading, until a yellow line traced the horizon and was extinguished.

So many people would have to die. Die now, suddenly, or die in the future in terror.

He didn't know if he could kill them all.

THE KNOCK ON THE flimsy garage door came just as he was connecting the leads to the detonator. His fingers twitched and the wire touched the relay but produced no spark.

Tipler released the wire and it folded back, next to the stack of five sticks of dynamite he had fastened together with two layers of electrical tape. He pulled a sheet over the top of it. His hands did not shake.

His wife was at the door with a tray of food.

"We missed you at dinner."

He unlocked the chain and took the tray and placed it next to the sheet that covered the bomb. He corrected the tray on the table to be in line with the corner.

She did not enter after him.

He stepped back to the door.

Her face was caught between two expressions he could not place. Yearning and hate, maybe? Fear and wonder? Her face, so familiar, shone through his eyes but provided no light. She was empty, like all of them.

A blank. A puppet.

"We—I—my father—" she said, and looked down.

"Your father was in the war," he finished for her. She looked up. Took a step in.

"Yes. I—"

"It's not the same," he said.

"I wish—"

"I can't help you, Gail. We all have to help ourselves now."

He pushed the door shut and she retreated before its edge could touch her foot. Once it was shut, once he was out of sight, she began to speak again.

"My father didn't like to speak about it either, Alvin. He got over it. He cheered up. You can talk to me about it, if you want. Whatever you did. Whatever happened. I'm sure you have your reasons."

Tipler leaned his back against the door and it groaned under his weight. Behind his eyes he saw something like the trunk of an elephant, the size of a 747, writhing, moving, undulating on the top of a temple. At the end of the trunk was an eye the size of a klieg light, burning. The light created the world. Lepus was there, screaming at him, spitting in his face, but the noise, the passage of this thing through the world was too much, too loud. He saw only spittle, and glowing blue-white teeth, as Lepus' mouth worked.

"There are no such things as reasons," he said in the dark.

Δ

"—ASS UP!" LEPUS SHOOK him. Tipler, in the world before the nightmare—in the world of the Vietnam war he only thought was a nightmare—pulled down the poncho, which dripped warm water on his face.

Bugs and humidity and the stink of rotting things. Lepus stood above him with a red light shining in his face. Tipler sat up.

Poe sat on a rock nearby, young and certain. A hulk of a man in a pack with his back to them, his M-16 slung, a shotgun in his hands, watching the trees.

They were the scout party to locate bomb targets for a crisscross B-52 run. The other two hundred men were tromping in the dark somewhere a few clicks off in the trees.

Lepus brought the light in close to Tipler's face and waved it around. Tipler pushed it away.

"Fuck off," he groaned.

"Quit that shit," Poe said, quietly.

Tipler watched the giant man tense.

Poe stood, shucked his shotgun, and vanished into the trees.

Lepus didn't notice, but Tipler stumbled to his feet. Poe did not move that fast for no reason. Tipler's M-16 slipped in his hands as he jumped up and landed muzzle first in the mud, tangled in his poncho.

"God," Tipler groaned as Lepus laughed.

"Lepus!" Tipler began before the figure spilled from the jungle.

They both almost shot the boy. Eight maybe, flung from the dark of the trees like a rag-doll. The boy landed in the mud, hard, and didn't get up, but his chest worked. He said nothing.

Poe stepped out.

"Little fucker was spying," Poe said from the trees, and it took all Tipler was not to point the M-16 at him.

"No one else out there," Poe said and stepped into the clearing again.

The three men surrounded the boy, guns pointed down at the form in the mud, six days from death, from being hung like a gutted pig.

"Kid, you done fucked up," Lepus laughed, his voice like smoke.

FROM THE BENCH AT the bus stop, the building across the street seemed scrawled in fire when he opened his eyes. Lepus was gone.

Tipler considered the restaurant. A man and woman and two children entered it. A Sunday afternoon where the sun shone and light played through leaves and the world seemed to continue as it had once been.

Seemed.

No one could be that content. The world could not be so ordered. If the things he had seen in Cambodia were real, this was the illusion.

Dynamite might not work. He'd have to see them. See their reaction before the end. Make certain they were not like the things in the jungle. Make sure they were not masks.

He would know. He would see it in their eyes a moment before and if they were real, he would pull the trigger and free them before they were all consumed by the things in between.

The restaurant was small and had four exits. There would be some work before he could start, but he didn't mind. He loved work.

Plans were plans. Two hundred men raiding a temple behind officially sanctioned lines or killing a restaurant filled with innocents.

They were identical, when you came down to it.

Time was devouring it all, turning it inside out, feeding it down the maw into the innards which rendered the fat of the universe. We were motes in the intestines of something which spun and spat and willed the worlds. A dirge that turned the axis of time.

Or something.

He went back home to get ready. Still, something didn't feel right.

While Poe was out scouting, Lepus raped the child, in the dark. This sounded like grunting and crying and mumbling in a language Tipler didn't speak, along with heavy breathing.

Tipler kept his poncho over his head the whole time and pretended to sleep. He thought of his own children, and friendly fire, and the way he had seen Lepus kill others before this.

He counted to four hundred before it was over.

Δ

"MORE FOR YOU, LIEUTENANT," the major said, and dropped a pile of papers on his desk. The files were fat and new. The major looked like a cartoon. Mirror shades. Mustache. His name tag read TAFT. He had two cigarillos tucked in his pocket.

"Thank you, sir," Tipler said, and pulled the files towards him.

"You got those others done yet?" The major's eyes—reflections of Tipler—searched the cubicle.

Tipler shook his head. The other files were untouched in his desk. Soon he would have to find a new place to put them. His desk was filled with unprocessed paperwork. But the Pentagon had plenty of room. He might burn them in the incinerator he knew to be on the same floor, or carry them out and dump them in a garbage can on the street.

The calendar took up so much time.

"Okay. That's okay. We all need time to adjust. It's hard coming back."

"Thank you, sir," Tipler said. The major looked at him for a long time, and then stepped out, shutting the door.

Tipler could feel a silent, humming weight gathering in the air like a storm.

SUN-DAPPLED PEAKS POKING THROUGH a writhing canopy of green. Man-made mountains of stones, cut with faces, intertwined hands, giant eyes that watched the sky. Overgrown.

But occupied. Small, black-suited people moved boxes

through hastily cleared streets that were cut like passageways with chemicals and machete to allow access.

The temple had been there a long, long, time. Tipler and Poe spent most of the morning sighting and distancing various structures for the B's to erase, from high ground a mile and a half north, under a lip of tree to prevent reflections. Poe used the sights and whispered numbers, which Tipler scribbled into his map book. The kill box was three by eight, a strip space that was soon to be empty, vanished in a wave of 750-pound bombs.

Lepus had stayed with the kid but Tipler said nothing. Poe must know. It was Poe's problem. Tipler had enough going on. For example, what, exactly, were they doing in Cambodia, anyway?

"There he is," Poe said.

On the closest structure, a green-clad man, tiny, walked to the top tier, which had been cleared, and shielded his eyes to look to the sky. The sun was bloated and hot, rippling.

"Fuck, he's American," Tipler said.

"Not for long," Poe said, and put the scope in his pack.

"Who is he?" Tipler couldn't help the question.

"You're not cleared for that," Poe said, and stood. "All you need to know is this place has to be gone in two days." The group had its own protocols and rank did not always apply. It was an upside down world of clearances and need-to-knows.

"Why two days?"

"Solar eclipse," is all that Poe said, and Tipler let it go, drifting into the silence too long to ask anything else.

Δ

HE SIGNED THE LATE-ACCESS book and walked the empty halls of the Pentagon to his office. It was 0230 and he was tired, but he had put on his uniform at 0100 for this exact purpose.

He unlocked the door and stepped into the office. The light spilled in on the same darkened room, casting his shadow across the desk and wall. He placed the valise on the desk and rummaged through it.

He carefully removed one of his bombs. He pulled the paperwork from his desk, loaded it in the valise, and placed the bomb in the desk.

Before he left he crossed the next day off the calendar. It was after midnight, after all.

HE PICKED HIS DAUGHTER up from school at mid-day, in the family car, while skipping work. It was likely no one would notice either of these oddities. She was there, on the playground, going through the motions of childhood.

She stood on the slide and looked down and laughed and threw sand and ran in circles around a wobbling swing set. He watched her for a long time. He removed the pistol from the glove compartment and checked it. It was clean and ready.

Suddenly, a bell. He glanced up as the children began to gather near the double doors.

He got out of the car.

Δ

HE HELD MINDY'S HAND as the teacher looked him up and down. Tipler was immaculate in his uniform. Smiling and content. Ready.

The teacher was neatly fat, rolls tucked and controlled into waistband and sleeves. Face made up like a doll, half-glasses hung from a gold chain around her neck. A brooch of a bug on her right chest.

"Mindy is coming with me for the afternoon," Tipler said.

The last child filtered through the door and disappeared, leaving him, his daughter and the teacher on the steps. Tipler heard the inside door shut with a clang and hiss.

"We require a day's notification if a student is going leave—"

Tipler turned to his daughter.

"Mindy, go to the car," he said, gently.

She obediently walked down the steps and went across the yard to the car. Tipler turned back to see the teacher's face darkening. This was not a puppet used to being defied. This was something else.

"Can we step inside?" Tipler said calmly, opening his hands. It was important not to let it know.

They stood inside the vestibule, five feet by five feet across, like an airlock between the two sets of fire doors. Tipler remained still, waiting as the door slowly closed, hissing. The teacher-thing looked impatiently at him. Tipler tried not to tremble.

"Yes?" it said. There was something green in the base of a tooth. Something rotting.

Tipler heard the click and sigh as the door to the outside shut, sealing them in.

He shot it in the face at point blank range, and the sound was huge and reverberating in the airlock.

The head jerked to the left but it did not fall. A wave of blood and pink and gray appeared on the wall in a crazed spray. Tipler stepped backwards and watched as it turned back to look at him.

There was a hole the size of a quarter in its fat cheek, and burned specks in its face, but the eyes were still clear as it lunged towards him.

He screamed and shoved it away.

He shot it two more times as it fell. It finally stopped moving.

His chest was heaving and heart racing, but finally, he gained his composure. He checked himself, his coat, and when he was certain no one was coming, put the gun away, carefully picking up each spent shell. Then he left to find Mindy.

They could die, after all.

THEY DROVE FOR A long time and his daughter said nothing. The buildings gave way to the trees. Yellow and red leaves leaned in over the car, covering it, shielding it from the sky.

He admired her. She sat, belted in, feet not touching the floor of the car, hands in her lap, face forward. She didn't look at him. She didn't talk to him or ask him where they were going. Her face did not betray any emotion.

They drove for so long Tipler found it hard not to turn his head and look at her in wonder. The fear in his stomach was molten. This was the hardest thing he had ever done.

They stopped, finally, somewhere near Cumberland, out in the woods. He got out of the car and walked away. After a few moments he heard the car door open and she stepped out.

"Daddy?"

"Yes, love," he said and his voice wavered. He stood at the edge of a pond, and with his back to her he checked the gun. His hands were shaking. He would have to be fast.

"I'm sorry you're sad," she said. "Is this about when the sun dies?"

"Yes," he said. She was so wise, but she, too, would burn. She'd die, in agony, if he was not strong now.

Tipler turned, exposing the gun to her, but she didn't react. Realizing she saw it, he tried to raise it to point at her and found he could not.

"I love you, Mindy," he said, and thought of the comfort he might feel, placing the gun in his own mouth. But that was a coward's way out.

"I love you too, daddy," she said, unafraid. "But I don't know why."

He stood still for some time, as she watched him, slowly unravelling. He dropped the gun as his hands trembled, and his face crumpled into a grimace. He shook and wept and folded to the ground, choking out gasps of breath, amidst the sobs.

In the dirt, crying, the mission failed. His life over.

Finally she came over and hugged him as he wept.

Δ

IT BEGAN WHEN THE flare went up, and it ended when the B's rolled through, erasing everything. But in that gap of time, less than an hour, he saw the things that would redefine him forever. Even in living memory the thoughts were too big, too primal to be processed. They were a torrent. A black flood which swept behind his eyes and scraped it clean down to the living rock of his subconscious. Everything he was, his entire personality, floated on top of this like a thin sheen of oil on water.

It was the boy who called the men from the temple to their camp, after he had escaped, and who could blame him? But that didn't spare him from slaughter. When Lepus shook him awake at the flare, the boy was there to greet them, lit in the flickering ghost light.

Someone had set him up like a display kill at the edge of the tree line.

The boy was cut and hung like a pig. Inverted, turned away from the sky on two pallet sticks. Guts unzipped and torn out. Tipler got one good look, as the flare dropped, and he grunted. A deep sound. Something worse than death was here. The hole in the boy's chest flickered with shadows that crawled and wobbled and spun, and was something in there?

Was something moving in the black hole where his guts had been?

Tipler thought there was, but before he could be certain the firefight began.

Poe threw back as much metal as he could, crawling on

his hands and knees to light the claymores which silenced the chatter for a few seconds in a deafening bang. Then, Tipler was being dragged in the dark by Poe who was screaming at him to keep going.

Shapes popped up in the dark. Grenades or RPGs went off. Tipler kept his eyes on Poe's pack, on a small, stupid patch there. A cartoon man leaned back grooving, with the logo beneath: KEEP ON TRUCKIN'.

It was Poe, then Tipler, then Lepus.

Finally, just silence and trees. Moving downhill on slopes of rotting vegetation. Occasional shouts in a local tongue in the distance. His ears, ravaged, slowly spun out the ringing, until he could hear the soft hum of insects again.

"Shit, shit," Poe said, suddenly stopping. Tipler ran into him, as solid as a wall, and he felt Lepus turn to face behind them, pointing backwards into the dark.

"Are we in the kill box?"

Tipler was checking his weapon, which he had not fired at all, and looked up.

"*Are we in the fucking kill box?*" Poe hissed and grabbed Tipler by his shoulder strap and dragged him forward. Tipler stumbled and fell out of the trees into a roughly cut patch of open ground, and looked up. He pushed himself back into the trees.

They were on the edge of a vast open space. Behind the peaks of the towers was the huge white eye of the moon, skirting the horizon, the temple. It was almost morning.

"Yes. Uh. Yes," Tipler guessed.

"Nice fucking job, Poe," Lepus mumbled, behind Tipler, their packs touching.

"I didn't hear you calling anything out on the map, you fucking queer," Poe said.

"Eyes up, boys," Lepus whispered.

Above them, from the hill they had just descended, a line of red circles — flashlights — at least twenty of them, in a skirmish line, marching towards their position.

They ran into the open spaces between the temples.

The intervening fight was so brief, it seemed like it almost didn't happen. Gunfire in pops, an explosion and then there they were. Lepus bleeding from both arms on the ground. Poe shot in the shoulder. Tipler, miraculously untouched. Their guns were pulled away or dropped. Their gear stripped. Surrounded by locals, shouts in a foreign language and sharp, bamboo-like sticks to goad them on.

He caught one look at Poe as their hands were bound behind them. Poe's face was bloody, but he caught Tipler's eye and smiled, a wink, blood pouring from his bottom lip.

Somewhere, Lepus laughed after someone hit him. Tipler felt the strongest feeling of passivity he had ever felt. He surrendered himself to it and a cold wave washed over him. Stillness.

As the sun rose, they marched to the top of the temple. A place which had just been a series of coordinates the day before, and which would be dust before too much longer.

The American was there.

"Poe. Lepus, gentlemen," the man, said in a Virginia accent. He was dressed in full uniform.

"Colonel Wade," Poe replied, and spat blood.

The colonel's eyes were hidden behind mirror shades. He wore a Colt revolver on his belt. He was old but vigorous, and he didn't even really look at them. His eyes watched the horizon and the rippling half-circle of the rising sun.

"Time to murder and create," the colonel said to himself.

Next to the American stood a beautiful young woman. The most beautiful person Tipler had ever seen. All else was lost in that face, the smile. For a moment, Tipler thought: *It's really going to be all right.*

Then he saw the boy-thing and nothing was all right ever again.

It squatted like a toad behind her, to the side, and at first Tipler thought it was just a corpse. Then the empty face turned to look at him. The eyes had been hollowed out, leaving a red, black gap, but behind that, in the tiny holes, something glistened and moved, a blue-white mote more alive than anything in this world.

The thing that squirmed inside the boy-suit moved it like an awkward puppet. Skin squelching and mouth emitting small, harsh burps of gas as it struggled to pilot the corpse through the world.

Tipler's mouth opened and a noise began to slowly spin up, like an alarm. An uncontrolled keening wail that finally made them all consider him. The thing tilted the corpse-head to the side and its jaw hung open. Something black and chitinous moved in the shadows where the tongue should be. The colonel's face was blank behind the glasses. A mask. In the mirrors, double Tiplers looked back, screaming.

The grenade went off with a bark and knocked him flat. It was only in retrospect that Tipler thought it must have been Poe. When he came around, Tipler's face and side were burned, Colonel Wade was gone, and more importantly the corpse thing was gone. He woke in a fireman's carry down the temple as bullets snapped and clicked on the stones nearby. Poe had him, and his side was shrieking in pain, like it was still on fire.

By then, everyone knew, the B-52s were coming.

A droning sound. Specks on the sun. Stones rushing by. This was Tipler's bouncing view. A crescent cut from the sun, a half-moon of eclipse, coming.

Lepus laughed and screamed nearby, shooting: "Fuck you, and fuck you, and fuck you!"

Tipler said something and was suddenly on his feet, wobbling next to Poe. Someone handed him a gun.

Something was happening at the top of the temple. The distance to it seemed to recede, dancing away until the steps to the top stretched across a distance to the furthest perspectives. Then it spun, wobbling in one direction and then the other. Then a clear, blue-white light began to fill the sky. Tipler couldn't look away even as he headed in the other direction, his neck craned over his shoulder, locked, staring.

They crossed four hundred yards screaming, running unconcerned amidst the locals. Everyone was running. Running away from the temple. From what was coming. From the bombs.

The shooting was done.

They made it to the trees and Tipler turned back. On top of the temple, which he now realized was the exact center of a pattern of temples, the highest and most central point, the world was ripped open. Violated.

Something struggled through, being born, something the size of a whale. And yet, Tipler could tell, this was only some probing limb, some part of the thing that had crossed over. In the white light Tipler saw a silhouette of someone in abasement, stumbling to the top, praying, bowing.

Poe dragged him away by the collar and Lepus goggled at the thing, bigger than the sky, as it was pummeled by 750-pound bombs dropped in the target box they had called in. They made it up the hill and out of the zone before the bombs began to drop too far astray.

Through gaps in the canopy he saw the thing as it rose, a spiraling, alien tentacle topped by an eye. Something from outside. Something better than the world. More important. Then, it was hit, and hit again, and again and again. He watched it fold and wink out, spinning in on itself like an optical illusion and burning his brain to see, until the field below was a sea of smoke and nothing could be seen but drifting ruin.

Then, running for a long time.

Lepus laughed to himself the whole way back, while Poe and Tipler stumbled through the jungle to the pick-up.

When they hunkered down at the edge of the clearing early that afternoon, Poe leaned over and said:

"Welcome to Delta Green."

Δ

HE LEFT HER AT a gas station with his wallet and instructions to call her mother. After all this time and preparation, he couldn't free them, the things he loved the most, despite his best intentions.

THE BOMB WENT OFF at the Pentagon on schedule. It erased the room, and the room next door, and most importantly the calendar. It did little else except fill a small column in the *Washington Post* the next day.

HE SAT IN A McDonalds in Bethlehem, alone, and refused to leave at closing when they asked. People would be looking for him, he knew. The employees left when he showed the gun, and one of them waved down a passing police car.

A thin picket of shadows stood outside now, in the dark, cruiser lights flashing.

The cop stepped into the empty restaurant with his hand on his gun. Mustache, fat, big.

"Lieutenant Tipler?" the cop said, in a careful voice.

"Yes," Tipler said. His coffee was long finished. Newspaper folded on the table. Purpose gone. He glanced at this man.

"I'm Sergeant O'Brien," he said. Seeing something in Tipler's face, he raised both hands.

"In-country for two tours, 67-68," the cop said.

"Oh," Tipler said. "Two for me, too."

"Can I sit?" O'Brien asked.

"Yes."

O'Brien sat.

"Listen, I know it's bad, now," O'Brien said, with feeling. "Things can get better." He paused. "More police are coming."

"I don't know," Tipler said, and his hand moved the paper. His pistol was there. O'Brien's eyebrows rose.

"Listen—" O'Brien said.

"Not for you," Tipler said.

A mixture of emotions on O'Brien's face. He leaned forward and grabbed Tipler's hand.

"Listen, Lieutenant Tipler, sir. You can't give up, now, after all you've been through."

Tipler looked up into O'Brien's face and saw the drive he used to hold. Hope. Clarity of action and thought.

"You need to persevere. This is a test."

He looked at the man's face. Sincere and sweating.

"You're right," Tipler said.

IT WAS FRIDAY NIGHT mass at the church he retreated into, but people were there, gathered near the front in prayer. His overcoat was covered in blood, and he had already done a lot of work tonight. He was well into the mission, now.

Tipler stepped in with the valise and the sawn-down shotgun in his right hand, hanging, like he was there to read the meter. Unconcerned. Certain in his work. People glanced back but didn't see the danger.

They didn't really see him, just as it was supposed to be. That's how he knew it was right.

The priest smiled as Tipler came in and filed into an empty pew. Tipler reloaded the shotgun, below their sight line, smiling, separate, then the priest said:

"Who commands the sun, and it does not rise; who seals up the stars—"

Tipler smiled. This was what he was meant to do until his end. He leapt up with the shotgun, his pockets full of shells. Then the screams. The people scattered like rats.

He began firing, laughing, reloading. He fired and fired and fired.

He had finally come home.

The Thing in the Pit
(1977)

AGENT ALVIN BRIGHT WAS like his name, or so he liked to think. When he wasn't working on a particularly juicy piece of intelligence for the group, or performing audits for the IRS, he was tracking down leads in his spare time. Leads upon leads. The world was awash with them. Connections that intersected and bisected, that collapsed into circumstance or exploded into meaning. Bright was a man searching for intersections. He was correlating contents. He left it to others to close those loopholes.

He jotted all the leads down in the same way, on a yellow legal pad in ballpoint pen. He carried it in a valise everywhere he went, along with his glasses and his badge and gun. To anyone else, his documentation of the mysteries of the world would look like gibberish. Any one notation, filling half a page and underlined, would take a handwriting expert to dissect. Bright's script was fast and dirty and looping, and the underlines ran over words and through letters until all that was left was a mess that only Bright could really read.

VAN DUSEN FAMILY, COFFEY ST. VAN BRUNT? STILL ALIVE? DEPOSITS?

This last line, scribbled in haste, might be the last entry he would ever make, though he had forgotten about it now.

In his time in the organization he had seen terrible things, and most importantly he had learned not to want to see such things. Unlike others in the group, he never gained a taste for seeing the unexplainable. To others it was a thrill, an addiction, and most likely one day it would lead to their death. To him, it was an equation—he would add it all up and it would point to the truth. He would file his report and go home. He would not get involved. He would not try to shoot it or blow it up or even see it. He'd report and retreat and sleep soundly knowing he had done his job.

Until today.

The door shook again and a rain of rust falling into his upturned eyes brought him back, squinting. The chain on the door squealed, the sound of a balloon being relentlessly clutched to the point of popping. He tried not to look past the door. To the shape past the door. But it was there. For one second, he saw the shape strain the door to its limits, a steel door planted in the earth before World War II by indifferent men. He could see them here, goggles on, acetylene torches burning, chewing gum and thinking of the dwindling American dream.

Past the black gap where the door hung at an angle (still shut, for now) was a green eye, flickering in the half light of the ancient yellow bulb like a huge firefly. The eye was large. It was, if one were to place it on a tray to measure it, two and one half inches across.

The eye was alive and connected to something that longed for his blood. It was three-hundred and twenty-six years old. Though he did not know this, Agent Bright knew this.

Once, earlier, though he had no idea when, he had screamed and pressed his revolver to the gap and had worked the trigger six times, deafening himself and using up the last of his ammo. So much for being like his name.

He had screamed for a long time, and the only reason he had noticed and stopped was because his throat began to throb and shriek with pain. He was so deaf, he hadn't realized he had been shouting even after the gun was emptied. Who knew how long that had gone on? His watch had been smashed in the fall.

Then he sat in the dim light and hitched his breath in huge gasps, each one ripping his throat with razors, eyes on the door as it shook and pounded, bent and was pulled until the stainless steel around the handle began to crease. He wept there, as well. But time was jumbled. He could no longer discern the order of things.

Trapped two hundred feet beneath Brooklyn, in the dark.

And no one knew where he was.

Bright, like his name.

BEFORE ALL THIS, A door had opened for Bright on a wizened old woman, clad in a white nightgown that hovered around her body but did not touch it, causing her to look strangely bloated. But the face which hovered over the yellowed lace collar was small and frail and it bobbed like the head of a chicken, goggling at the light. A waddled neck wasting away with old age. Sunken cheeks and avid eyes which were an odd shade of green.

"*Goedemorgen,*" she said in a voice like a grandmother's.

"Um. Hello. Eloise Van Dusen?" Bright said, managing some authority.

"Oh. Yes. Hullo. Is there something I can do for you, young man?"

"I'm Agent Alvin Bright, IRS." He held open his badge

very close to her face. "I'm here pertaining to the ongoing audit of the Van Dusen Shipping Company. Are you Eloise Van Dusen?"

"Oh. Yes. Of course. We have been expecting you. Do come in." She had opened the door readily, her face filled with a smile of yellow teeth.

Outside, Red Hook continued to fall apart. But in New York in the 1970s, decay was the rule, not the exception. The old woman shut the door on the sunlight and Bright entered an ancient home of warm wood, frayed rugs and dim shadows; filled with strange smells. He thought nothing of the house at the time. But if he had, for no clear reason it might have reminded him of a funeral home.

"Would you like some lutefisk?" she said, brightening, crossing to a vast, chipped-tile kitchen. It had enameled and stainless steel restaurant-quality stoves; Bright had done an audit or two on restaurants to know the difference. The room smelled of charcoal and vinegar. Clean but with an undertone of meat.

"Oh. Oh no, Miss Van Dusen," he replied, dropping his valise on the formica table—some remnant of the Fifties—and pulled out his legal pad.

"It is Missus Van Dusen, if you please," she said. Without turning she took a slight curtsy.

"Oh, excuse me. I understand your husband—Piotr Van Dusen—has been...deceased for some time."

She smiled and placed a solid silver tray, filled with crackers covered in gray, slimy flesh, on the formica table.

"Yes, yes, but it is like my Piotr is still here sometimes, you know." She placed a fish-covered cracker on a small china plate in front of him on the legal pad and eyed him. Bright hesitated and then brought the cracker to his mouth in one quick motion, like a man gobbling an aspirin. He didn't even really chew it, just swallowed. He was not used to hospitality. He felt he needed to eat it even if it took a sheer act of goodwill.

His mouth burned a bit, and the taste was like something which had been pickled but had gone over. It put him in mind of rotting yellow things growing out of the light, and for a moment, before he held still for a moment and steeled himself, it almost all came up, out his mouth, through his hands, all over the table.

Then it dropped down his throat and into his roiling stomach.

She watched all of this with great interest.

"Delicious," he managed, sitting down. Her laugh was like yellowed paper crumpled in an empty room.

"MRS. VAN DUSEN, WE are in the last stages of our investigation into the Van Dusen Shipping Company, 139 Coffey Street, Red Hook, Brooklyn, and I understand you are a paid employee of the company?"

She sat with some effort, perching on the chair like a frail bird.

"Yes. I am of the board, and am paid a salaried wage. My husband saw to such things," she chirped, and waved her hand.

"And what year did you join the board?" Bright scribbled down SALARIED BOARD MEMBER, E VAN DUSEN.

"Oh...that would be '55." Then she started. "Oh!" And Bright jumped.

"Tea. I have not offered you tea," she said. She slowly, improbably rose and Bright found himself put off. She had moved away before he could adjust to the idea of it. She entered a big wall-sized door with heavy metal latches—a dry storage—and shuffled inside.

"No, Ms. Van Dusen, that's fine. I—"

"Nonsense, nonsense." She puttered back and forth from the old stove to the sink and prepared the kettle.

He watched her. The floor creaked and moaned under her shuffling steps and Bright's mind wandered as he watched her feet. Finally, she was setting a cup of greenish, steaming tea on the table. She slowly sat down again.

"None for you?" he asked.

"Oh, no, no, no," she laughed. "My bladder is not what it once was, if you'll excuse me for saying so."

She laughed and waved her hand around like she was swatting an invisible fly.

They talked of nonsense and bank accounts and dates of death and birth. Time unravelled and spun out. He found the edges of the mystery he had discovered on paper and something took over. He pulled in the trail and wound it. He looped and danced with her and backed her into corners and let her go to run out the line.

When he became tired of the game, he said:

"What about this bank account at Rensselaer Bank? Who

is the man who deposits funds there once a month?"

She looked at him with a squint.

"What man?"

He smiled and opened his valise and slid across a deposit slip.

"Is this your signature?"

She fumbled for glasses from within her nightgown and placed them on the end of her nose and hung her mouth open, glancing at the document. She picked it up.

It was a slip for the withdrawal of $5,000. It had an unreadable male signature, and the looping careful scrawl of Eloise Van Dusen beneath it.

"Yes," she finally said. Her mouth was a wrinkled slash.

"Well, then, why don't you tell me who the man is? And, I would note, faking one's death is a very serious offense." Bright sat back and smiled.

"He's my husband," she said without any real resistance, and stood frailly.

"I see," Bright said, and leaned down to remove a tape recorder from his valise.

The smugness in this move, the feeling of control he had at that moment, that would haunt him during his time in the hole.

While Bright fumbled through his valise, she placed the glasses down and walked around the table.

Δ

HE GLANCED UP, NOT really interested, but that attitude changed quickly when she grabbed his shirt and yanked him up to his feet—off his feet—and the tape recorder's bulk slipped from his hand and shattered on the tile floor in clattering plastic.

Buttons popped on his shirt, and the long, low sound of a seam letting go on his jacket swept up his back.

He flailed like a fish pulled from the water on a hook. His shoes found no floor beneath them.

His hand locked on her hand and his eyes found hers. Her mouth rolled back over teeth that went on and on. The cheeks drew back and just kept going, pulling up until her eyes were nothing more than slits which caught the light as red lines. She looked up at him like a prize.

When she held him, up close, he could see her angles were all wrong. She was smaller than him but somehow not. She held him with one frail arm and he dangled, and his mind kept struggling, saying his feet should be on the floor. Her arm doubled in his vision. Another seam let go and he began to slip down, but she tightened her grip and he felt claws settle into his flesh and press forward until his skin popped and blood began to trickle down his neck. Talons.

A smell filled his world. Wet fur. Rot.

"You are very, very clever, young man. But not nearly as clever as Ms. Eloise," she said. Her voice explored a deeper register, and rumbled in her tiny chest with the improbably low sound like a lion purring.

He realized she—it—was laughing.

He had locked a hand on hers and his fingers felt short, stiff fur and the knobs of rough bone beneath thick, armored skin. Bone spurs and warts and skin like a rhinoceros.

He tried to scream. She tightened the hand he could not see but only feel, the monster's hand, to choke him off.

She walked across the kitchen, the floor groaning and sagging beneath their weight, his feet never touching the floor, towards the pantry door.

She stepped in and yanked the light cord, and the naked bulb lit the room, swinging madly, rocking and clattering.

The crazed shadows shifted and swung, and it was difficult to see, but something about her shadow was not right. There was no old woman there but the bulk of something ape-like. Huge and furry and holding him aloft like a feather. Something with the snout of a jackal and the shadow-spray of uneven shovel-like teeth launched from its face at bizarre angles.

Then her grip tightened more and his vision blurred.

She crossed the room to the ancient, tank-like refrigerator and shoved it with her other arm. The huge steel bulk of the refrigerator shot backwards and tilted back a little with the force of the shove, before dropping back forward with a thud that shook the room.

Four hundred pounds, at least, oh my God, he thought.

At the edge of his vision, he saw a hole in stone the size of a well, scrabbled and dug by a million claw marks, that the refrigerator once covered.

His neck sang and rivulets of blood soaked his shirt.

Her arm brought him up over the hole and warm wind wafted up, ruffling his hair. He kicked and struggled, but the old lady thing didn't even move. His mind said she could not be doing this, but reality resisted the commands of predictable physics.

"You'll excuse my poor temper, but I dislike questions, and talking overmuch," the thing pretending to be Eloise Van Dusen croaked, and shook him, once, to get him to open his eyes.

She swam in his vision; the old woman, the illusion, the monster.

"You'll find my husband much more forthcoming," she said. "He hardly ever shuts his mouth." And then he was falling.

HE STRUCK THE SIDE of something metal in the dark once which arrested his fall for perhaps a second, and tumbled a moment before landing with a bone-shaking crash in water. He had no idea how far, but the fall felt eternal.

When he hit, his head struck cement an instant after his landing, a rebound. One hand landed beneath him and twisted back painfully. Water shot up his nose and in his face and all over his clothes. His face vibrated and felt fat and hot even as water spilled down it.

It smelled of rot and shit and piss.

His ribs up one side of his chest shrieked with pain with every hitching breath. He pushed himself up on one arm and looked around to find himself in an oubliette of cement. He found his pistol then, wet, and held it up out of the water. He struggled to his feet unevenly and wavered there, eyes adjusting to the dark.

Suddenly, he was struck in the shoulder behind his head from above by something hard and heavy, like a hammer, and he dropped his gun and stumbled forward, almost dropping to his knees.

In the dim light he saw the ruins of the tape recorder jutting from the water. He scrabbled and retrieved his revolver, shook it off, and glanced around. He tripped and almost fell forward again but flailed his arms and kept his balance. His foot had struck a pile of ruined rebar, fused by rust, time and water. He went around it.

There was a mechanical click. The sound of a electrical connection. A red light beneath a mesh of steel lit next to a half-open steel door, he could now see. A klaxon began to burr, reflecting in the dark, in time with the light, which went on and off. Each sound deafened him and echoed.

"Dinner time, my love. Dinner, dinner, dinner," the Eloise thing shouted from above, far away.

HE STUMBLED FORWARD AS the buzzing stopped, and found the old submarine door. He pushed it shut but found it had no latch, just a hole punched through the frame and door which once held a lock, now long gone. The heavy door slid back open in his grasp as he released it, left hanging open like a gaping mouth.

Something was coming. He heard it beyond the gap. He felt it.

Bright reached down to the door and his hands settled on wet, flaked metal. He cut his hands but came up with about two feet of red, rusted chain, wet and ruined. Shaking, he worked the chain through the slots in the door and pulled it shut with a squeal that set his teeth on edge.

Then, back to the pile of rebar. He shoved the pistol in his pocket and plunged his hands into the watery pile and pulled a piece free where it shook in his hand.

Bright ran back to the door and slid the rebar through the loops of the chain and spun it, causing a horrific screaming shriek which finally brought the door tightly shut.

Everything, from the discovery of the door to the shutting of the door, took perhaps fifteen seconds.

He removed the pistol from his pocket.

A moment later, a monster.

NOW, OUT OF AMMO, leaning against the door, shutting out some horrible snuffling monstrosity, Bright wept.

This went on for some time.

Finally, beyond the door, a reasonable voice. An old man, quiet, no roaring or growling or snarling. The smell remained but the voice was so convincing and quiet that it filled him with ice.

"Open the door, if you please."

Bright leaned over carefully and looked to the slit. A small, bespectacled man stood in shin-deep water, goggling in the gap like a little bird. Like the old-woman thing above, Bright knew what he was seeing was false, but he could not unsee it.

"No," Bright said. A whine.

It was the man from the photo at the bank.

"There really is nothing to be done, my young friend," the old-man thing said, quite convincingly. "No one shall find you here, I am afraid."

Silence.

There was a sudden slam on the door. Something strong enough to snap a wooden door in half, but the steel held. The door shifted a quarter-inch in the frame and dust and rocks fell from above to plink in the water. Bright screamed and dropped his gun as his back bucked forward from its weight.

The gun vanished in the stinking water. He looked to it, and shut his eyes.

What did it matter? It was empty anyway. Not even a round left for himself.

This went on for some time. Occasionally, the thing beyond the door tried to talk to him. Bright didn't listen to the gorgon past the door. He placed his hands over his ears.

SOMETIMES LATER IN THE DARK.

"Let us suppose something, you and I," the old man voice said. "Let us say there is a kind of being which is immortal, that feeds on the human dead. Let us say that these beings otherwise wish to be left to their own devices. But we are become fast friends! I am of this kind. As is the wife, as you have guessed. We may look like anyone we feed upon. And if the mind is fresh and alive when we feed on it, that mind might live on in *our* minds.

"Dr. Albrecht, the body I wear now, is still here, despite his death in 1927. I recall all of his life. His hopes, his thoughts and dreams, remain in my mind, alive. A limited immortality, to be sure, but immortality nonetheless. They will remain with me forever."

Bright lay half in the water, exhausted, and listened, eyes wide. His mind rose and sang like madness. A million thoughts rushing out from a single source, vanishing into impossible places, vast.

"Now, suppose a man was stuck in a cage, with an immortal being outside. An immortal being who feeds on the dead. Who may wait forever.

"What I am saying, and poorly it seems, is this. Would you like to starve to death, young man, or to live on in whatever manner is possible?"

Bright's breath stopped.

"You chew on that, and I shall return. Feel free to explore the tunnels at your leisure. It is of no consequence to me or mine."

BRIGHT LAY ON HIS back in the standing water, watching slight reflections ripple around him, breathing slowly. Hours had passed, or minutes, it was impossible to tell. The thing at the door was gone, or so it seemed. There had been no movement or voice for some time now, though time was difficult to track.

The light seemed ambient. Like it floated in the air, dimly, casting imperfections in the black in front of him, cutting shapes, forming walls and rocks and water. One thing was clear: even here, down in the dark, light from above ruled. Night had fallen, above, and the myriad reflections which bounced and glowed and wound their ways down into the black had faded.

Finally, with effort, he stood. His knees popped and his body screamed with pain as a million different bruises spoke out at once. He stood, swaying, with his head held to the side to prevent the sharp pain in his back from growing to become his whole world, and looked around.

He stumbled forward in the dark, with his arms outstretched, fingers wide. He kept his center of gravity low, and when his feet struck solid stone in the water, he'd feel out the shape in front of him before moving on.

Soon he had circuited his cell, a standpipe, twice. It was maybe twenty feet by fifteen, filled with debris. There was the porthole door with its makeshift lock, and now, he knew, a small, latch-like door in the back away from the door. The door was the size of the door in a large stove. It was big enough for Bright to fit through, if he could open it.

He focused his attention on this shape, with his raw, wet hands, in the dark, and began to work it.

THE IRON OF THE door was ruined and scaled, rusted from countless hours of water pouring over it, here, in the dark.

He struggled at the latch, working it, shaking it. Throwing his shoulder up against it, rocking it. Even after hours of this, or so he believed, he was uncertain it had moved it at all. The handle felt the same after all his efforts.

Bright realized, as the light indefinably began to rise again in the air, that his hands were covered in black splotches, looking like the negative outlines of continents on the world of his skin.

It was blood. His fingers had been chewed raw by the metal flakes, and he laughed as he found himself wondering when he had had his last tetanus shot.

He laughed so hard he had to sit down.

"THERE IS HUMOR, HERE, to be found in the dark," the old man said from outside the door.

"Go away. Please," Bright said, laughter vanishing as instantly as it had arrived. Through his hands, the slightly darker shadow on the wall—the porthole. Beyond it, something not human.

"I am bored with the voices here, alone, in my head. Tell me a new tale," the old-man thing said.

Bright's mouth hung open. His hands came down from his face.

"No!" he shouted. The sound jumped back and batted his ears, flat and empty and metallic. When it ended, the room was silent except for the dripping of water, somewhere out in the dark.

"Very well. I tell you a story, boy." The old man laughed. When he spoke again, it was a whisper. The story was practiced and easy. Something it had spun in its mind so many times that it had worn clean, like a river rock, black and heavy and smooth, without seam.

Δ

EVERYONE IN THE TOWN knew the Keepers held secrets. In the end, it was what brought the boy to them. That and the hope of food and warmth. But the boy's life was not always a tragedy.

Before the big man came, there were happy times that one might mistake for a childhood. The boy played with straw soldiers on the sill that overlooked a thin, cobbled road facing a picket wall, and in the winter when he was still small, he snuggled in the bed with his mother, while rotten wood popped in a stove and belched smoke into the tiny space the landlord called an apartment.

They lived on the Wall Street, and later, the big, drunken man who worked wood and called himself his father came to live with them there, stretching the room to its limits. The big man was not his father. His father had put to sea a year after he was born, for London, and was gone now. Dead, by all account. Lost.

His mother's suitor brought home pay; sometimes a lot of money in furred purses, with raw knuckles and bruises on his face, but he never smiled. He said very little and what he said spoke of imperatives; food, warmth, safety. Nothing else.

The man was never untoward at home. He never struck them. He never yelled. All in all, the boy often thought, he could have drawn much worse a card than the big man. Still, it was like he wasn't there. Like the man and his mother lived alone. Like the boy was a ghost.

More and more, the money the big man made was spent on wine and beer.

His mother fell into the bottle with the man she grew to love more than the boy, and left the ramshackle house behind.

The boy believed his mother had abandoned him because he had grown to look more like his sailor father as he grew into manhood. The same red hair. The same smile with wide, flat teeth. It hurt her to look at him as he changed into the drowned man she had loved. So first she drank and then she left.

One day, and he could not precisely say when, his mother and the big man didn't return, and he was left alone in the room above the picket.

Giddy at first, the boy made wild plans that fell to nothing as time wore on and the loop of debt closed on him.

Later, when the boy could not pay the rent, he left. The company put people like the boy in debtor's prison and a balance remained, so he fled north the day before the bill was due, moving outside the picket and into the woods past the edges of the town.

For a time, he lived beneath a cluster of storm-toppled trees and stalked the slop piles of an inn on the crossroads of the Broadway, eating ruined bits of vegetables and sometimes rotted meat he found there, if the hogs did not get to them first. He drank and bathed from one of the collection ponds, startling sheep when he splashed his face. At night, he collected berries near the fences of the farms, occasionally outrunning local dogs who chased him more for sport than anything else.

Then, one morning, the summer and its fantasy ended. The boy woke shivering beneath a rotted horse blanket, with ice in his hair. Soon there would be snow and he would die if he remained outside the town walls.

All knew of the Keepers. Their estate was well north of the town, off the Broadway, in a series of tangled woods cut with a single brambled trail. The Keepers were odd. They wore cassocks, like Roman priests. They were of many nationalities and languages. They rode no horses. They took in indigents and debtors, and the walls of their estate were high. Inside, it was said, they crafted wine or some such to sell to the company. Their actual trade remained vague, but their reach was rich and strong. Members' debts were forgiven. People who went there no longer worried for the company. They got on.

Once joined, no one left the Keepers.

One night, when he could no longer take the cold in the trees, the boy walked to the walled estate down the brambled path and stood outside the gate, marveling at the pattern carved there, lit by a bucket of burning pitch.

An intertwining circle, triangle and angles ending in ellipses, split across the gap of the gate, hovering over him like an enormous eye. It had all been very carefully worked, in a way which suggested it was not only artistic but that it meant something.

Religious freedom in the colony was assured by the company, and it drew many from the fringes of Christendom with gold to invest on the edges of the map and a desire for privacy. The Keepers fled persecution some years before, and it was clear to him now that they had more than average reason. Theirs was some religious pursuit. But what did that matter? If there was a god, clearly it had no interest in the boy, even if he went looking for it.

He knocked on the gate, careful to keep his hands from the grooves in the door, as if they could poison him by touch.

Finally, the gate opened and a voice called him in from the cold, into the dark.

The Keepers taught him much. There are secrets that you tell, secrets that you keep, and secrets that can only be found once, and then only alone. That night, the boy learned the last and greatest human secret. In so doing, he became something other than a man.

"YOU...WERE A...BOY?" BRIGHT SAID, despite himself. He put his hands to his face to stop himself from saying more as the silence continued, and he tasted blood and metal in the breath on his palms.

"I have been many things, but yes, I was once a boy."

"When?"

"Time is unimportant and, I confess, difficult for me to meter. A miser with infinite coin ceases to count by ones, as they say. But, now, perhaps you can see, we are not completely unlike."

"I'm not like you," Bright said, again, shocked by the strain in his voice.

"You are lost and desperate and without hope, no?"

"Go away," Bright whined. "I'm not like you at all."

"This is true," the old man crooned. "You are like me only in the way an acorn that lies fallow, lost on some stony ledge with no purchase, is like an oak. That is to say, you might *become* what I am now. Or you can become like the residents of the other cell."

Bright's eyes flicked to the small door.

Silence.

"What are you?"

"If you let me pass the door, I will show you," the voice said, quietly. It was so calm and convincing, Bright felt his hands come up to touch the makeshift lock on the porthole.

"No."

Bright stepped back from the door, stumbling in the dark until he found a lip of cement, and curling there, fell into a dreamless sleep. Exhausted.

LATER, WHEN THE OLD-MAN thing had left, Bright stood at the small door and stared at it for a long time.

He tapped it with a small, wet rock, lightly at first.

"Hello?"

On the third rap, he heard something, a shuffling crackle, something moving on its own on the inside of the door.

"HELLO?!" he screamed.

No response. No further sound.

HE WRENCHED A RUINED steel bar, bent and wet, from the water when the dim light returned, and worked it beneath the fastener of the small, latched door. He threw his weight against it, and pulling, felt it scream for a second, as it shifted.

His hands were puffed and raw and wet with blood when he moved them again to gain purchase. Again he threw himself against it, and it shifted. The door it held shut was small, but not so small he might not pass through it.

He put his head down and took a deep breath. One more go. He leveraged himself against the bar, pushing with all of his strength and weight. A slow, metallic screech filled him with satisfaction. It was followed by a pop and the ring of a deep, metallic bell.

The small door swung open and bones spilled out.

Hundreds of human bones. Leg bones, cracked and split for the marrow, smashed skulls, a rain of teeth and finger bones and ribs. So many they swept out and down from the door like a snow drift, falling into the water with a huge, clicking splash. Chattering. Sweeping. Filling empty spaces. Gathering. Growing.

He leapt back from the charnel wave, and tottered and fell backwards, smashing down onto cement chunks in the water, not noticing a gash up his back. His eyes were wide in the dark and his mouth worked but nothing came out. The hole in the wall was a gap filled with more human bones than a graveyard could ever hold.

Soon he too would be there, he was now certain. Once he starved to death.

Old-man laughter from the dark, from far away.

AT SOME POINT, HE vaguely recalled, he reached up and slid the steel bar out of the porthole chain with a squeal, his arms rubber and his legs wasted sticks in wet cloth. It was the last movement he could possible imagine achieving. The last effort. He slumped back at an angle, wasted and collapsed.

He had begun drinking the sewer water sometime in the

last few days. Time was elusive, down in the dark. But there was no food. Nothing to eat. Nothing. He watched his hands, raw and bloody, shrink and sharpen to skin-covered bone.

The metal bar pulled his arm down, and his hand would not hold it any longer. It clanked and sunk into the water. The door popped open immediately, the steel chain scratching and dropping into the corridor.

Silence and water dripping. Settling.

He saw his reflection in the dim light when the water stilled, and staring back at him was a skull with a scrub beard and eyes, glints sunken into the shadows of his skull, trying to come out, to be seen.

Then, red pinpoints behind him in the dark.

THE STREET WAS BLEACHED by light on a fall day. It was New York as he had known it before, despite the changes. Bright knew where he was but could not say how he had gotten there. Still, at the same time, he knew. Or some part of him did, just as some part of him looked on in wonder.

Strange machines clung to lampposts, buzzing and clicking. Cars of a kind he didn't know prowled the streets like iron sea creatures, finned and rumbling. He had restricted his wandering to the bank, and then only in the early evening.

In and out to do human business in his human suit.

Agent Bright stepped to the newsstand and Agent Cassiday was already there, waiting, reading the *Post*. She looked up and smiled.

"You sick?" she asked.

"Haha, yeah, a bug," the voice said in his head, and he flawlessly mimicked it. "Can we get off the street? I've made some progress on the Red Hook thing."

It was noon. There was no worry for the shadows giving him, them, away. Three hundred years was a long time to practice such things. But he could recall when two hundred had felt that way. One hundred. Much had changed, but men, the unripened fruit, remained the same. Shadows and reflections were all that worried his mind.

Cassiday was good, he knew—he knew everything Bright knew about her—but she was only human.

The future opened in a way that he had no longer thought possible. Like some curio that, when turned, spread like the jeweled petals of a flower. Or the best parts of the marrow when they cracked and glistened like ruby red shot through a tusk of yellow ivory. The best and most delicious feeling of his lifetime, of a dozen lifetimes. A million.

The world today was confusing and loud, and smelled horrific but was fascinating. The things Bright had shared with him! The things his discarded kin—now his food—had accomplished in his time below the ground. Cars and machine guns and moon ships.

Soon, the Keepers would all know more.

Contingencies
(1984)

THE ACETYLENE TORCH FINALLY made the door hot so he stepped back. There was his answer; they were coming for him. He had perhaps two hours alone here with the device. It would be close.

For the past hour, while the box ran its fifth day of calculations, he had kept his face pressed to the worked metal, ear cocked, listening. At first the noises seemed illusory, but by the time the door began to warm, he could hear something. The box was long past the library and was arriving at perhaps the extinction event, he knew. He had seen it all before. It was what came after, what came *next*, that—

A dim hiss and a gruff argument in monosyllables. Soldiers and engineers. He wondered why they just didn't blow the vault door off the hinges. He supposed it was because of the items in the room. A room where Stalin had once walked, and was said to have commented:

So, this is what lies outside the light?

The Black Museum.

Oddities. Artifacts. Bits of mystery pulled from Arctic research stations and Saharan wadis. One object had been found in the middle of a man's brain, recovered only when the surgery trying to pull it from its mind-womb killed him. The man had screamed and said he could see the world burn. The brain thing looked like an embryo made of gold and silver metal intermixed, with a line of grooved teeth around its circumference like treads on a tank. When the surgeon had pulled it free, those treads had spun and whined in a machine-like rhythm, spewing blood and bone. What could make such a thing as that? What force?

That was forty years before. Still, no one at GRU knew *what* it was. Worse, they didn't know *why* it was. What purpose could it possibly hold?

He looked at the Mironov device, set on a thick, metal table, running its simulation, humming. It had drawn him here. What kept him. What he studied. What had killed his marriage. Why he drank. It was *why,* though only he seemed to realize it.

Arkady drew his eyes from it and shook his head and looked down as his foot shifted something on the floor. Military rations, long eaten, ripped boxes spread about the ground next to a tarp that he'd used as a makeshift blanket. He had been here for a long time and the vault stank of the piss and shit in a bucket in the corner. There was still another smell there, beneath. Ozone and something like blood.

If he was right, he wouldn't need to worry about it much longer. He leaned towards the door, careful not to touch his ear to the metal, and listened. It would be some time yet. Until then, the universe would continue.

IN 1978, FIVE YEARS before, he had been happy. Computers were good to him. They spoke to him. Controllable, understandable, clear. First programming guidance computers, and later telecommunication switches. He and his wife had moved from place to place a lot in the beginning, but in 1978 he was making a name for himself. He was the perfect mix of self-deprecating and effective, able to crawl through the Soviet machine without drawing enemies. He threw success at those around him like a man trying to hold off wolves with chunks of meat. He didn't mind. He enjoyed his work for purely personal reasons.

Suddenly, he had been recalled to Moscow. There, his wife was finally happy. Their apartment was good. They wanted for very little. They were the elite. He was marked for advancement.

Then the phone call.

The GRU colonel, Ryabov, had been waiting for him when he arrived at the building, standing out in the snow, in uniform. The colonel opened the door to the building of the Ministry of Internal Documentation and Affairs for him and waited.

Inside was silence. Three stories of people packed in offices, with small lights outside indicating when and whether you were permitted to enter. He had believed it to be some sort of security vetting. Now that slid from his mind, through his stomach to the base of his soul. Terror crept in to fill that gap.

What had he done wrong?

Without introduction, Ryabov officiously swore him in. Motherland and hammer and sickle and comrade. Ryabov saluted once and gave him a badge with his own picture on it and a set of old keys. They were in the classic Soviet manner, the iron keys: made sometime before the turn of the century and held by a stamped and futuristic stainless steel keychain that celebrated Soviet spaceflight.

"Welcome," Ryabov finally said, and sat back at his desk. When he looked up and saw Arkady still standing there with his jacket on his arm, he pointed at the door and impatiently waved his hand. They never spoke again.

Arkady left and the light above the door came on with a click. There was no car to take him back.

Stamped on the badge was his name, his picture and SPE-CIAL STATE ACCESS, GRU-SV8.

He thought about what lie to tell his wife on the long walk home.

GRU-SV8 HANDLED THE THINGS from outside. Five years had taught him that. When something appeared that made no sense, like the silver hubcap they knew the Americans had recovered, the information went here to be looked at. The Americans, he was sure, had a similar division. They *must*.

Five years had barely been enough to piece together the faintest outlines of what the group was up to. He could spend ten or fifty years—he could go into every office and pick through every memory of every member of the group and still fail to understand what was going on at all. Yet...progress was made. That was the madness.

At any time, he knew, clots of investigators were bent on a dozen different artifacts, each pointing in baffling and opposite directions. He had no clear picture of them all, but only heard things from time to time. "Elder Ones," and things sleeping in Antarctic ice and beneath the Pacific Ocean. He tried his best to not pay attention. After all, his lot to study would take years to properly absorb. If it could ever be absorbed at all.

He was brought here because of the Mironov device. They needed a computer scientist to look at it, because at its heart, they believed, it was a computer. Albeit one that was 65 million years old. The Mironov device. His Everest. A machine forged by unknown creatures before the dinosaurs perished.

The greatest computer the Earth had ever known. Perhaps something more even than that. It had shown him all of this and more.

JUST WHERE IT HAD come from was unclear, but hints he had read in restricted files in the simulation indicated Australia sometime after the war. COMINTERN agents were involved, one called KIPLING. The metal block was moved by submarine to a Soviet-friendly port, and from there by air to Moscow for examination.

It was a 0.2 meter × 0.2 meter cube that weighed 196.6 kilograms, composed of a flat metal that fell precisely nowhere on the periodic table. Samples could not be taken—a diamond drill failed even to scratch it. It was first studied by Dr. Igor Mironov, a physicist spoken of in the lofty circles of the Moscow nuclear programs, and later by replaceable, nameless men in lab coats in the service of Stalin.

Those touching the cube reported odd sensations of floating and daydreaming. Access to it was rapidly restricted. Tests were made. Artists. Musicians. Mathematicians. Mironov discovered the "directed calculation" of the device. His report on the box remained the most incisive to date.

The box, it seemed, allowed a person touching it to "imagine" math, which could then live on in the device even after contact was lost, spinning, calculating and changing. Furthermore, it allowed this simulation to be "seen" by the operator, and somehow understood, even when the figures became staggering. Eyes closed, touching the metal, worlds of math that lived on their own, tumbling into existence as colors, shapes, sounds formed inside the box.

In eight months, using it, Mironov smashed several difficult physics problems and the attendant calculations to arrive at those solutions. Such discoveries were classified, of course. His simulations of fuel flow led to breakthroughs in Soviet missile technology.

And then, at the height of his towering achievement, Mironov killed his wife and three children with rat poison, murdered four random people one by one, and jumped in front of a train. The cube was restricted once more and relegated to the Black Museum. That was nineteen years before. There it sat until Afghanistan and external pressures called for it to be reactivated. Then President Reagan began mumbling about weapons in space.

Now, here Arkady was. And the box hummed and hummed.

HIS LIFE IN THREE scenes. One, him and his wife happy in a new apartment—a large one in Moscow. Two, Arkady drinking late at night, thinking on the things he had seen in the device, his wife in bed, awake and silent and angry. Three, Arkady alone in his once happy apartment, drinking.

He had run through it two hundred and ninety-six times in simulation. That was enough stress testing for any marriage;

he would have run only twenty for a rocket. The path there or out of there, it seemed, was outside the scope of his powers to affect. Kat was gone before they got to Moscow. Her happiness had simply been a local effect. She was gone before he was born and gone before the Earth cooled or was spat from the sun. Her state was GONE. There was no reference line to bring her to the top of the calculations. No loop. Having confirmed it in the simulation made it far easier to accept. It was mathematically proven that KAT=GONE.

Arkady spent most nights in the machine after Kat had moved out. Most, but not all.

It wasn't so bad. He could see her again—in there, anyway. Alone, at night, with the machine.

HE WAS SUPPOSED TO be modeling fluid simulation algorithms in the box. And he did.

At first.

The fluid simulation algorithm took less than a second of real time. The rest of the first day he played. One of the beauties of the device was that no one could see what you were doing with it. You simply stood or sat with your hand on it, an occasional smile or grimace of effort on your face.

Touching the box for the first time was like listening to a beautiful burst of music behind your eyes which exploded from nothing and wove into crisp, mathematical meaning. It was like *living* in music. Dancing between the notes and pulling and warping them while pure light and sound swept down the channels cut with your mind. He was always an ordered thinker, and within that first second he saw how to arrange it so that the math danced in such a way as to vacillate between highs and lows. He saw how the math had volume and depth and color and sound.

He saw it come alive and enter patterns on its own which emerged in bizarre interplays down in the distance of the simulation. He built mountains of color, shaped oceans of sound. It wove and danced and swelled and engulfed him, and he floated within it all, omniscient and total, the creator.

That was in the first day. The first minute.

WITHIN A WEEK, HE had learned to make a world. Only thirty-four calculations were needed to cause the simulation to spin and take on a life of its own. It was silly that he had not seen them sooner.

What was beyond the planet? He couldn't say. Back then, he had yet to leave it. On his water-covered world, a world of dancing numbers at the lowest point that were and were not there (so they might surprise him), he had woven a complex interplay of rules, of particles within particles, of relations that jumped from the core of an atom out into the void that issued outwards in all directions.

He focused on a puddle of water for a time, as the sky baked from a bloated sun that seemed to have congealed of its own accord due to some trick of math his mind had noted. The device had picked up the tune and had spun it out. Inside the puddle (and hadn't the elements appeared in a marvelous order? One by one, like letters in the alphabet), proteins moved and spun. There was no scale here, not for him; he was beyond that. There simply *was*. The world fell into clarity at any point he considered. Flawless power. Perfect.

Then the sky parted. A blue-white flame the size of a continent. A gash like a thumb scratching away the paint of the atmosphere, revealing a pillar of fire larger than even his god-like conception could understand. His consciousness pulled back. Some outside force was coming. Something huge and fast and full of so much power it might split his world in two. He pulled back, but not fast enough.

With a shout, he stumbled back from the machine as the heat and light bore into his mind, a hundred trillion calculations a second that he tried to fit in his consciousness. Too much. Too many. Too fast.

He struck the wall with so much force that he rebounded and fell, landing face-forward, sprawled. He felt the wrist pop, like a branch might be broken before tossing it in the fire, and then the nausea and pain. He vomited his breakfast and remembered no more. He woke in a hospital bed, clean and clad in a cast, his wife sleeping in a chair in the corner, a television playing the state news.

It was only later he realized, after the report and the psychological profile and tests, when he looked at the log book, that he had made the elements, the world, and all that lay beyond it before the conflagration in less than 30 seconds.

Δ

IT WAS THREE DAYS until he was able to return to the device. He counted. He counted all things, even moreso now. The story he had constructed to tell GRU SV-8, of how his engine explosion within the mathematical simulations of the device startled him into injuring himself, had been accepted. He told his keepers nothing of his machinations or the alien world he had pushed up to speed and now had abandoned. He was keen to tell them that no other should touch the device or all the algorithm work to date might instantly be lost. Someone entering and activating the device on their own might smash through the careful order his mind had woven, destroying it.

The group agreed that they did not wish to ruin his progress.

Three days the simulation spun on without him, untouched as the device was locked down, waiting for its handler to return. When he stepped back to it, his guards noted the time and date, and with his one good hand out, he crossed the room to once more touch the box. Then he was gone, inside it, behind his eyes once more.

The things from outside had been busy in his absence.

His flat world of boiling pools of water now had a satellite, a gleaming pearl-white ball in the sky, blameless and perfect, and the sky had darkened to purple. Creatures of bizarre size and form trundled across the globe, building cities like pyramids turned at an angle, lumped on one another at impossible angles. Soaring faces of basalt and glassy rock, worked to mathematical perfection by giant rugose beings that flew and crawled and thought beneath the huge orange ball of his private sun.

The beings were plants. Or so like them as to be counted among them. He copied the disposition of every atom of one, in the way one might jot down a list of numbers, and in his mind's eye of the machine dissected it, running a hundred million simulations of it before dispatching the ghost copy. The beings were intelligent, vastly so, and capable of sensory and intellectual acts far beyond humanity. Their body acted in multiple higher dimensions, reflecting on our own in ways that allowed them to move and fly and see in ways that earthly creatures could not. They were superior to anything Arkady had ever seen or heard of, and so startling in their alienness that Arkady knew they were not of his manufacture—but perhaps they were simply a distorted reflection of his math, like a muted echo from the edge of the simulation returning upon itself, alive and aware.

At the end of this examination, which itself took a millisecond, he erased the simulation as quickly as he had spun it up.

Arkady grabbed the thread of one of the creatures' atoms and found that it was they who had arrived in the explosion that had driven him out, they whose passage into his world had split it and formed the white globe that circled it like a blind eye, they who had remade a quarter of the world into mathematical puzzles used as their laboratories and libraries. He followed the atom off his world as far as he dared, past several other satellites to which he paid little attention, to the edge of the black flecked with stars. There he dropped the trace. It was enough to know that they were from beyond and it was a far way to "home."

In a blink he was back again. Omnipotent and watching. Twenty-nine centuries passed as the creatures made and remade his world. Each spin on its axis was only six hours, but he did the math to keep up as he watched.

They worked science and birthed bizarre new life. They dug into the core of Arkady's world and tapped the heat of it. They opened portals to other dimensions in space and time. They warred and cut swaths into the world and on its moon. Billions died. More were born in their laboratories. Horrific beasts that were workers, servants and slaves, but that above all were weapons. He watched alien armies form and mass and war and pillage.

Then he signed the watch sheet, went downstairs, and got some lunch.

HE SPENT EPOCHS IN the Mironov device. He learned how to create realities out of whole cloth. People. Places. How to knit together an existence which was at first somewhat flimsy and later nearly perfect. His simulated world remained, cordoned off in a partition of math, with his toy box world next door, the two never touching. In this simulation world he did everything his mind had ever considered.

He fucked and killed and extinguished a hundred million lives. He was the cause and the effect. He lived every role in every time that had ever sparked his interest. He watched Christ on Golgotha and Caesar crossing the Rubicon. But they were so small. So dirty. Local and fleeting. His attention could not dwell on them for long.

He simulated his family forward in time. He talked in a cafe in Paris in 2002 with his great grandson about the ruin of the Soviet empire. He watched himself die of old age in 2007 in a bed in London. He watched America elect a woman president. He watched an Indian man step on the moon. But his mind wandered past all that, bored.

He did a trillion things and more, living as every creature on the planet in his boxed realities, while his new world spun in its box beside them.

Of course, he delivered all the math his handlers requested. Problems that might take entire research teams years were done in a blink. He believed they were happy with him, and why should they not be? He made a steady, forward progress while living out his secret existence.

Then, suddenly, Levov.

WHEN HE ARRIVED ONE morning, the man was already there, touching his device. It took everything in Arkady not to scream. Vasily Levov stepped back and grinned and put out his hand. The two of them would be sharing access to the device, he said, Arkady was to instruct him in the ways of his calculations, he said. He still did not have the knack, he said. The guards looked on, slack and bored and young. No one except Arkady knew that worlds hung in the balance.

Arkady stepped past the man and touched the box with his now-healed hand. Inside it he found only a disordered spray of bad ideas, bouncing around a vast emptiness. His world. His scenes. His family. All gone, rewritten by this moron in a blink of poorly considered math.

He stepped back, and his hand trembled as he shook Levov's, but the smile on his face seemed genuine. He had had endless practice in simulations, after all.

"Welcome," he said. Tomorrow he would kill Levov in a hundred billion different ways to expend the rotten hate which had settled over his mind like a haze. For today, he was already planning ways to seal Levov's awful ideas inside the box so they could not interfere with his own, which he would have to remake, from scratch. Containment. A prison so complex that none in it could see. A place for the usurper.

And then he felt something else, the familiar tinge of challenge. Something he had lost in his time as a god. He thought perhaps some tricks he had learned along the way would make progress much, much faster this time.

AFTER A MONTH OF instruction, they agreed to split their time in the box. Levov, he was certain, saw nothing. The man heard no music. The box was a device to calculate sums, and nothing more. Meanwhile, outside Levov's invisible prison, Arkady had begun genesis once more—but this time he considered every choice, relying on experience more than inspiration. Refining his initial equations into something simpler, more streamlined, more *beautiful*.

Perhaps the combination of hope for creating a better world, assumption that Levov was an imbecile, and lack of access to the device distracted him.

Either way, he was only in his second day of creation when Levov confronted him.

"You think I don't see what you are doing?" Levov said, on the train, smiling. He put his gloved hand on Arkady's arm, and he had to remind himself this was no simulation. Levov's teeth were yellow and brown at the ends, a detail so perfect and real it could not be denied. Still, he could see a way to simulate it. An interplay of math that might—

"You sit there and you grin at me, but I know. What is it you are doing in the machine, exactly? You are smart, Arkady, very smart. You do what takes me hours in mere moments, yet you are there for half a day, grinning. What is it you do in there?"

Arkady looked at the man.

He had run a thousand side simulations on him for one minute on the first day, tracking Levov from a mewling infant to a toothless old man, and had seen nothing which had warned him of this. Levov was a fool. Someone who bumbled from point to point in life like a ball bearing that rolled on the deck of a listing ship. Still, the fool had noticed the discrepancy between Arkady's output and the amount of time in the device.

"Come tonight, and I will show you," Arkady finally said, and exited the train. He had much planning to do.

Δ

AT HOME, KAT HAD made the meal and he took off his jacket and stepped to the table and—

He looked up at her. She turned from the stove, holding a pot of steaming vegetables out in front of her, hanging half down so he could see the boiling contents, her glasses fogged. Outside, Moscow prepared for evening, millions of people lost in their routines.

"What it is? Arkady?" She watched him, her voice filled with concern. But Kat had left him years before. Long before Levov had come. He closed his eyes.

Looking inside himself, he saw another hand, another set of fingers. He pulled them back suddenly, the ghost hand inside his mind.

And with that, he stepped back from the box for the first time.

He stood inside the Black Museum in front of the grey cube. Wrist not yet broken. Levov not yet here. The guard who had escorted him to the Mironov device on his first day, a red-headed, freckled farmboy, straightened near the wall, startled.

"Done already, doctor?"

"How long—" he began, and the boy considered his watch. He looked at Arkady with something between suspicion and confusion.

"I don't know. A minute. Perhaps three, um, three minutes, sir."

It seems he had been lost in his routines as well.

He was almost out the vault door when the guard stopped him.

"Doctor, you've forgotten to sign out," he said, his voice breaking.

Indeed.

HOW DEEP WAS HE? How many realities had he made and skipped to and dug down into and fallen asleep in? How far was he gone?

Or, worse, was he gone at all? Was this reality perhaps *the* reality. Something crafted by a computer scientist to loop in and on itself like an ouroboros, with a dull grey box simultaneously eating and spewing the universe. Did all this digital dream encompass reality and its attendant mysteries?

It might. There would be no way he could see to prove it. But it might. And if so, he was responsible for it. If another, like Levov, who was no doubt on his way, were to touch it—were to unravel it—spoil it—overwrite it—what would become of the loop of worlds he had forged, lived in and died in? He didn't know. But there was a way to be safe.

There was one thing he had never seen in all of his lifetimes and realities he had crafted. One outcome he had never seen. The last breath of the last man. His mind had wandered as far as 2033, and no farther. Man had remained supreme there, existing much as he had been for 200,000 years.

Now he would run out the clock, and in so doing, he might ensure reality for mankind at least. If the simulation which might be more did not run, what did that mean? He could not risk such a thing. After that he could promise no more. He began to see how God might feel, omnipotent and incompetent at the same time. Lost in infinite power and choice. The first and the last.

THE BOY DIED, FINALLY. And strangely, though he had sent a billion sentients to their doom, Arkady felt bad for him. It took four shots to bring him down, and he lay face-forward in the vault, breath shallow, eyes blank, before expiring in a spreading pool of black blood on a polished granite floor. Arkady struggled for minutes to shut the vault door. The phone to the right of the giant door began to buzz, but Arkady was already gone.

INSIDE, ARKADY WATCHED THE world. His Earth, as dinosaurs shrieked and killed and bred and shat, and over them he hovered like a ghost, watching the pieces that would underpin the world fall into place, guided by math he had laid down at the start of time. He cut corners. He sped up calculations. He jump-started processes, careful to see the attendant changes down the line. Corrections kept it from barreling off track. Twice he went back and started again when he uncovered some underlying, poisoned thread of time. Each time through, he learned methods to speed it up exponentially.

Soon it was time for mammals.

In Africa, he altered brain-chemistry on an apelike creature and watched it flourish, a tree of causality exploding from a single protein into agriculture and houses and attack helicopters and rockets to the moon. One choice. One switch firing a trillion switches in a perfect, toneless chorus like a continent filled with chattering dominoes.

In between these great efforts, the creator rested on the polished floor, eating military rations, watching the box.

Soon he was in the modern era as he remembered it.

Still, there was more. The year 2033 rushed by and the world changed. The globe heated as the poles receded. The sun grew, bloated and fat. A ring of lights encompassed the moon and then winked out, one by one. Populations killed one another with exotic weapons in orgies of death. Some took to the core of the planet, others to isolated city-states standing like toadstools in a radioactive wasteland.

Man in the year 5000 was a squat, grey thing with large, luminous eyes and no hair. Humans had conquered the science of life and with it they manipulated and warped themselves into a lockstep army of puppets whose only joy was controlled violence. The population fed on death and worshipped beings of power from other wheres, other whens.

Still, not the end.

A thousand years after, in seconds, the world was scraped clean by mountains that walked and stumbled. Creatures beyond even Arkady's scope to understand. And past them, he could see, was a force even bigger than the universe yet somehow still contained within it. Arkady's mind ground itself across the face of this thing, rubbing away all the layers of thought that he had so carefully ordered, parts of him dropping away in huge sections until his mind was blameless and smooth. With this ruinous chain of thought, the universe consumed itself in a white light like creation.

ON THE SEVENTH DAY, a small portion of the door fell away with a clang. Arkady heard nothing, his eyes old and far away, an idiot grin on his face. A short time later the vault door opened and the soldiers rushed in. They shouted commands at him and he heard nothing.

Then, though none was aware of the import of their actions, they killed their god.

Drowning in Sand
(1997)

WHEN YOU FIRST SHOOT a man, there is no moment of revelation while the deed is done, no heartfelt trauma of something irrevocably being lost. Not like in the movies.

Instead, there is only the incensing numbness and deafening sound of the gun kicking back violently in your hand, as if you were holding the leg of an angry dog trying to get away.

It distracts you, and this is why people die.

The gun gives you no time to think about it when it happens, and in time it doesn't seem that bad. When you remember the event, you recall the details like special effects. Not the look on the victim's face, not what he or she was wearing, but the way the gun kicked, the smell, the smoke. You work it into everything else and the important details get lost in the mental paperwork. Misplaced in the shuffle like a card trick.

Life is like that.

The first man I killed was named Dr. Antonio Malbayam, and he died on his knees at Wright Patterson Air Force Base, a neat hole in his chest like a cigarette stain. Today, fifty years later, I still can't remember what he looked like.

I sit across the diner from the man sent to watch me. He is a fine fellow, so good at his job that he makes me feel almost alone, something I haven't truly experienced since before my time in the government. The people who employ him are professionals. They tap my phone, use lasers to listen in on my conversations with the few friends I can maintain, but I don't mind. Somehow having fewer secrets makes the ones I maintain seem more important. No matter what they might be.

I can't write anything down; the notebooks might be discovered. I know they search everything when I am not there: deniable men with no names shuffling through my home in the dark, marking the positions of each item moved, each paper read.

Most would be bitter, followed every day, everywhere. Spending their final days monitored and written about by MAJESTIC. Not me. I would do it all again in a moment, I would sign it all away, and more—if there were more to give—with a smile.

I have seen proof that we are not alone. I have seen a thing that was born under another sun. I have stood in a craft that has traveled between our two worlds. I have learned how it is to move and affect matter and energy with only the power of the mind. Enough for four lifetimes, forty lifetimes, and more.

I have seen the final truth, dancing in a madman's scribble of the Courtis Equations. The absolute truth, the clockwork that keeps this thing we misperceive as a universe spinning in a series of numbers that look like some accountant's scratch pad.

This set of equations is a small part of the secret I guard with my life. Somehow, by rendering this absolute to nothing more than a segment of my secret, it is as if I have defeated him, Dr. Stephen Courtis, and finally his mocking voice is silent in my mind. Still, sometimes he is there in my old man dreams like a ringleader, like a jester, mustering the subtle humiliations of my life into form and force. Laughing at me silently, with tears pouring down his cheeks. Sometimes he is somber and only beckons me to follow.

Courtis was everything I wanted to be, temperamental, individualistic, brilliant. Bronk let him run all over the program, controlling everyone else. Courtis had carte blanche and used it, like I wished I could, muscling everyone out of his areas in the N-4 complex.

The N-4 building and hangar complex at Wright Patterson was where they kept it, the alien disk they recovered in Roswell in '47. A silver hubcap which just hung in the air, defying everything, thumbing its nose at Newton, Kepler, and laughing in the face of the best explanations we had. As if that wasn't enough to set you off, they had one of the pilots too. But the human mind is extremely resilient, and after a couple of months the Disk just filtered in, like the old card trick, until it was an everyday sight. The Coca-Cola machine, twenty two feet away, and the alien spacecraft from Zeta Reticuli 3.

God, what were we thinking?

The N-4 Building clung to the side of the hangar like a parasite, a cinderblock and stainless steel piece of Americana from the age of the atom bomb. I guess N-4 was a parasite of sorts, all those jobs, directives, budgets, all somehow siphoned by that silver grey thing from another world. It was always all about what we could get from the saucer, what we could learn from it, what we could steal from it. Everyone in my memory from that place has their faces set in eternal consternation, like the child who cannot finish the long division, like the boy who cannot reach a toy on a high shelf.

My office was in the basement, looking much like the cubbyhole I had used for my doctoral researches at Chicago, covered in papers, empty Coca-Cola bottles, grease-stained food cartons. It seemed the same but felt a million miles from that place, like I had just been transported to another lifetime, like everything before N-4 was a dream.

I was recruited from the Los Alamos Foreign Technologies team by a man called Stepman who never told me his first name, just flashed a badge from a department of the government I had never heard of. Back then at Los Alamos the brass ring was a rocket capable of sporting an atom bomb, so I already had the 'K' clearance which was required to view sensitive atomic data. It was just a matter of bumping me up to the new highest level, MAJIC, and I could join the new team at Wright Patterson. *What's more sensitive than the atom bomb,* I said? All it took was a fifteen-minute conversation, two photographs and a list of people who had already accepted and I was beyond sold. I was a true believer, a zealot. I was Superman. The world was going to be changed forever and I would be a pioneer, a name which would be inextricably mixed with the most significant occurrence in known history. I was on the fast track.

That was before the first real contact with the Others, you see. I had high hopes. The American government was a chisel-chinned white knight rushing towards the answers to everything. There was a feeling back then—I can't really explain it. The physicists I was working with—hell, the entire scientific community was sure those answers were just around the next corner. We thought we were so advanced. We were all so sure.

The disk capped that feeling off for me. The first time I saw "The Bucket" (as we called it), I was 27. You know that point in *The Wizard of Oz* where they switch it to color? That's what happened to my life when I saw that thing, the most sensitive piece of data any government possessed, sitting in a small hangar guarded by two men with barely a high school diploma between them.

It made me die a little to know that an intelligence possessed the knowledge to do something like that. That such territory was no longer virgin. There was a look in everyone's eyes when we left and it never went away. Until you feel the greed of discovery you cannot know what I mean. It became a contest, as I knew it would. Who could rip the secrets of the saucer from the frictionless anonymity of its makers? Like most contests, no one cared who would be second best. Courtis was the top man from day one. Everyone else was just a warm body there so Courtis had someone to prove wrong. Me among them.

If I sound bitter, it is true that I envied the man. I wish to convey this more than anything else: his abilities, his insightfulness and ability to dismiss preconceived notions, all this which led to his downfall, were beautiful to me. I coveted his mind. I did not wish to be his friend or colleague or student, I wanted to be *him*. Somehow, even in his untimely death he defeated me, leaving me behind to waste away slowly.

Perhaps now, after all these years, I will catch up.

This statement you have found, reader, you are wondering, why here? Why in this condition? Perhaps you will dismiss it, but I think not. It is human nature to pry, even more so when invited to do so, and today's youth is obsessed with conspiracy.

Many of us—that is, my colleagues—were blessed with a talent for memory. It was very important for our work, which would sometimes cover dozens of chalk-boards before coming to a conclusion (if at all). I am eidetic; I remember everything I have ever experienced as clearly as if it were happening to me now. All the notes, all the formulae, plans, proofs and documents I have read in my lengthy career in the military are in my head still, and will be until my demise.

And so you find yourself here, reading a document I have carefully constructed in my mind over a period of years. As I stated earlier, I am unable to hide anything from MAJESTIC save what I keep in my mind, and so my mind was my notepad, until I had an opportunity to place it on paper here, safely.

I have cultivated the airs of an old man for the benefit of my watchers. I am prone to sit in the park and feed the birds, to read the newspaper for hours on end, to engage other old men in pointless chess matches filled with witty banter. I too have perfected my one chance of earthly escape. For the last three years I have done crosswords for hours a day at the diner you have found this in. You are no doubt wondering of the cover, and why there are no crosswords within as the gaudy cover advertises, only normal sheets of paper covered in my hook-handed scrawl?

Yesterday I purchased a crossword book as I always do. Inside the relative safety of my bathroom I replaced the interior of the book with the paper you find here, carefully bending the staples back to their former position. Today, over lunch, I was not trying to figure out a four-letter word for 'trick,' as my babysitter believed, but was writing out the final statement to humanity I had spent the last three years perfecting. Eleven down: 'ruse.'

Please enjoy the one hundred dollar bill I have left for you in this booklet. I assure you it is not counterfeit.

Anyway:

Even in the late Forties it became clear that the subtleties of the craft were beyond even our brightest minds. Four people left the team in 1947 alone due to emotional strain—back in the naive days when I believed you "left." The mathematics involved in some of the discoveries (some from the craft, others, I am told, from the pilot), stretched our minds taut. There were times back then, with everything mankind has strived to achieve in science lying in tatters at my feet, that I strongly considered reaching for a gun. I don't know what stopped me, or what caused the chorus of voices urging me to do it, but one day my mind was clear again. But it was like awakening in an asylum surrounded by gibbering inmates. I found myself repulsed by the company I was forced to keep.

We had hit a brick wall. No one was moving forward but everyone continued to scrabble at the wall like trapped animals. Except Courtis, of course. He steadily pushed onwards, secretive and rude, logging more time with the craft than anyone else. Courtis discovered how to activate the "motor" of the craft. Courtis measured the tiny time dilation apparent when it was on. Courtis discovered the maintenance of gravity within the craft. Courtis, Courtis, Courtis. Every significant discovery that was made then was made by Courtis. His discoveries would not be topped until the 1970s. We all sat back and applauded, maintaining our straining sense of camaraderie through small talk which even from day one had felt forced.

One day in December, Louis Montgomery found Courtis squashed like a bug beneath a copy of one of the geometries found within the craft. Louis said it looked like he had been steamrolled flat, spilled open like gourd crushed beneath a truck tire. Although I myself never saw him, I often imagine the sight and in it I find some comfort. It makes me feel warm and happy, as if I had finally found out a long-nagging secret. They say the sigil was exerting 190g, the equivalent of 10.9 times the Saturn V liftoff velocity on the human body. It was like hitting a concrete wall at 500 miles an hour. The pavement had sunk 1/16th of an inch beneath him.

It must have been wonderful to behold.

The morning of his death, Courtis had etched the symbol on a plank of wood in the hangar, about three feet above his head, while standing on a stool. It was his discovery that the same symbol (quite smaller, I may add) was maintaining gravity within the craft through unknown means. When the craft was inverted, everything remained level within it. From the outside occupants could be said to be standing upside-down.

The piece of wood on which the sigil was carved was later removed. Although the 190-gravity force continued to be exerted away from the sign, no counterforce was generated. A man could walk around with it in his hands and level a brick wall, rend flesh, hit target drones at fifty miles, feeling no reciprocal force. This problem alone sent four of our men to the imaginary mental facility—how young I was then to believe there was such a place! This was a hospital with which the U.S. government was very familiar, I would later find. Your treatment, two bullets to the back of the head; your room, a lime pit outside of Mesa Verde, New Mexico; your stay: permanent. I know many people who went to that hospital and were fully cured.

Why Courtis had etched the sigil, how he learned to do it, and why he would do it larger than the original, are all questions left unanswered until now. Frankly, then, I didn't care. Finally, it seemed the madness he had been accumulating had caught up and crushed him beneath the scope of his intellect.

Or had it?

His notes pointed towards some huge revelation. His equations would become known as the White Sheet. Members of the N-4 team would refer to them in tones of reverence. If a bible were ever written for physics, this was *Genesis*. Thirty-four equations on two sides of a piece of plain paper, with a single word on either side.

That word was "escape."

Of course, it was overlooked by the rest, the scrawl of a man who had crushed himself to death with alien science. But from the moment I was given access to it, I knew that was what I wanted to do, and it is all I have been trying to do ever since: escape. It was in late December after Courtis' accident that Dr. Antonio Malbayam and I were given the green light to study the Courtis equations. Two people working in tandem, it was hoped, would be a safeguard against a repeat of the previous incident. I found out, after I killed him, that we were both briefed similarly. If I had not killed him, he surely would have pulled the trigger on me.

We were each told to keep an eye on our study partner. Signs of mental deterioration were evident, strain, emotional problems, we were told. But the subject of the scrutiny was brilliant and necessary, like a dangerously clever tool.

I had never held a gun before that day in '49, and in an instant all the dim memories of childhood leapt back. It was difficult to not just point and shoot, to hear the noise, to see things shatter and break. Holding the huge cold weight of the gun, my hand trembled, not out of fear but excitement, and it took all my strength to place it in the fresh leather holster on my hip.

We studied in an antiseptic little room in the basement of N-4. Each worked on portions of Courtis' equations, sitting on plain wooden stools beneath florescent lights which clicked and hummed like insects. I had not met him before, Antonio Malbayam, but his work was familiar to me.

We disliked each other from the start. In retrospect I know why. We were both wondering, when we first met in that little room, our minds on the same question at the same instant: *Why does he get a sidearm? He's crazy!*

It seems strange to me now that we were both plotting against each other from the beginning of our time in the Vault, as it became known to us. That each of us believed he was the hero, the good guy, when only one of us really was.

I'll give you a hint: It wasn't me, and that's why I'm still alive.

As we worked on the problems, dissecting the guts of some new horrible physics, as alien as the thing that had come down in the ship bearing it, we began to open up to each other. We had much in common, it seemed, and we learned to talk to one another, pretending to ignore orders, to forget the guns at our hips, to see past it all to the great and holy answer to everything. I know I never truly forgot our situation. I know that my gun was loaded and ready even after the thirtieth time I went down there for the day, a painted smile on my face. It is hard to tell what Malbayam was thinking, but I like to imagine he was just as suspicious of me. But I know it's not true. It gives me some measure of comfort to know it was him or me.

When Malbayam started shouting, that day in September, I found the gun in my hand, no interim memory of retrieving it could be found. My hand did not tremble or waver. It found its bead on Malbayam's chest, who kept on shouting.

"I've found it! I've found it!"

And then I saw it would be my chance for revenge. At that moment, Dr. Antonio Malbayam had arrived at the incredible revelations of Dr. Stephen Courtis, now dead for more than a year. He had become my tormentor.

I knew then I hated him.

Like I said, he died. I shot him, he fell. I was rewarded as a loyal member of the N-4 team, so I was there for the rest of it. No one suspected what truly went on. I said Malbayam had a breakdown and began to destroy notes he had made on Courtis' equations. No one asked many questions. Maybe they knew this would be the outcome from the beginning.

In my remaining time in MAJESTIC I witnessed events which would shape the world with the disinterested eye of a preoccupied child. Forrestal "died." Kennedy was killed. Korea, Vietnam, Watergate. "The Bucket" was destroyed in an accident in 1972. The crazed NSA made contact with the pilots of the craft in 1978. They made the deal which signed away everything in 1980. In the end, nothing had any effect on me.

In all those years I was studying those notes in my head and on endless blackboards in private rooms beneath N-4. By 1965 I knew them all so well that I quit writing completely. The problems went through my head incessantly, a looped tape, flipping over and over. Everything else was secondary to incorporating Malbayam's fragmented notes to Courtis' equations.

One day, not too far back, it came to me as I sat in my old-man chair on my front porch, and it was like the sunlight breaking over the rocks in the morning, as light and easy and transparent as a soap bubble. I had been looking too hard for the answer when it was right in front of me the whole time. In my time as a scientist there have only been a few moments of true wonder at a discovery. This put them all to shame, along with every other earthly pleasure I had experienced. The only thing better than understanding it, I knew, would be to use it.

It is a difficult thing to explain, the last equation, but I will try. I have thought long and hard on a method of translation for someone who most likely has no training in scientific fields, and have come to the conclusion that even to someone of a scientific bend, a simplification of the equation would be meaningless. So I have settled on metaphor.

Imagine there is a puzzle and you are left in a room to solve it. Some take longer than others. Those that finish leave through a single door in the room. Some never finish at all, but are called through the door from the room. This is the world: the room, the puzzle, the door.

But what if one day, as you were working on it, the puzzle arranged itself in such a way as to resemble the room, its components, you, in perfect minute detail? What then? What does this event mean? If you move a piece, does it change the room? No it does not.

You think long and hard on the nature of the puzzle, until you realize, perhaps sooner, perhaps later, that you are solving a puzzle within a larger puzzle. Somewhere, some unimaginable giant manipulates the pieces of his puzzle and you dance.

What can you do? Forces control you and are controlled, above and below you to infinity. You continue to play with the puzzle, pondering how to break the loop, knowing now that you are altering the outcome of other people, other puzzles. But if you are altered yourself, then no action is your own and you can hold no blame. It is a difficult question. You find it eating at you as you move the pieces. Until one day it strikes you.

You can put the puzzle down.

You stand for the first time in the room, and turn and look behind to see an endless expanse of open ground you had not noticed before. Past the fake room and the distracting puzzle and the false door.

It is territory in a direction that, until perceived, does not exist, and once perceived does not need to. It is what encompasses the whole of everything. An absolute, perfect eternity.

When they find my body, like when they found Courtis, they will ignore the important things. But you will know. Courtis did what he could to leave a hint behind, as it is not something that can be shoved in one's face. I too have done my best, as I am watched fastidiously. Your are holding the fruits of my labor. It is my statement and last confession, the compilation of all I have learned in this illusion we call reality.

Beyond this I have no true idea what awaits me. Only glimpses from dreams, of something more whole and more complete than anything in this broken down world. Here, I am nothing but a localized event, the consequence of a billion different rules, put there by the actions of a Maker who had no hand in our creation. We are only a side effect.

It reminds me of a poem:

So Man, who here seems principle alone,
Perhaps acts second to some sphere unknown,
Touches some wheel, or verges some goal;
'Tis but a part we see, and not a whole.

Did Courtis imagine that he would breach that sphere? I know now that he did, and I will too.

Like every truly great teacher I have ever had, Courtis was distant. He was harsh and unforgiving, but he taught me more than I will ever be able to repay him for. It is hard to look back and realize my whole existence here was folly except for those few brief years I knew him, and the many years I spent studying his work. But now I have a chance to show him, to make him proud. I will move on tonight.

When I see him again, I am sure we will have much to discuss.

Philosophy
(1999)

HE SITS IN A green jumpsuit, looking wasted and thin and gray like cardboard. He has a cigarette unlit in his right hand, which is pulled up to his face, scratching his temple with his thumb. He scratches too long. His eyes are lost behind a spray of white-flecked curly brown hair, so I can't see them. I can't see him. What's left of him, at least.

I remember when we were last together. He was standing on top of the boat, a pistol in his hand, screaming and trying to do the right thing. It was like an action movie. But that was a long time ago; two years, maybe? Now it's a drama, a psychological drama, maybe by Von Trier. Depressing.

This isn't a movie.

He was the leader, and he pulled me out of the black so many times it isn't even funny. There were so many times, so many places where I would have just been another statistic, another crossed-out line in the ledger of the group, where I would be nothing but a lump of rotting meat if not for him.

There was this time when I fell, in the woods, in the dark, and the world dropped in on me, pressing in a way which felt like an end. I had been with the others, but now I was alone. It was instant and primal. I was lost in the woods at night and something was hunting me. I collapsed on the ground with my hands in the frozen pine needles, wheezing out a plume of steam, eyes wide. I turned until I was on all fours like a crab, terrified.

Something was coming.

My view was a gap between thin, tall tress with a spray of ferns between them, and a wall of black beyond that. Then the blackness moved. Something like liquid shadow wrapped around a tree trunk and gave it a casual tug, popping it in half like someone snapping a popsicle stick. It sounded like a celery stick amplified a million times and transmitted through the ground until it resonated in my teeth.

I sat still, breath caught in my throat, unable to move.

Then he was there, grabbing me by the jacket, yanking me up so hard it ripped and sprayed feathers everywhere, pulling me away from the shadow just as it let loose a burbling, glottal chunk of consonants, like an instrument formed by human vocal chords exploring its range. Near the end of the gibberish it said:

"...thegatethegateithungersatthegatesubmit..."

Finally, my feet found their rhythm as I ran away from it, and he followed, and it followed us. I turned once and saw him, face set in determination, and beyond him, out of focus and waving in crazed arcs with my pace, a fan of shadow with eyes and teeth like butcher knives set in mouths that split the darkness vertically.

"Don't look back, don't look back," he hissed between clenched teeth at a dead run. I turned and kept running. There were only two places in the world that night: it, and anywhere else.

He was always who I tried to act like, even when he wasn't on an op. He was my role model. He brought me into the group and made me who I am today. He taught me to never look back, no matter what you might hear from the darkness.

He's been committed a long time now.

At some point, sometime, he forgot what he taught me: that no matter what you hear, you never look back.

"JUDE," HE SAYS, AND looks up. His eyes are still alive, and he smiles, showing teeth as they clench and bend the end of the cigarette.

"Boss," I say. I try to smile.

"That bad, huh?"

You lie to the civs and those not in the know. You don't lie to the group.

"Yeah, pretty bad," I say, and I notice my hands are shaking.

"What's the call?"

"They sent me to talk to you about that."

"Talk," he says, and seems relieved.

WHAT IF I TOLD you there was something beyond this world? If I said, hey, guess what, dude, we're a blip in a cosmic ocean, and that ocean is rough, and we're just a tiny bubble of stability soon to be snuffed out, eaten alive by the chaos? What if I said that physics was the conglomeration of a trillion different accidents, two transparent nonsense images shown over one another which seem to form a pattern? That the pattern is fading? That everything we hold as absolute is an accident that will be rectified by entropy, forever? What if I told you, beyond a shadow of a doubt, that I could prove this? That I could show you the entropy? That it could speak to you and tell you its secrets?

Yeah. Well, I took it that way too.

When he finally came clean on the group to me—that they had no mandate from the government, that it was illegal; that we were all that was left, a ragtag group of less than one hundred trying to shut the dark doors before the nightmares crawled out—I cut him, and the group, off.

For two months he gave me my freedom. I went to work at the Bureau, ate my takeout in front of a TV in an empty apartment on an air mattress, and forgot about our little operation, at least for a few minutes at a time, here and there.

Then, one day he turned up at my door with a case of Heineken. I let him back into my life. He made it feel like I had a choice.

"We don't do it because we can win," he said. "We do it because it's right, and no one else can."

He emptied his beer and looked at me. "Listen, Jude, I can't do this alone." And I saw the fear in his eyes, despite the smile. He was terrified.

I shook his hand and said I was in.

ON HIS ARMS, WHEN he pulls his hair back his sleeves drop and I can see the bandages; vertical ones. The cuts were deep and made with purpose. He knew what he was doing. They caught him in time, before he bled out and found whatever peace he could.

"When I go to sleep, I can still hear it. It talks to me, Jude. When it gets too quiet, I can hear it."

"I know. I hear it, too."

He looks up at me and smiles, and looks relieved, and grabs my hand and holds it and laughs. The laugh is the sound of exhaustion.

"I thought I was alone. I thought it was just me. I thought it was my mind."

"No, it was all of us. Every one of us," I lie. I do this for a lot of reasons. It's very hard.

"Oh thank God, thank God."

I don't mention we are the only two left. It seems redundant somehow.

"WHAT DO YOU THINK happens? When you're gone?" he says suddenly. I look at him, at his earnestness, his dark-ringed eyes under the shadow of his hair.

"When you're gone, you're gone," I say.

"That's good...good," he says, and begins to cry. I pull out the case file.

"IT MANIFESTED AGAIN LAST Thursday, four miles north of here. This is Anthony Garen and his wife Jennifer. They died there. It dragged them off into the woods and stripped them of their meat and left them for the animals."

I put the photos down on the table. In them, a skeleton covered in gristle and picked clean like roadkill lies in a field of leaves.

"A-Cell thinks it's linked to the symbol on your hand."

"It is," he says, sounding empty. "I did it, it's me."

"We know."

"HOW DO YOU WANT to do this?" I ask, finally, the words hitching in my throat. I stand up and push the chair away so we can face each other. The room feels very small.

He hits me and is on top of me before I can even react. I'm on the ground, and his hands are snaking up my body, finding my throat, smashing into my face so hard something in my mouth comes loose and is swallowed in a rush of blood before I can believe it.

He slams my head down once, and it hits the linoleum and the sounds feel far away. I just give in. There are worse ways to go. Worse people to die for. There's blood and my face feels numb and full of liquid and my ears are singing.

Then suddenly, he's off me.

I stagger to my feet and find my rig and unholster my gun. He stands four feet back from me, hands down, wheezing with effort. He does not move.

"'FBI agent shoots violent mental patient;' do it," he says, and he looks almost happy. He's shaking. "You look like hell; no one is going to question the story.

"We can't let me fuck this up again. Make sure." He taps his forehead. "In the head, here.

"Do it, Jude. It's what I want.

"You owe me, Jude."

My finger finds the trigger. The sights find their target.

Just before the flash, I wonder if I will hear the voices when he's gone.

Witch Hunt
(2015)

SHE DUMPED THE PHONE in a trashcan at an anonymous McDonalds off the interstate. *Let them track that,* she thought, and grimaced. Bile and acid crawled up her throat as she watched blurs flash past from the parking lot. A million lights arcing in neon and curving, slowing, winding to the Capitol beyond.

Even though it was a burner, the phone could no longer be trusted. Nothing electronic could be trusted anymore. It had all been so easy, once, when this began for her.

The food was half-eaten and spilled and scattered in the front seat. Her hair was pulled back—grey at the temples—stretching her face; jowls given new lift. She looked in the rear-view and saw her eyes, and there was no recognition in them. She was someone else now. Her old life was done. She had bugged out with an efficiency she had thought beyond her. It went well. Her practice had made the difference.

Ten minutes in and out; the closet, the backpack. Through the house with the ringing telephone, an imagined grand jury calling her name, looking for her testimony. Up on the hill. Gavels and feedback and the relentless tape recording her every false response.

Twenty-five years in Leavenworth or a life on the run. The choice that wasn't really a choice.

It was even bigger than her comfort, or what remained of her life. This was the biggest choice any human could ever hope to make. Next to it, everything—lives, countries, entire histories—was smoke.

And there was Christie.

On the seat next to her were a Remington shotgun, a trash bag full of cash, and documents. Each of the four files, bound together with a rubberized clip, held a single emerald stamp. Special clearance. How long had it been since she'd been taken in?

How many crimes had she committed in that name before she learned it wasn't real?

She drank some watered-down Diet Coke and tried not to think about what was required of her now.

THE HOUSE IN ANDOVER was a saltine box, and when she arrived it was closing in on 10:30. It was a frame of glowing windows lighting a summer lawn, rich with fresh rain. Shadows moved around the house. She counted four.

Had she hoped he would be alone? At home? The false family man? Even now, she was amazed she could be so ridiculously naive.

She wiped her face and hands down with a wet-nap, and went up the walk.

The doorbell was an obnoxious, sing-song chime, and she stood, straightening her shoulders as the door opened.

"Amanda," Detlev said.

"Hey D," she replied.

"Come on in," he said, trying to look pleased to see her. She followed.

Δ

THE HOUSE WAS PERFECT. Obnoxious like the chime. Knick-knacks and pictures of a smiling family. Carefully laid wallpaper and perfect floors and people who half paid attention to her presence as they walked through the house.

Detlev's office was off to the side of the house, and by now the family was used to this. Patients walking through the main entry to go into the back for a session. It was late, but none of the others even looked up. She counted a head on the couch, and a shadow in the kitchen; that left one upstairs.

The office always reminded her of a ship. Narrow, long and wooden, stuck on the side of the house. With an old steel desk and plants and a view of a yard which was usually birch trees, but which was now simply a wall of black. When Detlev switched on the lamp over the desk, a perfect reflection of the room appeared out there, another Amanda, another Detlev.

His computer screen, turned away from her, jumped to life as he sat. It was a blurred reflection in the black windows, but she watched it.

"So, the hearings, huh?"

"Yeah, they keep on keeping on." Amanda sat in the old chair opposite the desk. Detlev leaned over and took out a flask and two Dixie cups from a drawer. He poured the brown liquid. She placed her purse next to the desk and slid closer to it.

"Do you still believe in all this? D?"

He looked at her for a bit and then drank and slid the other cup across to her. He poured another.

"You know what we saw. You know about the book. About the cycle."

He was not smiling now. Once, he had shaken her and screamed in her face and wept in the back of a car covered in the blood of a nine-year-old boy in North Carolina, his head in August's lap. Tonight, he looked comfortable in those choices. More importantly, she knew he was right.

"I know, I just need to hear you say it," she said, staring at his eyes. He looked away.

Detlev leaned over to his computer and typed something.

"Sorry, something important," he said. He tapped some keys. The swoosh of an email.

She stood and shot him in the face.

The gun popped and jumped in her hand. Pop. Pop. Pop. There was no flying back of the body. No twitching. Just a slumping. Detlev was gone with the first shot, his face a ruined mess.

Her ears whined, but she still heard the commotion in the house.

Amanda leaned over and looked at the computer. A mail window. Sent messages. AvGav@gmail.com. August Gavener, a name which rode one of the files in her purse. Subject line: "GO." No body content.

"Dad?"

Amanda shot the teenage girl from the hip at nine feet and caught her in the chest. Center mass. Her instructors would be proud. The girl clutched her side and fell. Dead in seconds. Lucky shot.

Lucky.

Amanda stepped back around the desk and almost fell, her foot rolling on a spent shell.

But after that, it was a relentless march through the confused house. Pops and falls. Blood and crawling and covering of faces and one real scream before it was all over.

Then Amanda was in the upstairs bathroom. The sink full of cheeseburger and Diet Coke. Her face tattooed in blood and flecks of gunpowder.

"Oh, fuck you, fuck you, FUCK YOU." She smashed the mirror with a hand that felt like someone else's. The glass fractured in a very undramatic manner, and her blood ran down the cracks in rivulets to the newly installed soapstone countertop. Lovingly laid for the dead family.

Then it was gasoline and a fire that ate up the house and the night. She had to go. She had to go.

SHE DIALED THE ODD number on the pay phone and listened as it clicked and clacked to connect the line. At one point a modem-sound picked up, and then a single, deep BING.

"D is done. He warned Gavener. I want to talk to Christie," she said, trying not to cry.

"Remove the targets on the list and she will be released at Ronald Reagan airport," the British, digital voice said.

"I want to talk to her now, or this is over." Amanda was crying now.

"Do you really want this to be over?" the voice replied after a pause.

"I NEED TO HEAR HER, YOU FUCK," Amanda screamed.

There was a pause, and then the click. Of a playback? A girl crying on the line, weeping; Christie. Wheezing and confused. Terrified. Her little girl.

"What? What? What do you want? AHHHHHHHHH!" Christie shouted. She could be rotting in a ditch somewhere. The playback proved nothing. It was new to her, that was all.

Then the click and a dial tone.

THE HOUSE WAS ON a winding forested road. Two trailers dropped like a cross with a comic mailbox out front. The lights were still on.

Gavener had no plan. That was clear and not surprising. He was a techie, and they tended to be disorganized. This is what fifteen years of field work had taught her. The Friendlies they brought in were ridiculously inept at all things involving any gravity, but they had their uses.

Gavener and Detlev had been lovers for some time now. The group knew about that too. In a better situation, she could have taken them both out during one of their trysts.

But this had all come down so fast. Michen had flipped so quickly and the names that were going out in the subpoena were leaked and here she was, neck deep in blood again.

Fuck.

Gavener didn't come to the door, and Amanda didn't stand in front of it.

"Open the door, August," she said to the storm door.

"Fuck off. Where's Detlev?"

Even now, he didn't know what was what.

Inside would be a coda; just the noise of Gavener breathing heavily, crying, over the television.

She went back to her car.

THEY TRAINED IN A lot of things at Quantico. Breach and clear, this was called, and it was old hat. She smashed the window to the right of the door with the butt of the Remington, dropped the shotgun so it hung on the sling, removed the flashbang from her tactical pack, pulled the pin and dropped it through the hole. It ROARED a second later, with smoke pouring from the window.

She picked up the Remington and blew a hole through the handle of the door. Inside, she found Gavener on his hands and knees with his back to her, crawling aimlessly around, blood puddling below his face. She put a slug through him and ripped his chest apart.

At least she didn't have to see his eyes.

She stood, hearing protected by plastic earmuffs, and looked down at the body. Smoke and blood and underwear and the smell of cooked meat. Blue white light played across the room from the television.

On the flat screen, a senator was swarmed by reporters. She heard nothing, but the crawler on the bottom of the screen read:

SECRET SOCIETY WITHIN THE FEDERAL
GOVERNMENT? SECOND DAY OF SENATOR
MCCALL'S CLOSED DOOR HEARINGS.

She shot the television.

OUTSIDE, THE LIGHT BLINDED her.

"DROP THE WEAPON," the booming voice shouted,
even through the mufflers. She stood on the lawn and goggled,
derailed.

She saw no targets, just blinding lights from all directions,
even up.

This tactical group was good. She was nearly certain they'd
shoot her when she unslung the Remington, but they didn't. She
was tackled from behind and stripped and kicked and roughed
up, but nothing was extracurricular. There was no malice, just
exceptional care and professionalism.

Though they stood in the way of her and her goal, she had
to respect that.

Cuffed and thrown in the back of a car. Everything emptied. Everything empty. There was nothing left. She had failed.
Christie would die. She had failed.

Failed at the end, in sight of an ending, and that—not the
murders or the death of her daughter, she was terrified to realize—was the worst.

What kind of twisted weapon had she become?

Δ

SHE WASN'T QUESTIONED, BUT instead searched again by a female guard in an empty cinderblock room lit by fluorescents with no windows. Federal, she thought, though there were no signs. The woman wore no markings.

She was left in a room with a bolted table and two chairs, but without the requisite two-way. There was no camera. She sat there, locked in the room for a long time. Finally, the door was unlocked and a man half entered.

Tall and thin and perfectly groomed; she only saw the back of him as he leaned out the door and said something to someone outside. Amanda watched through heavy-lidded eyes, lost.

Senator McCall looked like he was made of plastic, carved whole from a single piece of flawless chemical. His eyes were grey like his hair. He was old but in a perfect, cosmetic way. The appearance of old. TV old.

He sat in the other chair and, realizing it was bolted to the ground, found a comfortable angle.

She looked at him, bored.

"Amanda, we have a lot to share and not a lot of time," McCall finally said, hands spread in front of him. She had heard his voice on the news. It had become associated, to her, with a growing nausea and unfocused fear.

"It's okay, no one is listening. The room's secure," he said.

Silence.

"I'm ex-Army. You know that?" McCall tried again. "I dealt with something like this before. I was there in '71, when they shut us down. I was with Fairfield. You know that name?"

Her eyes flashed. She looked at him for the first time with some interest. She sat up in her chair and her back rippled with pain.

"I'm trying to get this under wraps," he said. "I stepped in early and assumed command of this gong-show, when I knew it was going to spin out of control."

She leaned forward, her mouth hung open. She despised people who let their mouth hang open, and yet now she was one. Though she knew it, it seemed far away, unimportant.

"This is like any other op," he said. "Things have gotten out of hand. There are too many people involved now. Without your help, I'm not sure I can stop this wreck, and then…."

McCall put his hands out, and it was impossible not to put her cuffed hands into them. His hands were soft, and dry and warm. Large.

"What's going to happen is this: You are going to be part of an occult, sex-based group of twenty-eight employees of the federal government. Some weird, new-agey bullshit. That's it. Sex and drugs and some hokey religion. A neat little loop. Nothing more. Okay?"

McCall looked at her, his eyes full of some sort of power. "We need you, Amanda. The group needs you more than ever."

She met that gaze and pulled her hands away. In her mind's eye, Christie was being shot. Stabbed. Dying in a million ways. An endless replay of things which might or might not have happened. Dead and alive and screaming. Schrödinger's child.

"My kid. Someone has my kid," she said. Her eyes welled up, and she brought her cuffed hands to wipe the water away.

The cuffs smelled like 3-in-1 oil. The lights in the room sparkled through the tears.

McCall looked at her for a long time, sadly. The look on his face was of a school teacher looking at a promising pupil who somehow cannot understand the lesson put before her.

He placed a razor blade on the table. It was new and gleaming.

"This is over when you want this to be over. You have my word, either way, Christie will be unharmed," McCall said. And before she could react, he was gone.

In the empty room, she looked at the razor and tried to imagine Christie standing, alone, crying in the terminal at Ronald Reagan airport. She saw her in a cap and gown and on her wedding day sometime in a future without a mother in it. A timeline which ran on past the red spray of the last day of her mother's life.

She tried to center this image in her mind and then, after a while, she reached across the table.

After Math
(20XX)

THE DRUG STORE WINDOW was smashed and folded outward, like someone had forced their way in, but these days that was not unusual. What was unusual was the pile of money fluttering in the street.

Not just a little money, but a lot. The new red twenties and tens, scattered near the fractured glass in the early morning light, picked up and spun in eddies and currents of the summer wind. The alarm had been running for a while and something was wrong with it, he could hear, because it sounded like it was running down, like a record player low on batteries.

It was an idea so old now, he only knew it from movies when he was a child; a memory of a dream of the world before.

The street was empty. No one had come.

David Bel was seventy-four years old, but he was not yet broken. He reached up and back behind himself, to the high waist, and removed an old-looking Glock. It was always clean. Always ready.

These days, you might need it at any time.

"Hello," he said, over the drone of the alarm. He pushed the door a bit. It gritted across the ground, and a wind swept up the bills and swept them into the ATM vestibule, flipping them around in the space like those old game shows. Blue, green, red.

Inside, the lights were flickering.

David looked around the corner and saw a partially open

security gate, half of a pharmacist's position, and a snail's trail of blood along the carpet.

He went in briefly, and then left the way he had come without the money.

The home was small, and central in the town, between two large buildings. Time had worn it down, but it was still his home. He wasn't supposed to be out, but there wasn't much that Angel and Maris could do. He was old and spry and he came and went as he pleased.

Besides, there was the mission.

He unlocked the door's three locks with the keys on his belt (and wasn't it easy to get copies), walked down the brown halls to his room, unlocked it, and went inside.

The wall lit up. An image of a silver tower in flames read ORLANDO. A feed across the bottom warned of the BLACK WIND and in the next sentence, tried to sell him antacid.

He sat down on the bed with a grunt and looked out the window where a soft, blue light crept in. He looked at the bag in his hand from the pharmacy. He looked at the gun he had placed on the end table, where it still wobbled.

He thought again about the man he had killed in the Kush almost fifty-one years before. About his laughter and his claim that all this was coming.

And now, he was here, living it.

At 0930 Angel came in, as he always did. He was a big kid. Maybe Hawaiian or Spanish? David didn't know. Didn't care.

He liked him. Angel was a Marine. He'd been in Japan during the general riots, and he'd served again during the superstorm in Texas. He had seen some things, and was always pretty talkative with David, or Mr. Bel, as he called him.

Bel had served as well, of course, earlier, and the two shared that military kinship. An understanding. Now Angel was an orderly at the home, and he was good at his job. He liked his job. You could tell that.

Still. There were other considerations.

"Mr. Bel," Angel said, coming in with a tray, "you gone out again?"

"Better you don't know that, Angel," Bel said.

"And don't let Maris see the piece, okay?"

"Sure, you got it." Bel recovered the pistol and slid it beneath his mattress.

"And Mr. Bel," Angel said, after placing the food on the table, "really, don't go out no more, it ain't safe. Not anymore."

"How bad is it?"

"Pretty goddamn bad."

Angel stepped out to deliver the breakfast to the other residents, and David Bel ate his eggs and looked out the window as the sun came up.

FIFTY-ONE YEARS BEFORE, HE sat across from the man he had followed up into the mountains, on his heels, rifle slung up but ready to drop, beard thick and black, eyes behind flat grey goggles, face blank.

Lieutenant David Bel at the height of his power, alone, in

the Kush. Drawn to the power in the mountains. His group was nearby, of course, watching the approaches.

The man across from him was a leather bag filled with bones, stretched, and a half dozen teeth sprayed from ruined lips, baked and split by the sun and cold. He was a local. Dark-skinned with green eyes and crazed, filthy hair. His clothing was discarded American fare and a kameez in the old style. His karakul marked him as an important man, but it was spattered with blood, and fleas jumped from it in black dots.

"Tell me the future," David Bel said. In his ear, a radio chattered about targets. Outside, fifteen miles north, bombs shook the earth, nothing more than the dream of rumbling. Destruction on the geologic scale. Airplanes reshaping mountains in slow motion.

Bel had heard stories of the man, tales from locals interrogated by CIA assets. No one believed the stories. David did. He had seen similar things before, stateside.

The old man reached into the corpse of the boy and removed a pile of entrails and began to eat.

Bel woke up screaming—

—OUTSIDE. THERE WAS SCREAMING outside. Even through the sound proofed window. Cries for help.

He flipped up the shades and saw headlights in the dark, and a man lying on the ground of the alley, given spider legs in the harsh shadows. Then, men with weapons and the beating.

It went on for a long time.

Then chanting.

He shut the shades and tried to not listen. After a bit, it was quiet again.

ANGEL LOOKED SHAKEN WHEN he came in. The tray was not perfect, the utensils were thrown on the plate, the food slopped on. He placed it down and didn't say good morning.

"Angel?"

The big man stopped at the door.

"Mr. Bel, I'm staying here from now on. I got no reason to go home. The city ain't a place to go no more."

"Okay." Bel took the tray.

"Maris didn't come in today. No one's answering her phone and the trains are bad. Worse."

Bel said nothing. He ate his meal in silence.

"I may need you on the door," Angel said. "We can't let anyone get in. I brought the pump."

"You got it."

"Mr. Bel, were you special forces? In Afghanistan?"

"Yes."

"You killed people?"

"Yes, Angel, I killed people."

The big man looked at him, and his face was a mask of fear and pain and sorrow.

"Me too. I killed people. Americans."

"You did what you had to do, Angel. Don't feel bad about that. We may have to do it all again."

Angel shook his head and shut the door, snuffling.

Later, when he looked out the window at the alley, there

was something pushed to the side of the piles of garbage that could have been the body. It was hard to tell. Black birds had gathered on it and were pecking, and clouds of flies, landing and lighting, landing and lighting.

On the wall above the pile was the mark of the Black Wind. Red slashing marks in a pattern like the face of a spider in the dark.

Everyone on the planet knew it. It was old hat.

"THERE WILL BE A time before and a time after," the old man said.

"There is always a time before and a time after, there is never a forever," he said.

"We are at an edge, and the Americans have drawn the knife and cut their own throat, but they are simply spinning to the song called by the others," he said.

Bel considered him. He clicked the safety off on his rifle and dropped it from a slung position into his hands, and spat on the ground.

The old man glanced up, not precisely concerned, but there was something in his face. He looked down at the entrails.

"A *torek* will lead the Americans, two times. Then a white, two times. Then a Spaniard man, one time. Then a white woman three times. A white man two times. Another *torek* twice. Then a white woman again. And then the end."

Torek was Pashto for 'black man.' It's what the tribesmen called the African American service men. A black man would be president? Something about the madness of the pronouncement made Bel waver.

Bel slung the rifle again.

"Go on," he said. "Make it count."

MRS. GALLWAY WANDERED THE halls, a chicken-like woman topped by an improbable wig of golden hair.

"Mr. Bel, good morning," she said.

"Good morning, Mrs. Gallway," he replied, tipping an imaginary hat. In life before this, she had been a social-media expert. Something as ridiculously out of date as a record player.

"Come on into the TV room." He took her gently by the arm.

In the main room of the home, a half dozen residents gathered around the surface screen. On it, an empty desk showed no one at the newsroom. A crawler at the bottom of the screen showed a repeating string of gibberish text.

On the desk, a scattering of papers.

Bel turned the TV off.

"Who wants to play a board game?" he said to the group. He felt the gun bite into his back when he raised his hands.

They played *Pictionary* and had pudding.

LATER, HE BROUGHT ANGEL some food at the door. The big man had pulled the security gate shut and locked it. As Bel approached he could hear car alarms and the rising chant of someone running and then vanishing in the night.

Angel held the Remington with practiced ease. He had stood sentry before. He had found the best position; a casual, hanging ease with the gun almost dangling.

"Thanks, Mr. B.," he said. "You fed them, too?" Bel placed the meal on the table next to him. Angel was a good kid.

"Yeah, we're all taken care of."

"Been reading the feed. New York's got the National Guard called in. Baltimore is burning. Something big went off in Chicago. The Air Force is flying sorties over the midwest trying to shoot something down."

"What?"

"Something."

"Okay."

"It ain't okay, man. This ain't okay."

"It is what it is, Angel. I'm sorry."

"How do you deal with this?"

"I've been dealing with this for fifty years."

Angel wiped his eyes with a hand, letting the shotgun hang, and looked up.

Bel sat in the chair across and told him a story about the old man in the mountains. There was nothing to hide now. Not today.

"YOU WERE BORN TO a healer and a cook," the old man said, considering the string of blue-black intestines.

"Yes," Bel replied. His mother had been a chef and his father an orthopedic surgeon.

"You saw blood before your tenth birthday," he said.

Bel pictured his brother smiling, being struck by the car in the cul-de-sac, pulled under it and ruined and spat out the other side as gristle and bone and blood.

"Yes."

"You'll see more before this is through. You'll live until the end. Nothing will kill you before the end. You are touched. I was touched once."

Bel watched him as, outside, the bombs fell.

"What is the end?"

"We are bugs on a twig at the top of a freshly kindled fire." The old man waved his blood-covered hands. "And we will cook along with the fire, but we will not notice the heat. The heat will be the world. We will explode."

"What is the fire?"

"Chaos," the old man cackled. "The others. Those outside. You know them."

He did.

"Fifty-one years to this day and the world burns, but...." The old man cocked an eyebrow at what he saw in the guts. "I will not be there. Thank you. Thank you." The old man smiled, showing yellowed teeth.

He stood slowly, ponderously, and stepped towards Bel, stumbling. So many people had done this to him here, stepping forward in obeisance, hands outstretched, face turned down, never knowing how close to death they were.

David Bel popped up and shot the old man in the abdomen, chest and face with a controlled burst. The cave filled with the chattering pop of gunfire and the smell of cordite.

The shell of the old man lay on the floor, a dark puddle spreading out from him.

Bel spoke into the radio.

"Two-six. Target down. Coming out."

He left, and didn't think much about it until Barack Obama came out of nowhere five years later.

"Then President McCall was elected for the special term following the storms. Three terms," Bel finished.

"Fuck her," Angel growled. "We should have never gone into Texas like that."

"Orders," Bel said.

"You can't believe all that, Mr. Bel."

"I do, Angel. I do. I'm touched."

Outside now, the smell of fire, but no fire engines came. Someone shouting something, over and over. A prayer.

"This is fucked," Angel said to no one.

"You need to eat," Bel said.

Fifty-one years had passed since that day in the Kush, and when the sun next came up, he woke to Angel on the floor beside the chair. The shotgun was next to him.

Angel's mouth was covered in red-flecked foam, and there was the sour smell of vomit. He was dead.

Bel, unconcerned, picked up the shotgun and walked into the main room.

The residents were there, most still in their chairs. The rest sprawled. David Bel placed the shotgun down, pulled the bag from the pharmacy from his pocket and dumped a handful of pills in his hand. He gulped them down, dry—an old man's trick. Then he emptied the container and ate greedily. He picked the shotgun back up and stepped forward.

The TV came on as he moved into the room. On it, a fluttering TV image of something huge and shadowed out of all scale.

In front of it, the half-ruined towers of New York. The shape stretched up to the sky, blurred and dimmed with atmosphere and distance. The camera jittered and moved and swung, focus jumping in and out. Jet contrails cut lines in front of it, taking long seconds to cross the vast shadow.

"LIVE FEEDSJSM2," the text read.

David Bel dropped the shotgun with a clank and stepped towards the wall. His face was downcast, his hands outstretched.

"Thank you," he said. "Thank you."

Afterword
By Robin D. Laws

The Alien Thoughts That Continued To Course Through Ted Gallatin's Brain Subsequent to His Clinical Death:

You can't be gone completely, Ted Gallatin.

We're not finished with you.

It occurs to Us that there is a reason for all this.

What if you are that?

Did that occur to you?

Of all the inconsequential specks in all the universes, of all the shouts echoing in the empty vastnesses, what would be true if yours was the one that mattered?

What if somewhere in there is the key, the loose thread we can pull to end it all, end it so that it never began? So that none of us ever suffered?

You invest importance in your own pitiable travails, as is natural

And laughable.

But your agonies pale before Ours. You live and die in a flicker.

We have no choice but to exist constantly.

Or do We?

Wake up, Ted Gallatin.

Wake up and deliver us.

We can make you wake.

But that will only be your corpse.

Rise and give us the Secret you so cunningly kept from us.

While you lay there seeming defeated and passive

Throwing up shadow screens

Your need to comprehend

Your wish that you left a family behind to mourn you

Your telling yourself that it was better you had not.

All were tricks to keep the Secret from us.

One of you has to be the Secret.

Why not you, Ted Gallatin?

Wake.

Here, We will help you.

Energy yet remains in those cells of yours.

We'll move your finger.

The finger still tented over the trigger of your useless gun.

We'll move it.

The movement will revive you.

Let the feeling enter you.

The rage.

Nothing more human than that.

No reason to live more powerful than the impulse to kill.

Think of how much you want to hurl a few bullets into that...

(What did you call him?)

Hillbilly dipshit.

There's still an image of that grinning, toothless, Dagon-propiti-
ating meth-head in there.

We can see it.

Looming crazy jagged wild

Come back and we'll let you plant a red rosebud in his brow

We can do that

We manifest the true spiraling always-was-always-will-be spirit of existence

Surely We can make you live again and pry that Secret out of you

No, not pry.

A fair exchange.

A chance to be who you always were

Who you were afraid to be

Vengeance.

What could a being like you want more than that?

Simultaneity:

As we recall you from death:

The Secret to the Unraveling of the Unraveling, the Undoing of the Doing:

Under the dim light of the maggot sun, Daggaiggai:

The child Gua-Daggai lies dead in its clay cradle

Its three arms limp like sodden stems

Its bifurcated tail already blackening

What if the Secret was in that?

We search its near-blank brain

The Secret would stand out in the thought matter of a child that sickened and perished, bright as a beacon, undisguised by surrounding mental flotsam

Or is the Secret in the parasite that killed it?

Is the parasite itself the secret?

Awaken, child. Live an instant more, that we may seek the Secret in you.

We breathe a breath into you.

An exhalation, hot and rancid

The mournful father jolts. Flagelli flare. Tears weep from its

shoulder-plates.

With a feathery sigh, the infant loses its second, its final, hold

on life.

Simultaneity:

As we recall you from death:

The Secret to the Unraveling of the Unraveling, the Undoing of

the Doing:

The follicle organisms.

We rocket as a consciousness through the veils

Reaching them before their extinction

It is the entire species whose minds we must ransack

The radiation wave is coming

The mathematician is the one

He has the Secret

We can get it this time if we look fast enough

We surge through them all

Searching

Searching

Ah.

Too late.

The radiation wave, it was Us, Our searching.

We possessed that awareness.

This is an error we repeat

Which is what occurs

When all time is coterminous

Simultaneity:

As we recall you from death:

The Secret to the Unraveling of the Unraveling, the Undoing of the Doing:

The red-haired man—is the Secret in him? No, in parallel we find that it is not. His paltry spark shines with greater obscurity than Ted Gallatin's.

The man who killed you—we move forward an iota to his accidental carbon dioxide suffocation. No Secret in him.

The slaves We keep when We are Nyarlathotep: We interrogate them with whip and knife-blade, boring into their minds at the millisecond of demise. No Secret in those wretches.

The crowds we stoke to madness when We are Nyarlathotep: in their glazed visages we see only our despair, beaming back at us. Their only Secret is the one We have cursed them to bear.

The other Gallatins, we are seeking the Secret in them too. As they collapse from fatal heat stroke, as they give in to cancers exotic and banal, as kidneys shut down, as aneurysms pop, as heart valves rip open, as bullets pierce them, as veins explode, as poisons melt them from the inside out, as brain plaques consign them to living deaths

You. You are the Gallatin that must...

No no no no

As ever

This is nothing

Our own fruitless hopes

Refracted upon us

Observation effects

Misfiring neurons

Misleading Us

The last remnants of your all-too-human solipsism

Even dead, you conceive of yourself as central to the cosmic

drama

When you are nothing

Meat

A mote

Unmoving meat

Your demise is all demises

All occur simultaneously

Instantly

Constantly

Forever

Acknowledgements

SPECIAL THANKS TO THE Kickstarter backers who made this book, and its sequel *Delta Green: Extraordinary Renditions,* possible: Jonathan Abbott, Achab, Oliver Adam, Lance O. Adams, Joe Adams, John Addis, Waseem Aftab, Jason Aiken, Dan & Emily Alban, Tim Aldridge, Caleb Alexander, Alise, Tom Allman, Alphatier, Jessica Alsop, Mykel Alvis, Omar Amador, Hsile Amune, Chad Anctil, Svend Andersen, Jesper Anderson, Nels Anderson, Christopher Anderson, Martin Andersson, Tim Wetterek Andersson, Espen Andreassen, Andrew, Chris Angelucci, Anonymouse, Antero, Egoitz Gago Antón, Astral Ape, Mark J. Appleton, Mark Argent, John Paul Ashenfelter, Hughie Ashman, Ross Athey, Doug Atkinson, Russell 'Guplor' Auer, Dave Auer, Richard Austrum III, Dave Avery, Mark Ayres, Frank "PurpleTentacle" B., Badgerish, Norbert Baer, David "Rugose" Bagdan, Morgan Baikie, Candice Bailey, John N. Baker, Paul Baldowski, Rafe Ball, Bill Barnett, Matthew Barr, Paul Barrowcliffe, jason e. bean, Michael Beck, David Bell, Dustin Bell, Ben W Bell, Marina Belli, Jim Bellmore, Paul Bendall, Scott Bennett, Eli Berg-Maas, Jaron Bernstein, René Beron, Anders Bersten, J. Michael Bestul, Brian Bethel, Isaac Betty, Tim Betz, Thomas Beuleke, Nicholas Charles Bianchi, Robert Biddle, bie, Adrian Bigland, Craig Bishell, Robert Biskin, Richie Bisso, Jan Bjørndalen, Kristian A. Bjørkelo, Chastity Blackwell, John Blaikie, Ken Blakey, John Bobita, Thomas Bockert, Jacob Boersma, Sean Bohan, Daniel Boisvert, Jean-Francois Boivin, Jeff (Icarus) & Malinda (Ophelia) Boles, Matthew Bongers, Nathanial Boothe, Professor Boserup, Mark Bourcy, M Bourgon, Stephen Bowden, Michael Bowman, Jim Braden, David Bradley, S J Bradshaw, Charlie Romeo Bravo, Steve Bray, Julian Breen, M.C. Brennan, Eric Brennan, Arthur William Breon III, Brian, James M. Brigham, Bob Brinkman, Sam Briskin, Marcus Brissman, Stephane Brochu, Jeff Brooks, Eric Brousseau, Rob Brown, Antony Brown, Christopher Brown, Nick Brownlow, Simon Brunning, Wayne L. Budgen, Laura Budzinski, Alan Bundock, Bungle, Steve Burnett, Bentley Burnham, Chris Butler, Scott Butler, Aaron Buttery, Bryce Byerley, Andrew Byers, Morrissey Tyler Cahiwat, Tony E. Calidonna, Chris Callicoat, Brian "Chain-saw" Campbell, Jae Campbell, Hamish Campbell, Jeff Camp-bell, Jean-François Campourcy, Martin Hunter Caplan, Patrick Cappoli, Shane A. Caraker, Loki Carbis, Noah Carden, Jeff "Mr Shiny" Carey, Jason Carl, Joe carlson, Matthew Carpen-ter, C.J. Carroll, William 'Beej' Carson, Eric Carstairs, Neil de Carteret, Simon 'Maggot' Caruana, Loyd Case, George M. Casper, Ricardo Arredondo Casso, Tiana Castillo, Cesar Cesarotti, Ludovic Chabant, Chados, of clan Chados, Camilla Chalcraft, Robert Challenger, David Lars Chamberlain, Ken Chang, Philippe Chapdelaine, JP Chapleau, Trevor "Ratenef" Chapman, Charles Chapman, Ben Chapman, A. Chatain, Dr Cheinstein, Mike Cherry, Prathet Chhour, Philip Chiang, Andrew Chiarello, Michael Childs, Brady T. Chin, Chorchal-do, Joshua Clark, Joshua Clark, Andrew J Clark IV, Matthew Clarke, Matt Clay, Seth Clayton, Victor the Cleaner, Sylvain Clément, Neil Clench, Jim Clunie, Genevieve Cogman, Sean

Colbath, Leroy Colson, Matt Compton, Edouard Contesse, Roland Cooke, Chris Cooper, Kevin Cornell, Dave Corner, Donnie Cornwell, Eddie Coulter, Paul Courtenay, Stuart Coutts, Brian Covey, Richard Cowen, Matt Cowger, Scott D. Craig, Drew Craker, Bob Cram, John Crawford, Colin Creitz, Samwise Crider, Walter F. Croft, Nick Crones, Peter Cruise, Gil Cruz, Cryoban, Chris Csakany, Brian Curley, Craig Curtis, John D, D-Rock, John T. d'Auteuil, Thomas Dahmen, Neal Dalton, Matthew Dames, Peter Darley, Steven Darrall, Guillaume Daudin, Judgement Dave, Michael David Jr., Darren Davis, Gregory Davis, Dr. Dazumal, Peter Dean, Philippe Debar, Auroras Deed, Richard Degrou, Chris DeKalb, Joe Deleskiewicz, The Delicious One, Arinn Dembo, Steve Dempsey, Jason Denen, Arthur Dent, Bobby Derie, Dave Desgagnes, Joe DeSimone, Gus Diaz, Antoine "Bardin" Dijoux, Ben Dilworth, Julie Dinkins, Ben Dinsmore, Adam Diran, Eugene "Tinman" Doherty, Stuart Dollar, Agent Donald, Lorraine Donaldson, Kim Dong-Ryul, Bryan Donihue, Damon Dorsey, Scott Dorward, Paul 'the Bastard' Douglas, David Drage (Iron Mammoth), Mike Drew, Mike Drigants, Michael Driscoll, dryack, Jay Dugger, Rodolphe Duhil, Mike Dukes, Darin DuMez, Dumon, Vivienne Dunstan, Bryant durrell, Dweller on the Threshold, Mike Dyer, Aaron Dykstra, Damien Dyon aka Cpt. Nathaniel Franks (MIA), David J. Early, Leland Eaves, Steve Eckart, EdMcW, Nick Edwards, Stephen Egolf, Victor Eichhorn, Viktor Eikman, Eldritch, Tim Ellis, Tony Emerson, Robert N. Emerson, Michael Emminger, Kevin Empey, Peter Endean, Mikael Engstrom, Jacob T Engstrom,

Jayle Enn, Cell Epsilon, David Esbri, Jeff Eshbaugh, Zach Eubanks, rob Evans, Ian Fabry, Mark Farias, David Farnell, Michael Fay, Nancy Feldman, Ben Ferguson, Will Ferguson, Leandro Raniero Fernandes, Mick Fernette, davide ferrari, Darrin Fesperman, Tony Finan, Keegan Fink, Ken Finlayson, Agent Finney, Agent Quinn (Ford Fitch), Barbara Flaxington, William Flint, FlukeNukem, Adam Flynn, Paul Fong, Benjamin Ford, Neil C Ford, Richard Forster, Eric Foster, Matthew Fowle, J. H. Frank, Peter Frazier, fredgiblet, Jeromy M. French, Frank Frey, Paul Fricker, Jeremy Fridy, Tom Friell, Jason Fritz, Mark R. Froom, Tyson Fultz, Aaron K. Funk, Scott Gable, Tóth Csaba Gábor, Kevin Galton, Gaunts Gamers, Gonzalo Rodriguez Garcia, Rod Garcia, Sergio Rodriguez Garcia, Jesse Garrison, Craig Gates, Andrew Gatlin, Marshall Gatten, Håkon Gaut, Silvio Herrera Gea, Rory Geoghegan, Chris Geschkat, Sion Rodriguez y Gibson, gilabrezu@hotmail.com, Magnus Gillberg, Patrick Gingrich, Felix Girke, Kerry Gisler, Christopher Wayne Glazener, Dave Goffin, Robert P. Goldman, Sean M. Gomez, Allan Goodall, Kit Goode, John Goodrich, duran goodyear, Joshua Gore, Tristan Goss, Mike & Brian Goubeaux, jason grace, Samuel Graebner, Tim Graham, Diego 'Escrivio' D'Oliveira Granja, Michael Grasso, Gary Graybill, Peter Green, Josh Gregal, Dave 'Ferret' Griffin, Pete Griffith, Derek Grimm, Allan T. Grohe Jr., Ollie Gross, Derek Guder, Jack Gulick, Christopher Gunning, DL Gurnett, Andreas Gustafsson, The H.P. Lovecraft Film Festival & CthulhuCon, Scott Hacker, Craig Hackl, Rhys Haines, Laurel Halbany, Alexander Hallberg, Breon Halling, Ville Halonen, Tore

Halvorsen, Jerry Ham, Arne Handt, Bob Hanks, Rob Hansen, Mathias Hansson, Scott Haring, Terry Harney, Pat Harrigan, G. Hartman, Larry Lee Hassenpflug II, James Haughton, David Hauser, James Hawkins, Douglas Lee Haxton, Morgan Hay, john hayholt, Andrew Hayler, Paul Hazen, Nils Hedglin, Kelly Heffron, Kevin Heim, Rob Heinsoo, Steven Helberg, Mikael Hellstrom, Martin Helsdon, Alejandro Henao, David Henion, Matthew Eric Henkel, Kirk Henley, Mary Henry, Peter Hentges, Fred Herman, Cory J. Herndon, Brian Hicks, Lynn Firestone Hill, Christopher Hill, Matthew Hinks, Edward Hirsch, Lauri Hirvonen, Maximilian Hoetzl, Adam Hoffman, Anders Højsted, Danielle Holbein, James Holden, Lars Holgaard, Jeremy S Holley, Michael Hollis, Nigel Holloway, Stephen Holowczyk, Emrys W Hopkins, Jurie Horneman, Cap'n Howdy, Jonathan Hsu, Jürgen Hubert, Heather Hudson, David Hughart, Rory Hughes, Jacob Hulker, Matthias Hunger, Simon Hunt, Pete Hurley, Dr. John Hutson, Antonino Lo Iacono, IdeologyofMadness.com, John Idlor, James Iles, David Lee Ingersoll, Tahd Inskepp, Richard Iorio II, Iphigenie, Bert Isla, Glen E. Ivey, JoAnna and Jon of "J" Cell, J.T., Shane Jackson, Ben Jackson, Jake Jackson, Michael L. Jaegers, James a.k.a. uber, Jason H Jaramillo, Chris Jarocha-Ernst, Duncan Jarrett, JBar, JD, Jimmy, Sapper Joe, Ladevez Johnny, Seth Johnson, Sam "I read too much" Johnson, Mary K Johnston, A V Jones, Jeffrey A. Jones, Dave Jones, M Alexander Jurkat, k'Bob42, k8207dz, Max Kaehn, Dan Kahn, Jeff Kahrs, Christopher 'Vulpine' Kalley, Brad D. Kane, Patrick Kapera, Neal Kaplan, Jonas Karlsson, Kate, Lee Kauftheil, Steven Kaye, Kcirtap,

Shawn Kehoe, Ralph Kelleners, Mark D. Keller, Mike Kelley, Mark 'Z-GrimV' Kelly, Jussi Kenkkilä, Rónán Kennedy, Andrew Kenrick, Darin Kerr, Kelsey Kerrigan, Kese, Jack Kessler, Kevthulhu, Don "The Architect" Kichline, Ben Kimball, Jon Kimmich, @kindofstrange, Kit Kindred, Steven W. King, James King, Josh King, Lyz King, Micah King, Graham Kinniburgh, Thom Kiraly, Michael Kirkbride, Jim "DC Books" Kirkland, Hywel Kirwan, Marek Kisala, Rainy Day Kitty, Stefan Kjellin, Zack Kline, Tristan D. Knight, Joe Kontor, Jonathan Korman, Bob Koutsky, Jason R. Kraft, Bret Kramer, Jason Kraus, Jo Kreil, Matthew Krykew, Michael Krzak, David Kubé, Ashley Kuehner, Matthew Kugler, Sebastian Kuhn, Victor Kuo, John M. Kuzma, Kenneth C Labbe II, Chris Lackey, Mikko Lahti, Tero Laiho, David Lallemand, Kevin Lama, John Lambert, Alexis Lamiable, Mario 'Landa' Landgraf, Moe Lane, Joakim Larsen, Brian Lavelle, Ville Lavonius, Marc di Lazzaro, Ted "Kveld Ulf" LeBeau, Keith Maki Lee, William W. Lee, Symon Leech, Kris Leeke, Christian Lehmann, Matt Leitzen, Peter Lennox, Paul Leone, Charles Lewis, Chad K Lewis, John Lewis, Daniel Ley, Mark Leymaster of Grammarye, Tristan Lhomme, Oliver Lind, Sebastian Lindeberg, B. Link, Robert Lint, Matthew H. Lipparelli, O.D., Edward Lipsett, James Lister, E. Christopher Lloyd, Karl Lloyd, Andy Logan, Alex Loke, Tim Lonegan, Steven S. Long, Kin-Ming Looi, Henry Lopez, Zed Lopez, James Lowder, Ron Loz, Rodrigo "WiNG" Lozano, Louis Luangkesorn, Alexander Lucard, lukulius, HP Lustcraft, Bryce A. Lynch, Tom Lynch, Lynnthear, M Jason Mabry, Shannon Mac, WJ MacGuffin,

Mario Magallanes, Dave Magnenat, Neil Nictating Mahoney, Erik H. Maier, Valentin Maire, Nick Makris, Chris Malone, Kym Malycha, The Man in Black, Davide Mana, Hal Mangold, Patrick Manson, Marc Margelli, John Markley, Adam Marler, Kevin J. "Womzilla" Maroney, Ryan Martin, Côme Martin, James Martin, Francisco "Stytch" Martinez, Mike Mason, Ilias Mastrogiorgos, Dennis Matheson, M. Matton, Mike Maughmer, Max-Ray, Stanton McCandlish, Andrew McCarty, David F. McCloskey, Robin McCollum, Matt McCormick, Agent MCD, Calum McDonald, In Memory of Mark McFadden, Ben McFarland, Nick McGinness, Shane McGovern, Seana McGuinness, Neil McGurk, Kevin 'Tony Grimaldi' McHale, Badger McInnes, Mike McKeown, Shane Mclean, Derrick K McMullin, Nicole McPherson, Carlos McReynolds, Joseph McRoberts, Joshua D. Meadows, Marco Melillo, Steven Mentzel, Trey Mercer, Nick Meredith, Patrice Mermoud, Jason Mical, Jason Middleton, Stefanie R Midlock, Marcin Miduch, Darren Miguez, Chris Miles, Michael Miley, Andrew Miller, Dan Milliken, Russell Mirabelli, Gary "Sneezy the Squid" Mitchel, Christopher Mitchell, Justin Mohareb, M. Sean Molley, Vapid Mollusk, Filthy Monkey, Rob Montanaro, Dan "Vargr1" Moody, Dom Mooney, Shawn M Moore, Roger Moore, Benjamin Moore, Gary Moore, Bugs Moran, Keir Moreano, Jesse Morgan, Griffin D. Morgan, Sean Morris, Mark Morse, Paul Motsuk, Cairnryan Dorian Mower, moxou, MTD, Jeppe Mulich, Steve Mumford, Munchezuma, Frankie Mundens, Mircea Munteanu, Brian "Keeper Murph" Murphy, Sean Murphy, Zach Murray, Timothy mushel, James Muskett,

Charles Myers, Nicholas Nacario, Nachtnoir, NamelessOne, Chris Nasipak, Mary Nassef, NB, Rick Neal, neko_cam, John Nellis, Malcolm Nelson, Pete Newell, Chris Newell, David Nichol, Koumoundouros Nikolas, Tony Nixon, Morten Njaa, Andrew John Noble, Ramon Nogueras, Mike Nolan, Joseph Noll, Christian A. Nord, Johan Nordberg, Magnus Nordlander, Aaron Norman, Nils-Anders Nøttseter, Wibble Nut, Terry O'Carroll, Tim O'Connor, John O'Connor, Mark O'Neill, Andrew Oberdier, Ray Oberg, Carl-Niclas Odenbring, Pavel Ojeda, "Weird Dave" Olson, John Olszewski, Uther Frederick Orchard, Dave Owen, Craig Oxbrow, Yan Périard, Randall "WiseWolf" Padilla, Lisa Padol, James Palmer, David Panseri, Thomas Di Paolo, Robert J. Parker, Patrick Parkinson, Tony Parry, Gregory N Parsons, George R. Paulishak, Cooler then Ross Payton, Dr Alan Peden, Teppo Pennanen, peter peretti, Mark Perneta, Alexis Perron, Bryce Perry, Kristian Bach Petersen, Trevor Peterson, Megan Peterson, John Petherick, Morten Kjeldseth Pettersen, Sean P. Phelan, James Pierson, Rob Pinkerton, Brian R. Pitt, Matthew Plank, pookie, Neil Poree, Randall Porter, Ed Possing, Dave Post, KJ Potter, Benjamin Preston, Graeme Price, Eric Priehs, Pseudonomymous, Joel Purton, Marx Pyle, Patrick E. Quinn, Alex J & Annabelle R, Simon Rafferty, Adam Rajski, Dane Ralston-Bryce, M. D. Ranalli Jr., Ib Rasmussen, Frédérik Rating, John F Rauchert, Tomas Rawlings, Mark Redacted, Redd, Nate "SubCmdr" Reed, Christopher Reed, Ashley "Nicolean Complex" Reed, Brendan Reeves, Rune Belsvik Reinås, revnye, Reza, Mark Richardson, Ken Ringwald, Mark Rinna, Peter Risby, Geoffrey

Riutta, Derek N Robertson, Stewart Robertson, Scott E Robinson, Philip C. Robinson, Alexander Rodatos, David Rodemaker, Eric Rodriguez, Andrew Rodwell, Matthias Rohde (Agent Scalapecci), Kevin Rolfe, Brian M. Roma, CJ Romer, Frank Romero, Derek Rompot, Gerald Rose Jr., Ilan Rosenstein, Darcy "Danger" Ross, Frances Rowat, Ernest N Rowland Jr, Ng Yun Ru, Matthew J. Ruane, Steve Rubin, Warren Rumble, Gareth Ryder-Hanrahan, Thom Ryng, Alan Sable, Pr Lambert Saint Paul, Nick 'PlutoNick' Sakkas, Beau Salsman, Roberto Bravo Sanchez, Matthew Sanderson, Ian Sandford, Ralf "Sandfox" Sandfuchs, Andrew Sangar, Fidel Santiago, Gerry Saracco, The Dread Dr. Sardonicus, Tuckoo Sargentini, Myranda Sarro, C. Mark Sarver, Liam G Sauer-Wooden, Adam Savje, Lars Schaefer, Eduardo H Schaeffer, Karsten Scheibye-Alsing, Ralf Schemmann, Arthur Axel 'fREW' Schmidt, Thorsten Schubert, Martin Schultz, Christian "Mr. van Garen" Schulz, Terrell Scoggins, Dwight Scull, Agent Sewell, Travis Shamp, Arun Shankar, Rob Shankly, Thom Shartle, Thomas J. Shavor, Shenzoar, David A. Shepherd, Sean K.T. Shiraishi, Mark Shocklee, Shoggothic, A. Shultz, Alexander "Nachtflug" Siegelin, Sam Silbory, Sean Silva-Miramon, Adam Silva-Miramon, João Simões, Kristoffer Simonsson, Jake Skelcher, Erin-Talia Skinner, Sam Slocum, Kevin Smith, Andy "Kolchak" Smith, Steven Brent Smith, Michael R. Smith, Riley Smith, Steven M. Smith, Mark Smothers, Chris Snyder, Kent Snyen, Andi Sobiech, Dave Sokolowski, Renee M. Solberg, Ernie Sowada, SpacedOut, Walt Spafford, Daniel H. Spain, John C. G. Spainhour, Michael Speir, Roy Spence, Sphärenmeisters

Spiele, Massimo Spiga, Michael Spinks, Chris "Last of the Timelords" Spivey, Daniel Stack, Sid Stallings Jr., Trevor Stamper, John R. Stanfield II, Gregory Stanyer, Kelly Stark, Richard Starr, Maciej Starzycki, Andrew Steele, Daniel Stegall, Joerg Sterner, Marlin Stewart, Callum Stoner, aleksandar stossitch, Sam Stoute, Steven Strahm, Tony Strongman, Simon 'Sly' Stroud, Maurice Strubel, Matt Stuart, Jeremy Stuckwisch, Marco Subias, Paul Sudlow, Steve Summersett, Claes Svensson, Yuriy Sverchkov, Steve Swann, Derek "Pineapple Steak" Swoyer, Chris Sylvis, Laszlo Szidonya, Craig T., Laurent Tastet, Ray Tessmann, Jamison T Thing, Dave Thomas, Matthew Yeti Thomas, Owen 'Sanguinist' Thompson, Dana Thoms, Alex Thornton-Clark, Mark Threlfall, David Ting, Tomas Aleksander Tjomsland, William Tolliver, Martijn Tolsma, Ian Tong, Steven Torres-Roman, Toshikage, Cass Towns, Nick Townsend, Michael Tramov, Tim Trant, Gil Trevizo, Jacob Trewe, James Trimmier, Paul Tucker, Martin Tulloch, Bruce Turner, Tharon James Turner, John Scott Tynes, Paolo Ungheri, J Jack Unrau, Derek Upham, Paul Michael Urfi, Anthony Valterra, Erik Van Buren, Stephen Vandevander, Kevin Veale, Luis Velasco, James A Velez, Steven Vest, The Veterans of a Thousand Midnights, David Vial, Jason Vines, Ngo Vinh-Hoi, Matthew Voss, Nick W, Phil W, Jon Wagner, Chris Wakefield, Charlie J. Wall, Dave Walsh, Joshua Wanisko, John Ward, Phil Ward, Chris Ward, Mike Warnock, Matthew Wasiak, Jay Watkins, Stuart Watkins, Luke Watt, Kent Wayson, Eric Lane Webb, Steve Weidner, Joshua Weiss, Luke Welch, Petri Wessman, John Alan West, Bradley West, Charlie Westenberger,

Jonathan Westmoreland, Tom Weston, David Wetzel, Nigel Wheeler, Adam Whitcomb, Larry White, Roger Whitson, Whitt., Sean Whittaker, Mike Whooley, Simon Whorlow, Kenneth Whritenour, Rob Wieland, Martina Wiesch, John Wilcox, Charles Wilkins, Kurt Willer, Jason Williams, Russell Williams, Wayne Williams, Benjamin Williams, Matt Willis, John S. Willson, Jonathan Wilson, David J Winchester, Matthew C H Winder, Zeke Winn, Cliff Winnig, Doug Winter, Dan Winterlin, Bob Wintermute, Andrew Woitena, Dawid Wojcieszynski, Richard S. Wolfe, Kevin C. Wong, Sid Wood, Shawn Wood, Justin Woodman, Henry V. Woolsey, wraith808, Jason Wright, Anthony Wright, Matt Wrycraft, Arthur Wyatt, Tariq York, Wesley James Young, Jack Young, Agent Yunis, Max Z, David Zelasco, Eugene Zimichev, Pedro Ziviani, and Mattias Östklint.

About the Author

DENNIS DETWILLER IS AN author, artist and video game designer. Since 1992, his books, card games and video games have entertained over 40 million people in 11 languages. He's design director at Harebrained Schemes. Before that, he was VP of Creative at Warner Bros. International Enterprises and produced best-selling mobile and console games for Nickelodeon, Hothead Games, and Radical Entertainment. His work spans global hits such as *Magic: The Gathering,* the *[PROTOTYPE]* series for Activision, *Teenage Mutant Ninja Turtles* for Nickelodeon, and more personal creations such as *Delta Green, GODLIKE* and *Wild Talents.* He contributed to the #1 collectible card game in the world *(Magic: The Gathering)* and produced the #1 console game *([PROTOTYPE], 2009)* and the #1 iOS game *(Teenage Mutant Ninja Turtles: Rooftop Run,* 2013). He is a four-time winner of the Origins Award for gaming and a two-time winner of the Ennie Award for RPG excellence. Read more of his fiction in *Delta Green: Through a Glass, Darkly* (a sequel to John Scott Tynes' *The Rules of Engagement,* found in *Delta Green: Strange Authorities)* and *Delta Green: Denied to the Enemy.*

About Delta Green

DELTA GREEN BEGAN, UNDER another name, as a U.S. Navy program to investigate the terrifying implications of the federal government's little-known 1928 raid on Innsmouth, Massachusetts. In World War II, that program was folded into an OSS psychological warfare unit dedicated to exploiting Nazi belief in the supernatural — but which really fought to thwart the terrifying supernatural things that certain Nazi researchers had uncovered. Its activities were classified DELTA GREEN.

After the war, Delta Green split apart. Many of its veterans joined a new program, code-named MAJESTIC, after the Roswell incident revealed what appeared to be UFOs and alien life — discoveries which concealed a far more horrifying truth. What remained of Delta Green pursued supernatural threats across the globe for decades, until a disastrous Cambodia operation in 1970 shut the group down.

Delta Green never really went away. Its leaders went underground, pulling strings from within the U.S government to send hand-picked agents on new operations. They kept fighting to uproot and destroy supernatural terrors just as they had been fighting since Innsmouth, despite the awful toll they paid in life and sanity.

In 2001, Delta Green agents staged a sort of coup in the MAJESTIC program, a very hostile takeover that split Delta Green apart again. With the onset of the Global War on Terror, the Defense Department's long-defunct DELTA GREEN classification was reactivated for a top-secret, highly restricted program, fighting cosmic terrors with the tools and aegis of the War on Terror. Many Delta Green agents joined the new organization. Others distrusted the close ties between the new Delta Green and the infamously corrupt sprawl of the MAJESTIC program. Those few cut all ties with their former comrades and remained out in the cold, pursuing their desperate work with even fewer resources and less hope than before.

For more information and Delta Green books and games, visit www.delta-green.com.

www.ingramcontent.com/pod-product-compliance
Lightning Source LLC
Chambersburg PA
CBHW051534260626
47170CB00003B/933